# HART'S RIDGE

## BOOK 1

## KAY BRATT

RED THREAD
PUBLISHING GROUP

RED THREAD
PUBLISHING GROUP

## ALSO BY KAY BRATT

# HART'S RIDGE DESCRIPTION

**If Robyn Carr and Melinda Leigh had a book baby, *Hart's Ridge* would be it. Join Kay Bratt in her new mystery series that is packed with cases, and a small-town deputy determined to solve them.**

*When five-year-old Molly walks into a gas station on the outskirts of town, alone and barely speaking, one sheriff's deputy is determined to reunite her with her missing mother.*

Nestled gently in the Blue Ridge mountains, Hart's Ridge is a small and yet undiscovered quaint town. That is until you dig a little deeper and learn that no matter how perfect things look, every town has its secrets. Taylor Gray has lived in Hart's Ridge since she was a preteen and has clawed her way out of poverty, foster care, and then the police academy to reach her dream of being in law enforcement.

However, the townspeople aren't the only ones that she is committed to serve and protect. She's also the unofficial caretaker of her father and adult sisters, a family fractured by tragedy.

Her role is heavy and rarely appreciated, but she'll stop at nothing to try to piece them back together one day.

Joni Stott is the mother of young Molly and is missing. Time is of the essence, and Taylor plunges into the investigation, determined to find her and reunite mother and child. When the sheriff brings a familiar face in to take charge, things begin to unravel at a pace hard to keep up with, and what they find is every law enforcement officer's worst nightmare.

*Hart's Ridge* can be read as a standalone novel and is book one of the new *Hart's Ridge* mystery series, written by Kay Bratt, Million Copy Best-Selling Author of *Wish Me Home* and the *By the Sea* series.

# HART'S RIDGE

∾

**A Small-Town Mystery**
**By**
**KAY BRATT**

# CHAPTER 1

*M*inor female, approximately four years old. Wandered unaccompanied into Leonard's Quick Stop out on *Boleman Hill Road. No name given.*

That's all dispatch had so far.

Deputy Taylor Gray sat behind the wheel of her cruiser, enjoying the warm summer breeze through her window as she headed to the call to see why or how a small child had ambled into a gas station alone way out in the country.

Lusciously tall trees loomed over each side of the highway, and the sky turned soft shades of pinks and golds, preparing to close the curtain for the night. But the gorgeous scenery could be deceiving. No one knew more than Deputy Taylor Gray how suddenly their peaceful little town nestled in the Blue Ridge Mountains could be unsettled, sending their small force scrambling.

Bernard whined, and Taylor put his window down a bit farther, letting more air pour in. She wasn't supposed to have her dog with her, but she also wasn't even supposed to be on shift, so beggars couldn't be choosers.

"We need to check this out, and I don't have time to take you home first," Taylor muttered to the dog.

He didn't meet her gaze.

The child was said to be barely dressed and hungry. The most alarming part was the store was at least ten miles out in the country, away from everything. Taylor thought of the wolves she'd heard howling a few miles from her house only the week before. Bear sightings were common, too.

Taylor couldn't count the times she'd been called to the scene of a local homeowner dealing with a stubborn bear. She'd gotten quite good at scaring them away, but not all of them were as obliging. Only a few years ago, an elderly man was attacked when he found one rummaging through the trash outside his back door. If not for his tiny eight-pound dog intervening and getting the attention of the bear, the man wouldn't have made it. Thankfully, the dog was too swift and cunning to be caught, and the bear finally took off.

Taylor cringed, thinking of a tiny girl out walking alone and all the things that could've happened.

Where had she come from? Who did she belong to?

She pushed the patrol car as fast as she could legally go, knowing she wasn't headed to a life-or-death emergency. The last thing she needed was a rambling deer to be coaxed onto the highway by her headlights. She'd already lost one car to Bambi's mother, cousin, or some relation. The sheriff would have her butt if she totaled another.

Patrol cars didn't come cheap. Not to mention that Hart's Ridge Sheriff's Department had a tiny budget to match their small-town feel. So far, they hadn't yet been discovered by the droves of people looking for an off-the-beaten-path place to retire. Taylor liked to think of their town as a hidden gem. Though humble, the majestic peaks and wilderness that surrounded the town served as a backdrop that could make the most cynical stop and wonder who created it.

Bernard perked up, his spine going ramrod straight. Taylor followed his gaze and saw a majestic deer standing in the woods off the shoulder of the road, only a few feet away, the weight of his rack evident in the careful way he held his head.

"You don't want none of that stuff, boy," she said. "He'd tear you to pieces."

Carefully, she took her foot off the gas as she rounded Dead Man's Curve. She didn't want to be another statistic for that spot in the road. She'd learned to drive on the curvy Georgia roads, but that didn't mean she didn't respect the danger of them. She'd been at the scene of some ugly accidents all over her county.

She called in an ETA of six minutes, but she wished she could blink her eyes and be there instantly. Cases with children were her weakness. She thought of her youngest sister, Lucy. Or *Lucy in the Sky*, as she used to call herself, a nickname that came from the obsession their mother had with the Beatles.

Lucy would be twenty-three soon, and Taylor hadn't heard from her in eight months, the longest she'd ever gone silent.

Their late mother had given all her daughters names related to the Beatles. Taylor cringed at hers. *Georgia*. Thank goodness their father was a James Taylor fan. He'd at least given Taylor a middle name she could work with. Before she'd started junior high, she laid down the law and insisted they call her Taylor.

Lucy, on the other hand, loved her name and took her mother's fixation with John Lennon for her own. Taylor couldn't count the number of round—and fake—glasses her youngest sister had lost over the years, or the bottles of hair dye it took to keep her naturally auburn hair a dark shade of black.

While Taylor grew up dreaming of chasing bad guys from behind a badge, Lucy had sat in the closet, eyes closed as she swayed to the endless tracks from the Beatles albums pouring through her headphones.

They all had their quirks, she supposed.

*Where are you, Lucy?*

That was a question that Taylor asked too many times each day. As the oldest of the four sisters, Taylor had tried to keep track of them after they'd all sprung from foster care the final time and into adulthood. Two of her sisters were fine, and she could have them on the phone in seconds, if needed.

But Lucy... That was a different story, and the fact her youngest sister had fallen through the cracks never ceased to plague her with guilt. Losing your mom as a kid wasn't easy, and even though they still had their dad to bounce back and forth from foster care to, Lucy, the youngest, had taken not having a mother the hardest out of all of them. She tried to hide it with a tough exterior, but the pain showed in every wrong decision she made.

She realized she was holding her breath as she thought about Lucy, and her knuckles clutched the steering wheel so tight they were white.

Enough thinking of family, tragedy, and what-ifs.

*Concentrate on the dog.*

"Are you tired, Bernard? We're almost there. But you'll have to stay in the car."

No response. He sure wasn't too appreciative that she had recently granted his parole from the Harts Ridge Humane Society. More than once in the last week, she'd been tempted to put him right back behind bars.

That made her think of Lucy again.

Prison bars. At least once that Taylor knew of, and probably quite a few more times that she didn't.

Lucy wouldn't like the comparison, but Taylor was finding that her sister and Bernard shared a lot of similar traits. Ungratefulness was one of them. Sullen attitude, two. And the fact that Taylor still wanted to please them, despite their indifference to her feelings, three.

She just hoped the parallels stopped there so she wouldn't

wake up to find Bernard gone one morning and have to spend every waking day worrying whether he was alive or dead.

However, now wasn't the time to think about it because she had a job to do.

Someone else could've taken the call, but Taylor was pleased that the sergeant put her on it. He knew she was good with the young ones and had the most experience dealing with social services.

*Too much experience.*

The scenery flew by as she kept her eyes on the road, but mentally she was all over the place, adding items to the lists in her mind. To say she was a list kind of person was putting it mildly. With a childhood as chaotic and unorganized as hers was, she made sure as an adult that she was always prepared for anything.

And then some.

She hit the microphone on her phone and started dictating.

First things first. Was the child dropped off? Had she escaped unnoticed from home? How had she worked her way through the highways? Had she been abused? Was someone looking for her? Was her clothing out of style? Worn out? The right size, or hand-me-downs?

Supposedly, the girl appeared to be no more than four years old. She was minimally dressed and had bare feet. Not even a jacket, but she'd dragged a ragged stuffed sloth along with her.

The situation had alarmed the clerk enough that he'd called for help. Good thing he had, because it was a chilly day and letting a barely dressed child go back into the cold could've led to tragedy after dark.

Taylor passed a Dollar General and saw an old man pushing a shopping cart through the parking lot. It was full, blankets over-flowing, and bulging plastic bags tied to the sides. She waved, and he held his hand up for a moment. She always felt the most comfortable around others who, like her, were hungry for something more—a chance to climb out of poverty.

The police academy was her ticket out, and she was proud of the badge she wore. Not that it paid enough to make her rich, but her job made her feel as though she was contributing to the world. It also gave her the respect she'd always craved when she was young and felt everyone was looking down on her family for being poor.

She heard a beep and glanced at her phone.

It was a text from Clint McElroy, their senior deputy who patrolled the area.

I got this. No need to come.

Of course, he kept it off the radio where there was no record.

Clint hated her. For no reason at all that she could fathom. It was just one of those instantaneous disconnections you have when you meet someone. He'd wanted her out since day one when he'd been assigned as her FTO—field training officer. He'd told her after their first shift, *"You should just quit now."*

Then later, he'd pulled over and urinated on her side of the car, looking right at her. Taylor had stared him down, refusing to give in and look away. She should've reported him back then, but she didn't want to call any more attention to the fact that she was being treated unfairly because of her gender. The fact that she'd toughed it out probably ate him up inside. She was still there and not going any damn where.

She also wasn't going to text and drive.

He was probably ticked off that the sheriff was sending her to his area, but that was his problem. She was following higher orders.

Taylor dictated a reply, and the dog finally looked at her.

*You talking to me?*

"No," Taylor answered. "Not you."

It did give her heart a little flip though that Bernard acknowledged her. Even for a split second. She had resisted getting a dog for years. She wasn't home enough. Didn't want the responsibility for another living thing. Didn't want to get attached.

She finally gave in after the incident.

It shamed her that she was in law enforcement, carried a gun, knew all there was to know about keeping yourself safe, but someone had still gotten into her home in the dead of the night, and she hadn't known a thing until she'd felt his hot breath on the back of her neck.

Nausea rolled over her as that night came back to her.

He'd taken much more than her pride, and one day, she'd find him because she had his DNA. Even though it hadn't matched anyone in the system yet, it would eventually. And until then, no one could know what happened to her. Not even the sheriff. They would all consider her weak. And careless. She'd lose all the street-tough credibility she'd worked so hard for.

Taylor would handle it herself if—no, *when*—she found the warped pervert.

She couldn't lie, though. The incident had shaken her to her core. So much so that she'd set up her own therapy to try to help her get over the anxiety. And the fear.

Then she got the dog.

Because a gun didn't do a damn bit of good if someone was able to be right on top of you before their presence was known.

Literally.

She also couldn't afford a high-tech security system, so a dog was the next best option.

Bernard was also going to be her cure for a broken heart, because every dog lover she'd ever known had said they'd be more likely to re-home their mate before they would their pet. It sounded like a perfect solution to Taylor because she was lonely and tired of coming home to a quiet house. Since she was officially done with men, she was being proactive and going with something better.

Less work.

She saw Bernard sitting in the corner of his kennel at the shelter, his nose pointed at the corner in his concrete cell, as though he'd been put in time-out. He didn't want to turn around for her, and when he finally did, he looked sad and frightened. He'd given her the sad eyes—and she'd melted.

It hadn't helped that the attendant had spouted off statistics of how many black dogs were left in shelters and never adopted.

"What is he?"

"Mostly Labrador," she'd said. "But who knows? He's got too many possible breeds in him for most people to take him on. They want to know what they are getting."

Taylor had no idea that was a *thing*, and that people passed the dogs by because of their color, pedigrees, or lack thereof. All she knew was that he looked strong and more than capable of standing up to a coyote, bear, or any man for that matter. Living alone in the boondocks like she did would make him a good investment, and he'd be her first line of defense if an intruder ever came wandering around again.

When Taylor read the card on the kennel and saw the dog's name was Bernard, that had sealed the deal.

Lucy would be pleased and call it a sign. Her idol, John Lennon, had owned a dog named Bernard. Technically, though, the musician was more of a cat person and owned ten at one time when he was married to his first wife. Then when he was in New York with Yoko, one of his most beloved cats named Alice jumped out their high-rise apartment window to its death below.

Poor Alice had already used up her nine lives, it seemed.

The articles' said Lennon was devastated for months.

Lucy had adopted numerous kittens and cats when they were kids. Their dad wouldn't let any of them in the house, so her sister spent a lot of time outdoors with them, giving every one of them a name from John's previous feline entourage. She'd probably rather that Taylor adopted a cat or three herself, but Taylor wasn't sure how much company or defense a cat could offer.

And if anything, she was more of a dog person. Lucy would just have to be satisfied that she'd adopted Bernard.

On the way home, the dog had leaned on the passenger door, staring out the window, as though deep in thought. Same as he was doing now.

His attitude would change once he got comfortable, she'd thought, but so far, he still spent a lot of time daydreaming. It was really concerning, and Taylor wasn't sure just what to do about it.

Before she could put more thought into it, she arrived at the store. Clint's car wasn't there yet. She turned in and pulled up next to the door. She could see a guy crouching on the floor next to a little girl. She threw the car into park.

"Stay, Bernard," she said.

He whined as she got out and shut the door.

Once inside, she did a quick look, scanning all the corners of the building that she could see before focusing on the subjects of the call.

The child looked around three or four years old, unless she was just small for her age. She had ketchup smeared across her chin. Her huge brown eyes lifted to Taylor and took in her uniform, all the way down to her shiny black shoes. Then she looked away quickly.

Her expression was one of fright.

"It's okay," the clerk said, patting her on the back, his gesture awkward. "The police officer just wants to help you get home."

"Sheriff's deputy," Taylor corrected him.

The little girl was obviously guarded. She wore a man's jacket over her long T-shirt, and the leather hem touched the floor. The clerk had rolled the sleeves up so her tiny hands could be free. Taylor scrutinized her arms and legs, but there were no bruises or noticeable signs of abuse. Obviously, all abuse wasn't visible, but at least nothing physical had been done to the child recent enough to leave a mark.

"She was freezing, so I put my jacket on her," the clerk said. "But I promise she's been in view of our cameras the entire time."

Taylor smiled at him. He was a kind young man. Smart, too. In this day and age, you could never be too safe or too wary of protecting your own self.

"When I called 911, they said no children in the area have been reported missing," he said.

"Has she given her name?"

He shook his head. "She's barely said anything. Only asked for more food. She just finished her second hotdog."

Taylor noticed the tangled hair and dark circles around the girl's eyes. This wasn't just a case of a child getting out of the home by accident; she'd bet her badge on it. The girl looked like she hadn't slept in days. And who let their kids roam the highway and didn't even report them missing?

Yes, child neglect was going on here, and from what Taylor could see, it was probably long-term negligence. It always infuriated her that some women were so nonchalant about having a child, taking the gift for granted. She'd seen so much neglect and abuse out there that it had jaded her. Now she was afraid to even think of motherhood until she had everything perfectly in place so to never ever have a child want for anything—especially something as simple as sustenance and safety from all the horrible things that could befall them when they weren't being protected.

A car came screeching into the parking lot.

Deputy Clint—driving like a maniac to beat her to the scene, no doubt.

He was in the store in seconds and stomped over to them, a glare on his face. The negative energy he exuded was not helpful. Even Taylor felt on edge as he approached.

The girl reacted instantly, intaking a sharp breath as she stepped back.

"You're scaring her," Taylor hissed at him.

"You aren't even supposed to be on shift," he hissed back. "I'll take this."

"Sheriff sent me." With that, Taylor took the little girl's hand and led her toward the back of the store, away from Clint and the attendant.

She knelt and looked into her eyes.

"Hi, sweetheart," she said softly. "My name is Deputy Gray. But my sisters call me Taylor. Can you tell me your name?"

The girl stared through Taylor, not connecting.

"Let me guess. Is it Daisy?" Taylor teased, hoping to bring something out of the child.

She shook her head slowly.

*Progress!*

"Oh, okay. Not Daisy. What about Tulip?"

Another head shake.

"Well, I don't know, then," Taylor said, smiling widely. "You win. You'll just have to tell me. If you do, I'll get you a candy bar."

"Molly," the little girl muttered, her mouth still full of hotdog.

Taylor smiled. It was only a first name, but that was a start. She led Molly to the candy bar section.

Molly chose some Reese's Peanut Butter Cups.

"Do you know your last name?" Taylor asked, as she opened it for the girl.

Molly looked at her blankly. Then she took the peanut butter cups and started eating the middle out of one, her sloth still tucked under her arm.

Taylor scrutinized her tiny legs and arms again. Her neck. All without touching her. She'd also noticed the little girl walked fine. Still, she had to ask.

"Has anyone hurt you? Do you have any ouchies?"

No response.

Taylor had a feel for these things and didn't see any signs of physical abuse, though that would be up to social services to

11

determine if she needed a thorough medical exam. As for other abuse, that would take a professional's opinion because invisible scars were the hardest for a child to reveal.

The clerk and Clint approached.

"Her first name is Molly," Taylor said. She turned to the attendant. "Text everyone you know who comes in here as a regular. Describe Molly and ask them if they know who she belongs to."

"We need to call social services," Clint said, taking out his phone and dialing. "Then I'll take her in."

Taylor replied. "It's a miracle that something didn't happen to her out there walking along the road. Someone is going to have to answer for it. At the least, when we find out where she lives, they're going to face reckless conduct."

When Clint turned his back and began talking into the phone, Taylor took Molly's hand and led her outside to her cruiser. She buckled her up in the backseat, then got in and started the car and pulled out.

They had ten minutes to talk, and Taylor hoped Molly would give her another clue, but even if she didn't, the last thing the poor kid needed tonight was to take a ride with Creepy Clint.

# CHAPTER 2

*T*aylor swung through the door at social services, her hand clasping the limp one belonging to Molly. She left the little girl and a quick explanation with the receptionist and went straight down the hall to Wesley Wright's office.

He looked up when she stopped at his door. As usual, he looked harried and overworked, quite manic, reminding Taylor of a man about to jump out of a skyscraper window.

He was not happy to see her.

"I don't have time for anything else, so please don't ask."

"You always say that." Taylor opened her phone and scanned to the last photo taken, then turned it around to show him. "This little girl's name is Molly. Don't know her last name. Approximately three to five years old. She walked into a convenience store an hour ago, barely dressed and trying to buy food. Is she one of your cases?"

Wesley took his glasses off and squinted at the photo. "I don't think so. Where is she?"

"The lobby. I didn't want to wait all afternoon for you to get there, so I brought her in myself. Can you look her up in your system? Don't you have a way to pull up every child named Molly?"

He gave her an exasperated look. "That's a popular name. It'll take some time to sort by first name and then an age range. If you can't tell, I'm buried over here, Deputy Gray." He gestured to a pile of folders on the corner of his desk.

Taylor glared at him. "Deputy Gray, huh? Oh, it's Taylor when *you* want something, like an escort to a questionable home, but more formal when you don't have time for what I need. So, what do we do with this little girl in the meantime? She's exhausted. And I'm not even supposed to be on call until tonight. I need to get some sleep before my shift starts. Help me out here, *Wes*. What do I do with her?"

Wesley ran his fingers through his hair and stared at the ceiling. "I don't know. Seriously, this isn't a good time, Taylor. We have two on vacation this week, and I'm juggling some crisis cases here."

"*This* is a crisis," Taylor said. "There's a little girl out there, and someone might be frantic trying to find her."

He shook his head. "No. You don't want me to show you crisis. I'm talking some really bad stuff. A half-naked, hungry child has nothing on what I'm working on."

Taylor held her hand up to stop him. She didn't want any more details. She'd collected enough real-life horror stories to last her a lifetime. Some were even her own.

He sighed. "Does she appear to be physically harmed?"

"No. But she's still a half-naked, hungry child. Well, maybe not hungry now. She's stuffed with convenience-store food at the moment. What she needs is a bed in a safe place until we can figure out who she is."

"I don't even have transport today," he said.

They stared at one another, waiting to see who would break first. It didn't matter that there were policies in place. They'd broken them many times before. That's what small towns did. Whatever it took to get the job done.

"Fine. Tell me where you want her to go, and I'll take her. You can start the paperwork and search your files. If she's in the system, we could find out if she got out of the home by accident, and maybe it's as simple as taking her back and giving a warning."

Or reckless endangerment, depending on the situation, but Taylor kept that to herself.

"Maybe," he said. "But unlikely."

"Just tell me where to take her, Wesley. I need to get home."

"I'll have to make some calls, but it will probably be the Johnsons."

Taylor recoiled. "No. Not there. This little one is too fragile to go over there into that mess with all those teenagers. What about Louise Lansford? She has littles, right?"

"Can't. She's got a full house and is ready to pull out her hair. She told me last time I visited to not even ask her again for a while. And I could lose my job if the state finds out how many she already has."

That was disappointing. Louise was good with the small ones. Especially those who were traumatized.

Taylor tried to think of who else would be a good fit. She knew most of them. It was a small county, and unfortunately, law enforcement and children's welfare services worked on parallel lines most of the time. Top that with the fact that small towns never had enough approved foster homes, and it was always a struggle.

The paperwork involved to get her into a home across the county line made Taylor cringe. There had to be someone in Hart's Ridge.

He looked at her, his gaze hopeful. "Do you think you could talk Della Ray into taking her? Just until we find out who she is?"

"No way." Taylor shook her head. "You know she's retired."

15

Della Ray Hart was the best foster mom in the county, and everyone knew it. She'd taken in and raised a lot of wayward or just plain needy kids. She was firm but loving. Just what a child needed in such an upside-down world. She'd nurtured—and straightened out—a lot of hurting children.

Including Taylor and her sisters.

However, after decades of providing that safe place to land, Della Ray had finally agreed it was time to give up being a foster placement. Her fight against breast cancer was put as priority one, and even though she was now in remission, her doctor had recommended she stop taking on too much stress.

Taylor—and many others, too—was very protective of her.

Wesley pecked his pen on the desk, rapping louder with each second. "Fine. Then I'll have to put her where I can, and I don't want to hear anything about it. I'm a caseworker, not a miracle man. Give me a few minutes, will you?"

His phone was already in his hand when Taylor backed out of his office and returned to the lobby. She felt bad for him, but he'd signed up for the job. She had to give it to him. He was a hard worker and had lasted longer in his position than many of them had. It seemed like if the words *social services* were on the building, it came with a revolving door.

In the lobby, Molly was still in the chair Taylor had left her in, staring out the window as she clutched her sloth. The fleece blanket from the trunk of the cruiser was gathered around the girl's waist, leaving her arms bare.

"She hasn't moved," the receptionist said.

*And you haven't even tried to make her feel more comfortable*, Taylor wanted to say, but the truth was more than likely the young woman was a temp. She wouldn't know what she was allowed to do or not do with an intake. And it was probably better to say and do nothing than for her to do something to further traumatize Molly.

But this wasn't Taylor's first rodeo.

"Here. Let's fix this," Taylor said, approaching her and pulling the blanket up around her shoulders.

There was still a bit of ketchup on the girl's face, and Taylor rubbed it off with her thumb.

Molly didn't flinch at the touch, but she also didn't respond. Not even eye contact. She kept her impassive gaze on the parking lot outside, appearing resigned to whatever fate they decided for her.

But who was she looking for?

That's what Taylor wanted to know.

"Better yet, let me find you something to wear."

Taylor went down the hall to the supply closet. She pulled out a cardboard box from the bottom. It contained found items discarded by children who came through the building, whether there to be dropped off or scheduled for a supervised visit. It was always puzzling to Taylor how kids just discarded clothes and no one with them noticed. A sock here, a shoe there. Jackets and scarves. Gloves.

You never knew what you'd find in the box, and Taylor had rummaged through it many times over the years.

This time, she hit pay dirt when right on top she saw a tiny pink sock. She dug through and found a blue one, though a bit bigger. But when she spotted the small pair of stretchy purple pants with unicorns, she felt like she'd won the lottery. At the bottom was a thick sweater too. A few sizes too big, but it'd work.

No shoes or jacket, but she couldn't have everything on her wish list.

She gathered her bounty and headed back to the lobby.

"Molly, I know these aren't your clothes, but they'll keep you warm," Taylor said.

She went to the girl and gently pulled her off the chair, letting the blanket fall to the floor.

"Can you put these on?" She lay the pants and socks on the chair.

Molly didn't say anything, though she didn't try to move away.

Taylor sat in another chair and pulled the girl onto her lap. "Let me help you."

She pulled the socks up her skinny legs and then, with her arms around the girl's gaunt body, she worked to get the pants over her feet and pulled up to her waist. They were at least six inches too long, so Taylor set Molly in the chair, then bent down in front of her and rolled the pant legs up. The sweater went over her head, but Taylor had to work limp arms into each hole.

Working with her felt familiar, in a way that bit at Taylor's soul, and made her struggle to push memories away. She used to dress Lucy when she was little, too.

When she finished, she stood and turned to find Wesley standing over them. He looked earnest.

"Well?" Taylor said.

"Everyone else is full. Will you please call Della Ray? Or *you* could always take her home with you for the night." He raised his eyebrows.

A silent challenge.

Her move.

# CHAPTER 3

$\mathcal{T}$aylor slowed the car to a crawl when she turned off onto Della Ray's road. The enticing views of the lake guarded by a wall of mountains on either side grabbed her attention, and she immediately felt calmer. The water always did that to her—something about the silent world underneath soothed the constant worry that bristled in her veins.

She saw two kayakers moving through the water, their strokes long and smooth as they glided across it like it was glass.

It had been a while since she'd done that herself but seeing them now made her pledge to find some time to get out there soon. She needed to feel that welcome burn from exercise that brought her internal energy down to a manageable level.

She glanced in the mirror at the back seat. Molly didn't look up. She hadn't made a peep since Taylor had put her in and buckled her up. She had barely even acknowledged Bernard who still sat in the passenger seat, though the dog was interested in their little visitor, judging by the way he kept trying to look behind him to see her, his tail thumping against the seat.

Taylor told him to stay put, and thankfully, he listened. She didn't know if Molly liked big dogs or not, and now wasn't the time to find out.

"We're here," she said, pulling up the driveway to the house.

She shut the squad car off. She'd called in her location on the way and was going to have to deal with her sergeant breathing down her neck for getting off course.

But Taylor knew that Della Ray could muster up a firm no on the phone.

That's why a visit was in order.

Taylor hadn't been here in a while, but the house still looked as cozy and inviting as ever, though maybe just a little rundown. The grass needed mowed, and it appeared no one had gone after the weeds in a while. But it still gave Taylor a warm feeling to just be there.

The rocking chair on the front porch beckoned at her; the once-colorful jute rugs scattered around begged her to tread across them, and even from the car, Taylor could see a dainty hummingbird fluttering around a ruby-red feeder.

A weather-beaten sign still hung over the front door.

*Welcome To My Porch; Stay A While.*

Taylor had drunk many a glass of sweet tea up there, swaying in the porch swing as she worried about her future. Pots of over-grown ferns hung from the beams, just as they always had. They were the perfect pop of green against the faded whitewash of the house and the black shutters.

Della Ray loved her ferns. Taylor used to hate them. It had been her job to keep them watered, and those suckers were insatiable in the hot Georgia summers. To her teenage eyes, they'd looked like weeds.

Now that they weren't her responsibility, they looked less

hostile and demanding. She could see the charm now. Though actually, they could use some watering, and she was tempted to take on the chore again.

The land around Hart's Cove was beautiful, and Taylor had always wondered why Della Ray didn't sell some of it—at least enough to either build a nicer home or to renovate the one she lived in. There were a few other houses in the cove, too, and those belonged to Della Ray's daughters, who had invested in building nicer places on the parcels deeded to them. Their houses were of the small lake cottage style that was so popular, but Della Ray still lived in the plain white clapboard home that she'd moved into after marrying her husband.

Taylor had arrived here as a foster when she was fourteen, and the almost five years she'd lived with Della Ray off and on had been the best in her life. The woman had saved her, as she had many others just like Taylor.

The house itself had its own character and way of comforting a lost soul. Even a bit neglected, it was still a beautiful home set in an even lovelier place.

Della Ray Hart and her late husband weren't rich when they'd married. From what Taylor knew, they'd started their lives out barely getting by. Later they'd inherited the undeveloped land around their cove, and with its peaceful lake views and the ongoing scarcity of real estate in their town, it was now worth a fortune. Not that the wealth was anything Della Ray coveted. She was a woman of worth—but it was in her life lessons, not her possessions.

One nugget from Della had stayed with Taylor for all these years. She and her sisters had gotten into a terrible argument that Della had stepped into the middle of when the dirt slinging got too deep for them to sort out without her.

"Girls, be mindful before speaking, and let your words pass through three gates. Are they kind? Are they true? And most of all, are they necessary?" she'd said on too many occasions to count.

That was advice that had served Taylor well as she and her sisters had grown older, and their family issues had only progressively grown worse. She just wished her sisters had also heeded the advice. Some of the things that Lucy had said to her time and again still rang in her ears. Terrible words. Accusations. Most of it said on a cloud of alcohol or who knew what, but still hurt.

"Come on, Molly. Let's introduce you to Miss Della Ray and see what she has to say about loaning you a bed for a few days."

Not that she expected it, but Molly didn't react. Taylor climbed out and went around and opened the back door, guiding the girl out of her seat belt and the car. She felt guilty leaving Bernard in the car again, so she opened his door and let him jump out. He ran to the bushes next to the driveway and lifted a leg.

As they approached the door, Taylor heard children. Then barking. Well, yapping was more like it.

She smiled. The alarm had sounded. She wouldn't even have to knock.

Della Ray met her at the door, swinging it wide as she stepped out onto the creaking porch, two or three small dogs at her heels.

"I saw the car out the window and hoped it would be you," she exclaimed, then wrapped Taylor in a huge, warm hug. "Where have you been, and why haven't you been by?"

Taylor laughed as one of the pups jumped up and down like a little kangaroo, trying to get her attention. "It's been busy. I got a dog, too." She gestured at Bernard, who was now sniffing everything up the path. "He's had me tied down to the house when I'm not working."

Della Ray stepped back and gave Taylor a funny look. "You always said my little rats drove you crazy."

"They did—I mean, they do. I didn't get one of those. I got a real dog. He's at least sixty-five pounds."

Della Ray laughed. "I see that."

They had an ongoing banter about the small pack of rambunctious Yorkie dogs that were always in and out of the house. Della Ray's rescue efforts weren't just limited to those with only two legs.

"So, who do you have here?" Della Ray asked, looking down at the girl and smiling gently.

Taylor saw the way Della Ray took in the whole package, from matted hair to dirty face, and skinny arms and legs. She didn't miss anything. Never had.

As for Molly, she was finally showing some interest in something. One of the smallest pups, an old one from the looks of his solid white hair and the tongue that hung out the side of his mouth, was practically dancing around her little legs, begging her for attention.

"This is Molly," Taylor said.

"Hi, Molly. I like your sloth. And you know what? If you sit down on the porch, little Grandpa there might crawl in your lap and give you lots of stinky kisses."

"Grandpa?" Taylor asked Della Ray, raising her eyebrows.

The pup wore a tiny Superman shirt—an altered baby onesie, from the look of the jaggedly cut hem that hung around his bony hind end.

"Yes. Well, I named him Oliver, but everyone started calling him Grandpa, and it just stuck. He thinks he's the patriarch of the pack, and he's always first to welcome any visitors."

Molly crouched down, and Grandpa raised up and kissed her, his long loopy tongue brushing her cheek and causing a small giggle to erupt.

Taylor's eyes widened. "That's the first bit of life she's shown," she whispered to Della Ray. "She wandered into a convenience store a few hours ago, cold and hungry. Barely dressed. All alone."

"Well, no wonder Grandpa is bonding with her," Della Ray said. "I found him in a ditch a week before last Christmas when we had that cold snap. Cold and hungry. Just about starving to death. Like this little one."

Taylor sensed this was the moment.

"She needs you, Ms. Della Ray. We don't know who she belongs to, and she needs a place to stay while we figure it out," Taylor whispered.

Della Ray leaned in closer to Taylor. "You know I'm not taking any foster kids anymore. I'm just too old now."

"I know. And I'm sorry to ask you. But Wesley was going to place her with the Johnsons. Everyone else is full up."

That caught Della Ray's attention. She also didn't approve of the way Jessica Johnson ran her house or treated her foster children. It wasn't that the woman neglected or abused them, but she let them run wild, and per Della Ray, didn't teach them anything about how to overcome their trauma or any life skills to help them function once they left her home. Della Ray always said that fostering was a calling, and you had to be led to do it by a higher power, not a paycheck.

From inside the house, there was more laughter.

"I've got grandkids today and tomorrow," Della Ray said. "I guess it's a good thing, so this little Molly won't feel all alone with an old lady like me. But only a few days, Taylor. I mean it."

Taylor leaned over and kissed her. "You're the best."

"So I've been told," Della Ray said, winking at Taylor.

"I'll call you as soon as we find out who she is."

Taylor turned to Molly and crouched down to her level. "Molly, what do you think about staying here with Grandpa today? And maybe tomorrow? Ms. Della Ray will give you a yummy supper and maybe a bubble bath later. I'm pretty sure that little Grandpa will want to snuggle with you at bedtime, too."

Molly looked up and nodded, then went back to rubbing the belly of the little old fellow who had first done a little happy prance at the attention she gave him, then flipped over and put his paws in the air, his invitation to keep the love coming.

Taylor used her phone to snap a few close-ups of Molly, then stood and turned to Della Ray.

"I can't thank you enough," she said. "But I gotta run."

"Wait," Della Ray said. "Have you heard from—"

"No." She was off the porch and headed to her car when Della Ray called out, a warning tone in her voice. "Two days, Taylor."

# CHAPTER 4

*B*y the time Taylor returned home, she had less than four hours to get enough sleep to get her through her last shift before her weekend started. She was going to need to stand under some hot water to trick her body into being sleepy.

"Let's go, bud." She hurried Bernard in through the back door. "I'll feed you when I get out of the shower. And I hope you liked your field trip because that's the last time you'll get to ride along. Let's just hope Clint didn't see you. He'd love to see me get a nice, firm disciplinary slap."

Bernard looked disappointed. As though he understood he was going to be left home alone again.

"You're something else," Taylor said, shaking her head. "Sometimes you play deaf, and other times I'd swear you know exactly what I'm saying."

She left him staring after her, and fifteen minutes later, with wet hair and her softest lounging clothes on, she made her way back through the house.

"Bernard?" she called.

He was being awfully quiet.

She stopped cold in the middle of the living room, finding herself staring at a blizzard in her kitchen.

Seemed that Bernard had an affinity for Charmin Plus.

If it had just been the roll from the bathroom, that would've been easier to deal with, but no, she'd been in there, so instead, he'd found the entire family-size package from the pantry.

Sixteen glorious and expensive rolls of the good stuff.

Obviously, dogs didn't understand tight budgets.

The tissue was at least a foot deep, spread from corner to corner and trailing out of the room into the hallway.

"Bernard?" she called out. "I know you're hiding. Come out, you coward."

He crept up so quietly she didn't know he was there until he peeked around the corner, his expression as guilty as could be.

"Why? Couldn't you have at least left me one roll?"

She paused, as though he could answer her. But he slipped backward, disappearing again.

"In fifteen minutes? How is that even possible?"

Taylor cursed under her breath. She couldn't be mad at him. It was her fault for leaving the pantry door open, but that didn't take away the fact that cleaning up the mess was going to take valuable time away from the rest she needed.

"I guess you'll be eating the cheap stuff next week so we can buy more toilet paper. I hope you like Alpo," she muttered, an empty threat, and they both knew it.

After grabbing a trash bag from under the sink, she began gathering the tissue. She contemplated saving it—it was a splurge for the name brand anyway—but decided it wasn't worth the anxiety it would cause her to look at it for another month. As she stuffed the bag full, she could only imagine the expression on the trash guy lucky enough to pick it up, expecting heavy household garbage, and instead throwing what amounted to a puffy cloud over his shoulder and into the truck.

Finally, she finished and went to the bedroom.

"Crap, I forgot to let him out to pee." She was turning out to be a terrible dog-parent.

"Bernard?" she called. "Need to go out?"

He was waiting at the front door. He didn't seem to notice that his special project had disappeared and his path to outside was cleared again.

Taylor opened the door, and he slipped out and immediately relieved himself on the closest bush, then to another. He'd be busy for a while, marking as many places as he could.

She sat down on the porch steps.

In this place she called home, the mountain air was crisp and clean, the multitude of hiking trails a salve to her restless spirit, and her modest house on the lake, her sanctuary. Her tiny piece of heaven was only six acres, but it had a gorgeous view of the lake and sat on what was once Cherokee land. She swore she could feel the spirits of warriors and their maidens who roamed it many years before.

The house was officially hers now, bought at auction when her dad had failed to pay taxes for six years. Her father had brought them from Montana to Hart's Ridge after the big fire. Taylor was the eldest daughter at ten years old then, and she'd loved everything about their new place. Years later he abandoned it, running from all his mistakes he'd made there as a father. Now he stayed in a single wide trailer out by the old railway house, his pension never quite enough to pay rent after he bought a month's worth of cheap vodka to pour down his throat.

Jackson Johnson Gray used to be a proud man.

Those days were over, and now, he wasn't too proud to let his eldest daughter make up the difference to pay his bills, either. Taylor did it quietly because she never wanted him to feel less than.

The house and the land held memories that she never wanted to let go of, coveting the days of their childhood before her father took his evening glass of whiskey too far, and it took hold of his soul and took over who he was.

She loved watching the sun rise between the mountains. The rare times she was up for it, she'd drink her coffee looking out the same panes of glass, never failing to think how much her mother would've enjoyed it there.

They'd lived on a lake back in Montana, too, and it wasn't unusual for her parents to sneak off in their boat at bedtime for a moonlight cruise and hold hands as they danced down to the dock in their few minutes of freedom. When they returned, her mom would come check on all of them, leaning in to plant a gentle kiss on their foreheads, and Taylor would smell the sweet, strange scent of something she didn't understand.

Whatever it was, it was always a reprieve from the times that they argued, and things got scary. Most of the time, it started over money. Paying bills. Or not being able to buy groceries because their dad bought beer instead.

But they always made do. Somehow.

Her mom used to create all sorts of creative concoctions from the modest budget she had to work with. Taylor suddenly remembered the sun tea. Summer wasn't summer if there wasn't a gallon jar in the kitchen window with tea bags hanging inside, the warmth of sun rays turning the water a golden brown before her mom added a ton of sugar and poured it into the scarred Tupperware cups with two ice cubes each.

After her mother died, she had never had sun tea again.

Now the place was all hers, and she had big plans to make it nice again. One day, when she had more money. Right now, it was fine. Cozy and clean—nearly unrecognizable from the dump they'd grown up in, except from the outside.

Her sisters had begged her to let it go. To move on from the bad memories made there. But the house was just a house and salvageable at that. Her sisters refused to remember the good times made there.

Not to mention that Hart's Ridge was in Taylor's blood.

She felt protective of it.

Some people ran from trouble, but Taylor had always run toward it—in a good way. Not that she was any kind of super-hero, but she was serious about her job, doing what she could to stop criminals and prevent drug activity from becoming rampant in her town. She wanted Hart's Ridge to stay as pure as it possibly could in today's terrifying world.

Bernard returned to the small concrete pad and lay down, a long sigh escaping from him before he closed his eyes. He was going to need a little more stimulation before she could go to bed guilt free. With her luck, the second she lay down, he was going to have the zoomies around the house.

She went to the crate of dog toys she had sitting on the steps.

"Want the ball, Bernard?" she said, holding a ball over his head.

When he still didn't respond, she tossed the ball back into the crate. It was overflowing with everything a dog could ask for. Toys, chews, and even a bully stick or two.

He'd barely touched any of it in the two weeks she'd had him.

Bernard was a strange dog. What kind of Labrador retriever didn't want to chase a ball? That's what *retrieve* meant, after all, or was she crazy?

Her dog was broken.

She should insist on a refund. Or a replacement. Whatever.

He must've felt her stare because he slowly opened his eyes. She went to him and squatted, then rubbed his velvety soft ears. Her heart broke because she could feel his sadness.

"Bernard, we can't keep on like this. If you aren't happy here, I need to take you back. Or we could go to the vet. Get some medication."

Her threats didn't faze him. Not even an ear flick.

Medication sounded like a horrible idea. She didn't want to drug her dog to make him happy. She'd done a little online research in some dog groups, and the number of pets on Prozac was concerning.

"Everyone said rescue dogs are the most grateful in the world. This is a good home. You don't want to go back to the shelter, do you?"

He looked bored at her speech.

All she could figure out was that he just wasn't interested in being her dog. She wanted to bond with him. She wanted it to work so badly that it was all she thought about. She'd never failed at anything. Even when everyone told her she couldn't become a police officer because she was petite and could never pass the physical test, she'd ignored them. When she graduated, she never rubbed it in to the naysayers. She let the shiny badge and uniform she wore do the talking for her.

"Fine, Bernard. You don't want the ball. You don't want the toys. What *do* you want?"

He stared with those damn beautiful eyes. Eyes so dark and so deep that you could swim in them, giving true meaning to the phrase "puppy-dog eyes."

His eyes were what drew her to him and had landed him a spot in her car, riding home with her. He'd looked a little tall and silly sitting there in the seat, and much too quiet, but he sat up and seemed intent on seeing everything out the window as she drove him to his new home.

Looking back, it felt like he'd been searching. And every day since, she had gotten the same feeling. He was always at that damn window.

"Bernard, let's go," she said as she grabbed the leash from the hook next to the back door.

He ignored her.

"Want a walk?"

He turned to look, and when he saw the leash dangling from her hand, he perked up.

"I should've just taken you to begin with," Taylor muttered as she attached the leash to his collar.

It was frustrating that he barely batted an eyelash when she called his name. However, he knew the word *walk* really well.

They started down the path toward the dock, and he stayed close to her side. Someone had trained him to heel.

"We need to step it up, bud. I have to get some sleep before I go to work."

She could've sworn his shoulders slumped a bit at that statement. To be honest, it really made her feel awful to leave him alone for so long. The isolation couldn't be good for him, especially since he was showing signs of depression.

Either that or he was just a moody dog. Which would be exactly her luck to go in and out of dozens of possibilities, only to choose one who had issues.

"I'll try to come home early, okay?"

She rolled her eyes at herself. Now she was trying to placate a dog.

Taylor mentally checked off what she needed to do when the walk was over. She always did that. It was so hard for her to enjoy the moment of anything—because she was usually planning out what was next.

She needed to get her butt to bed was what she needed to do first. And she would, as soon as she checked her email for a message she knew most likely wouldn't be there.

But she'd never give up hoping.

Lucy had left angry. Taylor just prayed she was still out there somewhere, alive and thriving. Was an email too much to ask? One line? Maybe two?

They entered through the back door, and she released the leash. Bernard turned and looked at her, gave her a long sigh, then went back to the window. He wasn't happy, but at least she could try to catch a nap without guilt.

32

A glimpse of orange in a basket on the kitchen counter caught her eye.

Leftover candy from last Halloween. Taylor never got trick or treaters, but it didn't stop her from stocking up when the candy was marked down every year.

The Reese Cup that sat atop the pile beckoned to her, reminding her that a little girl was waiting to be reunited with her mother. Taylor knew what a terrible feeling that was.

There'd be no dozing off into a peaceful nap now.

# CHAPTER 5

*L*ater that night in the station locker room, Taylor looked around before dropping her towel. Bernard's sad face was still on her mind. Also, she'd only been able to grab a couple hours' sleep, and she was dragging.

On the other side of the wall, she could hear raucous laughter.

Admittedly, she was grumpy. Lack of sleep and dreams featuring the little girl running along a highway, scared. Unfortunately, Molly's face had kept her company all during the night. Today she'd canvas residential areas within the vicinity of the gas station Molly had wandered into. Hopefully she'd find who the girl belonged to and be able to close that case and get her big brown eyes out of her head.

Also, still no word from Lucy. Taylor thought of the empty email folder. Long ago, when she and her sisters had feared they'd be split up in foster care, Taylor had set up an email account and password that only they knew about. Their agreement was that if they wanted to reach each other, they should write an email, but not send it. If it stayed in the *DRAFTS* folder, no one could ever trace the IP address and find where that sister was.

Just in case they were hiding out for some reason or another.

Over the years, they'd used it often. Even Lucy had checked in, consoling Taylor when they had gone on too long without talking.

Another bout of laughter erupted behind the wall. You'd think the guys were at a frat party the way they went on over there sometimes.

Taylor remembered a night that her youngest sister had disappeared from the room they all shared at Della Ray's house. A few text messages later, and Taylor had an address. Another few, and she finally talked a friend with a car into coming to pick her up.

It was an out-of-control house party, and by the time Taylor arrived, Lucy was blackout drunk and had no idea who she'd been carousing with in the bedroom. Whoever it was had left her there to sleep it off, but in the state of undress that Taylor found her in, it was obvious something had happened.

With at least one guy, but who knew? Maybe more.

Taylor had struggled to get her clothes back on, then practically carried her out to the car and snuck her into the back door of Della Ray's house. She'd put her to bed, laying a bucket next to her for the sickness she was bound to have, and praying she wasn't pregnant.

They'd dodged that one, and back then, Taylor had thought that Lucy's drinking was the biggest problem in the world.

But it had got much bigger than that. The alcohol binges were simply a gateway to the next bad thing, then even worse stuff until her sister was in a spiral of self-destruction that all the love and caring in the world couldn't break her out of.

And now Lucy was MIA and had been for months. Taylor had turned her in as a missing person and followed every lead. Even personally verifying that each photo of every Jane Doe brought in was scrutinized, making sure it wasn't her little sister.

It was as though Lucy had stepped off the edge of the Earth.

The worry was killing Taylor slowly.

She took a deep breath, shaking off the memories and grounding herself back in the women's locker room. Her side grew quiet as the guys next door filed out and left the building, homebound for the day.

Taylor usually chose to get ready for her shift at work, because as soon as she walked through the doors, she felt like a different person.

Also, as the only female on nights, she had the place to herself.

She didn't mind the silence; it gave her time to prepare for a long night. Remaining alert and on guard was always her goal.

Expect the unexpected. Stay alive.

Admittedly, she missed the camaraderie and free-flowing conversation that happened in the sanctity of a busy locker room. Everyone knew that was where the bonding of partners and other cops really took place. It was akin to perching on barstools at the local bar, except with no tab at the end of the session. And they did that, too, down at the Bear's Den, but the locker room was where real talk was happening. That was where your peers sympathized with what it felt like to be shot at, or to lose a victim, or really any of the hard stuff one of them might experience.

To put it in perspective, the men's locker room was nothing fancy. Their budget couldn't afford anything like the bigger towns had. But it was an inner sanctum for the one-on-one peer therapy that they all insisted they didn't need. It was no secret that the last few years of civil unrest had made it even harder to be a cop. Officers were constantly exposed to all kinds of trauma, from domestic violence to deadly accidents, but even when they suffered emotionally from their work, they were resistant to formally admitting it. There was always the fear of losing their badges or being publicly humiliated.

Asking for help was rare, and instead, they supported each

other however they could with locker-room discussions, high fives, or a beer after their shift. Since Taylor was the only female deputy, she felt like an island to herself.

She shrugged. Let them leave her out of their talks. And their after-hours stuff. They still couldn't take away her badge. She was one of them whether they liked it or not.

Her slacks were so crisp she could hear them crinkle as she slid them on. As soon as the fabric touched her skin, she began to leave Taylor behind and become Deputy Gray.

She took pride in her job, especially since it came at a big price. Her own father had forbidden her to become a cop. He was still angry at her for disobeying him on that one. She should've told him her career choice was his doing, as she'd been privy to too many childhood scenes in which those in blue were the only thing separating her mother from his fists.

Taylor had loved her mom dearly, but she had no respect for anyone who would let someone beat them into submission. Her only thought as she'd gone through school was to get that badge and stop as many men as she could from thinking they were the almighty rulers over their wives.

Her pulse jumped erratically, so she switched her train of thought. She wondered what would happen that night. It was a full moon, and she didn't care what anyone said—more trouble was to be had during full moons. After three years on the job, she knew that all too well.

It wouldn't be a *routine* kind of night. Cops didn't even like that word. Just when you thought it would be an easy shift, something could happen. Some nights were crazier than others, and she could always hope she'd get called to nothing more serious than a barking dog, but that was unlikely.

That wasn't true.

She had to admit that a change in the monotony of cruising her assigned areas to watch for disturbances or traffic violations was welcome at times. However, she also knew that any simple incident could turn into a life-or-death situation. That was the nature of the work—try to maintain the peace but be ready for when it unexpectedly blows up.

After buttoning her shirt and ensuring it was tucked in properly, she put on her shoes. Then she slid into her vest and secured the Velcro, while she prayed for safety for herself and anyone else on shift that night.

Checking to be sure her handcuffs were on the final click for fast and easy administration, she attached them to her Sam Browne—her utility belt—then secured it around her waist. A quick check to be sure her firearm and taser were in place, and she braced her feet apart and adjusted everything until it fell into place.

Her piece and all the other equipment made it heavy, adding close to fifteen pounds and permanent bruising on her hips, though no one would ever hear her complain. Being a female in a police department meant if you didn't want a lot of crap thrown your way, you kept your mouth shut about any hardships, even if you heard the same complaint from the men day in and day out.

She slipped on her shoes and went to the mirror, turning to check her back. She couldn't have one little hair or loose thread out of place, or she'd be reamed out if it were spotted. The sergeant wouldn't cut her any slack and actually was a bit tougher on her than anyone else. The day he'd found that she missed a belt loop must've been the highlight of his year, the way he'd pounced all over it.

The memory still made her neck go red.

She headed to the conference room and stood in the back. Finally, after a fifteen-minute roll call with notifications of what was going on out there—a few more restraining orders than usual—Taylor went outside and inspected her car inside and out. She had to make sure the last guy she gave a lift to the "county motel" hadn't stashed anything, then she climbed in and pulled out of the parking lot.

Coincidentally, or not, Clint was right behind her. If he didn't start keeping his distance, she was going to have to report him. Some men couldn't take no for an answer, even if they knew that fraternizing in the same department was on the list of things to get fired for.

At the stop sign, she turned one way, and thankfully, Clint turned the other. Quickly, she notified dispatch that she was officially on duty, and she headed toward her first assignment.

On the way, she thought about Bernard. Though she tried to play tough, it was getting to her that they weren't bonding. He looked like a good dog. Intelligent. Friendly.

He wasn't old, either. You could tell that just by looking at his jet-black, sleek coat and his shiny white teeth. His shelter papers said approximately three years and healthy, yet he acted like a senior citizen.

She wasn't sure what to do.

It was Sheriff's fault. He was the one who had recommended she adopt a dog. He said it wasn't normal to be alone at her age.

At first, Taylor was offended and wondered if he said the same thing to the single guys under his command, but the more she thought about it, the more the idea had appealed to her. She'd never owned a dog as an adult, and it could be nice to have something to come home to. Something that thought she walked on water and spent its life waiting for her affection. She thought that on her days off, she could use it as an excuse to go hiking, something she hated to do alone.

A dog could be useful. He wouldn't stay out late and get drunk with the guys or get caught texting his ex-girlfriends. He wouldn't ask her to borrow money he had no intention of repaying, and he would do just as good a job of warming her bed as any man could. It all sure as hell sounded better than the last three lame boyfriends she'd had.

It was decided. A Glock and a good dog were all she needed in life anyway. Everything else was too complicated.

Being the thorough weirdo she was, she'd spent weeks researching the best breeds. A dog was a lifetime commitment, and she wanted to be sure she got the right one. But as she'd clicked link after link, devouring articles about different types of dogs for different personalities, she'd accidentally landed on a piece about the high number of black dogs in shelters and how they were usually left behind.

One thing hiding under her uniform was her overly soft heart and passion for fairness. A dog couldn't choose the color of his coat! Passing them by for being black was just cruel. It made her so mad she immediately closed the tab and went back to looking at stats about different popular breeds.

However, the black-dog-crisis article nagged at her for days until she was scrolling down her page on a social network and saw a post about a Black Dog Event at her local shelter. All adoptions for black dogs were free for the weekend.

She took that as a sign and headed down there.

Her friend Tina worked there and as it turned out, the discrimination-against-black-dog rumors weren't exaggerated. Black dogs and pit mixes made up the bulk of the shelter's dog inventory. She'd almost been tempted to give a pit mix a chance, but then she saw Bernard. Something about him drew her in for a closer look.

Tina had been thrilled that she'd taken Bernard, claiming that Taylor wouldn't be sorry because he was a gem.

The homecoming hadn't fit the fantasy she'd created. Instead of a deliriously happy and grateful dog settling in with her, she got a sulking pup. And he'd reminded her of someone.

She searched her brain, trying to remember who.

Suddenly, she was brought back to her first year on the job. As a rookie, she usually got the crap assignments, and one of those was constantly picking up a teenager who kept running from his foster home. She'd take him back, and one day she asked him why he was doing it because the people seemed nice enough.

"Because they aren't *my* people," he said. "I want to go home."

She wasn't ever able to fix that problem as his home was deemed unfit, but the memory stayed with her all these years, making her a lot more empathetic when she had to deal with rebellious teens. Of course, Bernard wasn't a kid, but what if he felt the same way?

Could he be grieving the loss of his home?

She wondered what the circumstances were that landed him in the shelter. She'd figured that like most dogs there, once he outgrew the cute puppy stage, his family had lost interest. In the back of her mind, she was tempted to start an investigation and track down where Bernard's beginning began, but for now, she had to get her head in the game.

Sergeant wanted her to canvas the area around the convenience store and try to find someone who knew Molly. The problem was that there wasn't anything close to the store.

Woodside Way was at least eight miles south of the store, but still the nearest multi-family complex. She pulled in and parked at the small building with the OFFICE sign in front of it. Next to the building was a small, defeated-looking playground. A swing drifted back and forth in the breeze, forgotten.

These complexes depressed Taylor. Too many memories.

She got out, secured the car, then went into the office. A man sat behind a desk. He looked friendly, if not a bit harried. A stack of folders sat next to his computer, and it appeared he was going through them one by one.

"How can I help you, Officer?"

Taylor approached him and showed him her phone screen. "Have any of your residents reported a lost child? This little girl showed up down at the store last night."

He peered at the photo, then shook his head. "I've been here

41

since daybreak and haven't heard a peep from anyone about a lost kid. Damn. She's little, too. I hope she's okay."

"She's fine right now. But we need to figure out where she came from. Do you recognize her at all?"

"I sure don't. I'm the property manager, but I'm only here in the mornings. Kids around here are usually at daycare or school during the day. It's mostly working families."

Taylor figured that.

"What about social services? They can't pull up her name and see if she's in the system?" he asked.

"We only know her first name is Molly. She hasn't given us, or doesn't know, her last name. But we're working on it. It's going to take time."

"Gotcha. Wow. Someone really dropped the ball letting her slide out alone. If she's not in the system now, she probably will be," he said.

"Maybe," Taylor replied. "Mind if I knock on a few doors?"

He shrugged. "Go ahead. Some of them probably won't answer even if they are home. It's rent day, and I've got some dodgers."

Taylor knew how that was. Too much.

She pulled a card from her pocket and laid it on the desk. "If anyone comes to you about a lost child, call me or the station. Don't give them any information."

"Definitely."

Once outside, she approached Block A. The complex was small, just two buildings of three floors of apartments. She had a plan to knock out a few doors at once. On the first floor, she went by six doors, knocking on all of them as she passed. When she got to the seventh door, only two of the previous six answered, and they stepped out to see who was there.

Taylor told the second one to wait, and she questioned the first, an elderly Asian woman, before moving on to the next.

With this strategy, she made contact with a total of sixteen residents, none of them claiming to have ever seen a child who matched the description of Molly or knew who she belonged to. Taylor was satisfied with those numbers, as she knew word of mouth would spread quicker than she could knock, and she moved on to the second building.

She thought she'd hit on something with one woman who at first appeared to recognize Molly's photo, but then decided it wasn't her after all. As Taylor knew was common, many of the residents were closemouthed and suspicious, but because it was such a young child, she felt like they looked a little longer than they normally would've.

More than two hours later, Taylor was confident that Molly was not from Woodside Way.

Hopefully, Wesley was having more luck than she was. Taylor was thinking more and more that Molly had to be in the state's system.

In the meantime, she had other orders to do besides Molly.

She peeked at her paperwork, memorizing the next address before starting the car. Restraining orders could be tricky, but Taylor didn't mind serving them, when she could find the perps. Most of them hid out or refused to answer the door because they knew what was coming.

She pulled up to what appeared to be an abandoned single wide trailer and called in her status, grabbed her clipboard, then climbed out. Two vehicles were out front, one with a flat tire and the other with the windshield busted out.

Dodging piles of trash and junk, she climbed the rickety steps and knocked on the door, then stepped back down to the ground.

No one answered, but she could hear a television playing inside. She stepped up and pounded this time.

That got someone's attention, and she could hear stomping coming toward the door.

"Who is it?" a woman called out.

"Officer Gray from Hart County Sheriff's Department."

"Whatdya want?"

"Open the door so that we can talk." Taylor's hand hovered over her weapon.

The door swung open, and a woman stood there, one pudgy hand around a can of Mountain Dew and the other on the knob. The stained purple nightgown she wore stretched too tight against her big bosom and only made it down to the top of her dimpled knees. Her hair was piled up in a scattered bun on the top of her head, a style that always reminded Taylor of a deranged pineapple.

She looked unfazed to see a police officer in her yard.

"Is Carter Anderson here?" Taylor asked.

"No," the woman said. She leaned against the doorframe; her body language irritatingly nonchalant.

"Are you related to Mr. Anderson?"

"I guess you could say that. I gave birth to the blood-sucking troll." She laughed; a sound that made Taylor feel like a screw was being driven through her ears with a high-powered drill.

"Is he in the home?" Taylor was starting to lose patience.

"I said no," the woman said and took a swig of her Mountain Dew.

"Where can I find him?"

She shrugged.

"If he is in there and you're lying about it, you could be charged with obstruction of justice," Taylor said, though the statement itself wasn't completely true.

Technically, he wasn't actually a fugitive. However, he was an abuser, so in her eyes, that was just as bad.

"I'm not obstructing anything. You want to look?" She stood aside, sweeping the air behind her with her arm.

Taylor could see the house was in worse shape than the yard. Going in would be a last resort. There was no telling what kind of creepy crawlies she'd have to fight off. The last thing she wanted was to bring home fleas to Bernard.

"Does he live here?"

"When he pays rent, he does," the woman said. "But if he ain't got it by Friday, he'll be out, just like his deadbeat dad."

"Okay, close enough. Consider him served," Taylor said, handing the paper from the clipboard to her.

The woman looked down at it in surprise. "You can't do that."

"I'm sorry to tell you, but I can. According to the law, I've used reasonable effort to notify Mr. Anderson, and if he doesn't appear for court, the judge will rule against him."

The trailer door slammed so hard it rocked the place. Taylor wondered how much flak Carter Anderson was going to get from his mom when he got home. The woman looked like she could take on a rattlesnake and a scorpion, all at once.

THREE HOURS, two traffic stops, and a lot of attitudes later, Taylor needed caffeine. Perfect timing because she'd just gotten a call for loitering around the Stop-A-Minute.

She could kill two birds at once.

Maybe three if she had time to use the loo.

She headed that way, still shaking off the insults from the last stop. The guy had rolled through a stop sign, failed to use a turn signal, and to top it off, was driving ten miles over the limit. Yet he hadn't seen the logic in why she'd pulled him over. It was exasperating that citizens thought cops just wanted to write out tickets. The truth was they just wanted them to obey the law.

She'd held out the ticket to him, and he'd snatched it from her hand and called her the c-word and some other lovely names. Because of her strict police academy training, she was able to keep her cool and walked off with her pride intact, though every fiber of her before-academy-training self would've liked to slap him with an open hand and a few more charges.

Back in the car, the radio crackled, and dispatch let her know her next stop after she took care of the loitering issue. A security alarm over on River Road. The address was familiar, and Taylor was ninety-nine percent sure it'd be a false alarm set off by raccoons or a bear, just like the three times she'd been there before for the same call. Still, it was her duty to check it out.

At the Stop-A-Minute, she pulled in slowly, scanning the building and parking lot for the suspects. It only took her a minute to see them leaned against the ice machine, no vehicle in sight.

Loitering wasn't that big of a problem during the day, but after sundown, and especially at a place with only one attendant working, they tried to keep a lookout for trouble and were better about enforcing the rules. Their town had its share of robberies, and they sure didn't want to encourage any gatherings at the all-night businesses. Keeping it from happening took too much time on their shifts. With a population of just over three thousand, their resources were low, and she was one of only six deputies.

She scanned the lot and then parked the car. She called in her status and climbed out. The two young men watched her, suspicion and distrust already painted across their pasty-white faces.

"Show me some ID, guys," she said as she approached them.

"Is it against the law to stand on a public sidewalk?" the tall one asked. He pulled a wallet from the pocket of his jeans, which were pulled down so far that at least four inches of his boxers were on display. He picked out an ID and handed it to her.

"Have some self-respect and pull up your pants," she said, taking the ID and examining it. He was local and over eighteen. She handed it back to him. "This isn't a public sidewalk. It's private property. And haven't you ever heard that nothing good goes on after midnight? Shouldn't you be at home playing your video games?"

"I don't have no ID, but why're you giving us trouble?" the other guy said, thrusting his hands into his pockets.

"Show me your hands," Taylor said, stepping back with her hand on her gun.

Hands in pockets were an automatic alarm.

"Damn," he said, throwing his hands in the air. "I ain't got nothing."

"Turn around and put your hands on the machine. Both of you."

Punk One complied, but Punk Two stared at her and laughed.

"And if I don't? You think you can handle both of us?"

"Man, just do it," the first punk said, his voice whining. "I'm almost off probation. Don't make this worse."

Taylor could sense trouble was coming, and she was ready for it. During her basic training, she'd always leaned toward the "police by consent" type of behavior. She had a knack for taking control of a situation with not much more than a discussion. She was never obnoxious and didn't bully, like some of the officers she'd trained with who usually resorted to physical power.

However, some people just hated anyone with a badge and were bound and determined not to cooperate no matter what. It was always dangerous territory when you ran into someone like that, and she knew she was facing one now.

She kept her voice neutral, but official.

"I'll tell you one more time. Turn around and put your hands on the machine. You are not being arrested at this time. You are being detained while we talk. For my security and yours."

The store employee and another couple came walking out.

"That's them. They've been here for over two hours. I told them to get out of my store. I'm pretty sure one of them was shoplifting, too," the employee said.

Someone in the crowd took out their cell phone and started recording.

"Step back and do not interfere," Taylor said to those moving ever closer to them, never taking her eyes off the two young men.

She considered calling for backup but quickly dropped the

idea. Both guys had at least thirty pounds on her, but she could handle it. She was trained for exactly this kind of situation, and there really wasn't an opportunity for her to step away.

All she had to do was remain calm.

"Hands on the machine," she warned again.

"You want me to turn around? See if you can make me, little girl," Punk Two said.

Calling her a little girl was his first mistake. His second would be his downfall.

Literally.

He raised an arm as though threatening to punch her.

Like lightning, Taylor stepped forward, and before he could react, she blocked his fist and then grabbed the front of his pants. He was a head taller than her, but she still jerked him up, knocking him off-balance just enough to kick his feet out from under him and send him slamming to the sidewalk on his back.

She kneeled over him, pushing her knee into his groin as she twisted the pants in her fist and straightened her arm, using the weight of her whole body behind her grip like a spear in his abdomen.

"Can little girls do this?" she asked him through gritted teeth.

He didn't speak.

"Dammmn…" Punk One said, sounding impressed as he turned slightly to see. He kept his hands on the ice machine.

Taylor leaned down close to Punk Two's ear and whispered, "Right now you look like a fool, and I can make it worse. But the other option is that you behave yourself and, in a few minutes, I get to use the bathroom and have a cup of coffee. Nod if you are ready to be good."

His eyes were bulging, but he gave one barely perceptible nod.

She jerked him upright, and he scrambled to get his feet under him, then with a little help from her, turned around and put his hands on the ice machine.

The small crowd gathering yelled appreciation for her efforts, and a few gave her applause. Taylor just wanted them to back off and give them some space.

"What the hell?" the punk yelled as Taylor brought one of his hands down and then the other around to slip her handcuffs on and give them a sound click. "What'd I do?"

Taylor dreaded the mound of paperwork he'd just caused her.

"You were stupid," she said. "And I hate stupid people."

# CHAPTER 6

aylor wished that Bernard's mood could match her own, but he was still sulky. As for her, despite the altercation the night before with the small-time punk who, unfortunately for him, was carrying a little baggie of hillbilly crack—their street name for meth—as well as a few items from the store, she felt great.

It was a good bust, and notwithstanding the paperwork, she was happy to get one more scumbag off the street, even if temporarily. Thus far, the town had mostly kept its innocence and avoided the onslaught of crime that other small towns were dealing with around the states, but a few small-time-wannabes slipped in now and then.

"You'll regret this. My dad's a lawyer," the punk had called out to her as he was being led to a holding cell.

She didn't care who his dad was. If Daddy Warbucks wanted to get him out, he'd have to pay a pretty penny to do so. Judge Crawford didn't go lightly on punks who tried to assault police officers.

Once she got home, she was thrilled to see that the only damage Bernard had done was to himself. His left foreleg was wet with slobber. Taylor examined it but could find nothing wrong, so she chalked it up to anxiety and went to bed, sleeping a full four hours before her first nightmare sent her to the kitchen for a glass of water.

Bernard padded around behind her, brooding as she told him to be quiet and let her go back to sleep. She wasn't sure if he'd slept at all.

He was going to have a better day today because she had the day off and had already finished her laundry, vacuumed the floors, and made a grocery run. She was trying to work fast, as once she made a quick visit to Della Ray's house, she had plans to do some sleuthing about Bernard.

First up, she tried Wesley at child services to see if he'd had any luck tracing a child named Molly. His voice mail picked up, and she left a message.

Next up, she dialed her friend Tina from the shelter.

"Hi. Don't tell me you're bringing Bernard back," Tina said, cutting right to the chase without pleasantries.

"Hello to you, too," Taylor said, laughing. "No, I'm not. But I am having some trouble with him."

"Has he bitten anyone?"

"No, of course not."

"Then everything else will fall into place when he's had more time. It takes a shelter dog anywhere from three to six months to come out of his shell and get comfortable."

"You haven't even asked me what the issues are." A little irritation was creeping in.

"Doesn't matter," said Tina. "I'm not letting you bring him back. I promise you; you will love that dog. Give it time."

"Look, Tina. This is the deal. He's sad."

"Of course he is! This place is traumatizing. He'll come out of it."

"No. He's sadder than he should be. I need to know where he came from so I can help him."

"I told you. He was relinquished."

"I need a name and address. Phone number if you have it," Taylor said, biting her lip. It was a long shot.

Tina laughed. Not an oh-that's-funny laugh. It was more like a you've-lost-your-mind laugh.

"Not happening," she said. "Taylor, you're too nosy for your own good. You should've been a bloodhound the way that you want to sniff out everything, but sometimes you end up chasing dead ends. Let it go."

Taylor considered. She hated to use up her favors too quickly. Tina only owed her one as it was. But this was important to her.

"Remember a few months ago?"

"Oh no, don't even go there, Taylor. I could lose my job," Tina said.

"He would've gone to jail for at least three days," Taylor said. "And possibly even had his license revoked."

"For reckless driving? I doubt it," Tina said. "And I told him not to tell you I was his sister. You shouldn't have let him off with a warning."

"But I did."

Tina was silent for a minute, then Taylor heard clacking against the keyboard. When she spoke again, she rattled off a name and address.

"I don't have a phone number for him. Most people dumping dogs don't want to be contacted again. And don't ask me for anything else, Taylor. I'll lose my job."

"Thanks, Tina. You're the best. I'll drop off some dog food later to show my appreciation."

"It had better be a premium brand," Tina said, then hung up the phone.

Taylor smiled. She wouldn't stay mad.

And now she and Bernard had a place to start. It was going to be an interesting day, to say the least.

"Bernard," she called out.

He looked up from his vigil at the window, his expression bored as usual.

"Want to go for a ride?"

That moved him. He jumped up and trotted to the back door, then sat down just as pretty as you please.

"You're something else," Taylor said, then opened the door and let him out.

On the way to Hart's Cove, she talked to him as he hung his head out the window, his ears flapping in the wind.

"I'm going to see if we can find out where you came from, Bernard," she said.

He ignored her.

It didn't matter. She was still going to see what she could do to find out what she could. Maybe if she figured it out, it would settle him down.

Maybe it wouldn't.

And maybe Tina was right—Taylor was just too nosy for her own good.

She finished the rest of the drive with the music up, tapping to the tune on her steering wheel until the Eagles trailed off and John Lennon's song "Beautiful Boy" started playing.

Taylor turned it up and let the music fill her senses.

*Was it synchronicity? Was Lucy thinking of her, too? Or just a coincidence?*

She arrived at the cove and flipped the radio off, parked the car, and she and Bernard headed for the porch. He acted like he owned the place now that he'd been here once.

"You are a visitor here, so behave," Taylor hissed at him.

His tail thumped on the wooden floor.

"Remember, I can always talk Della Ray into taking in one more stray," she threatened him.

He looked up at her, and his eyes danced mischievously.

"Oh, so now you're happy? What? You don't want to live with me?" She glared at him as she knocked again.

Della Ray answered and waved them inside. While Taylor sidestepped the little pack of dogs, Della Ray waddled off toward the kitchen as she spoke, her flip-flops slapping the tiled floor. Taylor noticed that she'd finally let herself go totally gray, the wispy strands struggling to stay put in the messy bun atop her head.

"C'mon," she called out. "Glad you're here. You can help set out lunch for the kids, and then we'll talk."

In the kitchen, there were five kids around the scarred, familiar table that had chairs enough for eight.

"You remember my grandkids? The three against the wall belong to Tricia. And there's the new one you haven't met yet, Olivia. She's Liz's latest. And of course, you know Molly."

Della Ray's grandkids were all in some stage of blonde hair. All blue eyes. Then little Molly sat there with her deep brown—and very sad—eyes. Dark, scraggly hair hung in her face.

She looked up at Taylor but didn't show much recognition, if any at all.

"Hi, y'all," Taylor said, smiling at them before directing her attention to the little lost girl. "Molly, remember me? I'm the sheriff's deputy. When you saw me last, I was wearing my uniform. I brought you here."

Molly continued to stare. She looked wary.

"She's not a talker, that one," Della Ray said. "But she is an eater. So, let's get some food on the table."

She pushed a big pot and wooden spoon toward Taylor, then slid a stack of plastic multi-colored Tupperware child's plates behind them.

The scarred-up plates had to be decades old. They were the original colors—brown, yellow, orange, and a few pukey-greens. Taylor's sisters Anna and Lucy had fought over the orange one, and Della Ray would award it to someone else every time. She didn't allow bickering in her kitchen.

Della Ray could easily afford new Tupperware or even the

finest China out there, but she was of a mind that if it wasn't broke, don't fix it. Things she owned were lovingly worn but kept until the good ran out.

The way it should be. Not like Taylor's sister Anna who had to have the latest styles of everything and spent money like it grew on trees to redecorate her home every other year, it seemed. She'd take it from rustic lake house to modern farmhouse, then back again when that didn't suit her well enough. She dressed her kids in clothes that were priced according to fad and the hard-to-get factor. She bought shoes that could feed a family of four for a week.

To a stranger's eye, Anna was the most settled at the surprising age of only thirty-one. She'd dropped out of nursing school to marry. Once a cheerleader, her looks and figure had attracted a fresh-behind-the-ears attorney from Atlanta, who snatched her up and immediately slid her into the role of a devoted wife and mother. Anna was ecstatic at landing a lawyer for a husband and had polished herself even more into the wife he wanted her to be.

Then she popped out two children in three years, joined the local country club whose members were never original locals, but instead was made up of those who bought property in Hart County and then built showy houses for weekend use until they retired there permanently.

Anna embraced them as her friends, but they only knew the improved Anna 2.0 after she'd shed all evidence of her less-than-modest upbringing. Anna liked to pretend that she wasn't part of a family who had beans and taters three times a week and had to share bathwater to keep the electricity bill manageable.

Taylor guaranteed that the ladies Anna lunched with and held book club with had no idea that their host used to hide in a closet with her sisters when their father was on a binge. Or that they'd learned how to bake before they hit puberty because sugar and flour and a few other staples were many times the only thing they had in their pantry. Or that in the winters when their father was too drunk to make it from his truck into the house, the four sisters rolled, pushed, and dragged him inside so he wouldn't die of hypothermia.

Yes, Anna put on a good show. She was a master of disguise, but underneath the smile, there was a hint of sadness. It was expected, actually. Their childhoods were tumultuous enough to leave a lasting impact on them.

Taylor looked in the mixing bowl and saw a hearty pile of steaming macaroni and cheese. The good kind—Kraft—not the off-brand cheap stuff her Dad used to buy.

"Jayden, get everyone a juice box from the fridge, please, dear," Della Ray said.

He jumped up and went to the refrigerator.

Behind them, Della Ray was plucking wieners out of a pot on the stove and putting them in buns before she laid them across a long platter.

Taylor couldn't help a chuckle that slipped out.

"Don't think I don't know what you're laughing about back there," Della Ray said.

"What?" Taylor asked, her voice innocent.

"You're thinking I've gone a little senile letting kids eat this kind of junk at my table."

Taylor raised her eyebrows. How did Della Ray always do that?

"That was exactly what I was thinking. Well, not the senile part, but you know what I mean."

Della Ray didn't turn around. "Taylor, this is the thing. I'm old. And I'm tired. And if a hotdog and a scoop of mac and cheese is going to fill those bellies up and put a smile on their faces for a little while, why should I kill myself putting together a meal that touches every food group? One that they will barely touch if I do! I'm going to give them what they want while they're at my house. I'll slip them a fruit snack for dessert, too."

"Got a point there, Della Ray. I'm not judging. I'm jealous, if you want to know the truth. I remember sitting at that table for hours one evening when I wouldn't eat my broccoli. It was a standoff to beat all others."

"Sure was," Della Ray said, laughing as she turned and set the hotdogs on the island, then began adding them to the plates. "And who won? You remember that?"

"I did," Taylor said, grinning.

She still recalled how good it felt when Della Ray finally told her to scrape her plate and put it in the dishwasher.

"Only because I let you," Della Ray said. "Each child was different. You'd been through so much. You always took on such a heavy responsibility trying to mother your sisters. You weren't ready to give up in front of them, so I let you have that one."

Taylor stopped, wooden spoon midair. "That's why you let me go to bed without eating it? To save face in front of my sisters?"

Della Ray nodded. "It sure was. I slowly eased you out of the role of authority instead of yanking you out of it like I could've done."

Taylor finished the plates, then helped Della Ray take them to the table. It was true. After their mother died, Taylor stepped in and made sure everyone did their homework, took a bath, ate dinner. Got up in time for school and didn't miss the bus.

It was a lot.

For the most part, she'd kept her sisters in line and doing what they were supposed to do. Until they all got old enough to be interested in boys. Then everything changed, and after they'd had to call the police too many times to settle their drunk dad down, they were gathered up and brought to Della Ray.

Only eight weeks the first time. Their dad promised he'd go to counseling and AA meetings and somehow got them back.

The next time was eight months, but that was after Taylor's sister Jo had been taken to the hospital by ambulance after she'd burned her hand helping Taylor cook.

While they bounced back and forth, Della Ray had done her best to teach them to be respectable young women. But hormones didn't always cooperate, and many nights Taylor had to sneak her sisters back into their room without waking Della Ray and Tom, her late husband. Or their daughters, who probably would've loved for them to get caught so they could have their home back, emptied of foster kids.

"I'm starving," Eli cried out, jolting Taylor from her thoughts and into helping Della Ray distribute mustard and ketchup.

When they finished, Della gestured for her to grab a hotdog and join her in the living room.

Taylor didn't need persuading. Hotdogs were her weakness.

Bernard was on her heels while she put one together on a plate and dabbed it with ketchup, then added mac and cheese, grabbed a fork and napkin, then joined Della Ray. She took a seat on the couch opposite her, while Bernard dropped down on the floor in a dramatic flounce, as though starving to death right before their very eyes.

"My knees are hurting," Della Ray said, leaning back in her rocking chair.

"Why are you still keeping kids, then?" Taylor asked between bites.

"The girls need my help occasionally. And I love having my babies visit."

Taylor nodded.

"Don't forget you dropped one off, too," Della Ray said. "And we need to talk about that. Any leads on who she belongs to?"

"Not so far. I left a message for Wesley, and he hasn't called me back yet. I went door-to-door at Woodside Way, too. Nothing. The sheriff submitted her profile to the National Center for Missing Children, and we've put out notices to all the surrounding counties in case she went missing from nearby."

"What about another foster?" Della Ray said. "I mean, I don't want to traumatize her more, but Taylor, you know I'm not even set up in the system anymore. We could both get in trouble."

"Wesley knows she's here," Taylor said. "If there was a better option, I'd take her. I promise. Can she stay a few more days?"

Della Ray rocked back and forth for a moment before nodding, filling Taylor with relief.

"How has she done so far?" Taylor asked.

"She took her bath and went to bed like a little angel. Today she's done everything I tell her to do. She just doesn't talk. Well, except to the dogs. They love her, and she just eats up their attention."

"Hmm. That's interesting," Taylor said. "They must have dogs where she lives because small children usually aren't that friendly toward big dogs, and she didn't even flinch when she saw Bernard in the car that first time. He even jumped out after her, and she didn't react. With his size, I think most her age would've been a little wary."

"I agree," Della Ray said. "I haven't really asked her too much because I don't want to scare her. But something tells me she understands just fine. She looks smart deep down in those dark eyes. Maybe she isn't telling us because she doesn't want to go back."

That thought disturbed Taylor because if a child didn't want to go home, whatever was waiting for them was probably something traumatic that they'd already survived at least once and didn't want to experience again. Thank God for Della Ray, who would gently care for Molly without causing any more emotional harm.

"Why do you do it, Della Ray? Or why have you done it, I guess I should ask?" Taylor said.

"What? Take them in when you say they need somewhere to go? How could I not, Taylor?"

"You could say no and really mean it next time."

Della Ray gave her a small smile. "Yes, I guess I could."

Taylor felt guilty for always coming back to Della Ray with some of the cases she came across. It had been a while since the last one, but she knew all along that she'd wanted Molly to come here and nowhere else.

In the kitchen, the kids laughed, and Taylor wondered if one of the voices was Molly's. But she didn't want to peek around and ruin it if it was. Bernard got up and rambled in there to see for himself what the ruckus was about.

Taylor looked back at Della Ray. "Does it ever hurt to say goodbye?"

"Oh goodness, yes!" Della Ray cried. "I've had my heart broken so many times that it's a miracle it's still beating in my chest. I wanted all of them. Every one of them. But that's not what I was called to do, Taylor."

"I don't understand," Taylor said.

She remembered the many times that she'd had to tell Della Ray goodbye before going back home again. How she'd wanted to stay there. To feel safe and loved. It hurt to leave. It hurt so very bad to go back to their house that was void of the mother figure she needed.

"You know that the wish of the state is always reunification if it can be done safely. No one wants to break apart a family, and sometimes the parents need a nudge in the right direction. Or a wake-up call. While they're getting their acts together, there are children who need a safe place to recover. And for some, we were the bridge between their previous upturned lives and another start with their parents—like you and your sisters with your dad. For others, we were the ones who prepared them for a new family to call their own. That's what we signed up to do, and who were we to take away the chance for a childless couple to finally get their dream granted and be parents? We already had our kids. I chose to help others get theirs."

"I can't imagine a harder place to be," Taylor said, blinking back tears.

"There isn't. Well, unless you are on the first part of that line and losing your child because you can't turn away from drugs, or alcohol, or you can't keep a roof over their heads. That is the worst place to be, in my opinion. Some of those people weren't terrible. They were just lost."

Taylor thought of her dad. He was one who couldn't walk away from the booze long enough to be anything other than a half-ass father to four daughters grieving their mother.

"I packed many diaper bags for visits and handed off babies or children to their social workers in the DCS parking lot for visits that scared me half to death. I'd return for them in an hour or two, relieved to have them back in my arms for however much time I had left before their last day with us. And I can remember every single one of them, Taylor."

"I'll bet you can," Taylor said, smiling at the old woman. "Nothing senile about you, Della Ray."

The back door slammed, and all the kid's voices dissipated.

"Darn right," Della Ray said, then popped up out of the chair. "I still got some get-up-and-go. Now, you get on out of here and enjoy your day off while I get these kids back in the house to clean up the kitchen. They have to do chores before they get their hands on some homemade popsicles."

Taylor groaned. Della Ray's popsicles were to die for. But she and Bernard had business to attend to. They rounded the corner into the kitchen, and Della Ray stopped so short that Taylor nearly ran into her.

"Well, would you look at that?"

Her grandkids were outside, but Molly was asleep, curled up in the corner behind the table, her head laying on Bernard's back as he pressed tightly against her.

"Bernard," Taylor said, ever so softly.

He looked up at Taylor, not moving anything but his eyes, as though he didn't want to disturb the small and needy body that he warmed with his own.

61

"You're a good boy. Yes, you are," Della Ray crooned.

Taylor wasn't so sure. She still had flashbacks of the toilet paper apocalypse that he'd left in her own kitchen. But she had to give it to him.

He had the touch.

# CHAPTER 7

*T*aylor pulled up to the corner and turned off onto Grouse Gap Road, then creeped along slowly. The change in direction sent a gale of wind through her open window.

As soon as it did, Bernard shrank back from his window.

"It's okay, boy."

He'd gotten a whiff of something he didn't like. Taylor didn't smell anything, but the dirt road was sure a mess. Way out here, the county didn't worry much about quality infrastructure, and it showed.

Her phone beeped a text alert.

> Not finding Molly in the system. Still looking. - Wes

Taylor hoped that something would come up in Wesley's further searches, but in the meantime, she hoped that Della Ray did her magic and cheered Molly up. Maybe even got her to talk a little. She'd always got through to Taylor when she was afraid. But never to Lucy. She was too guarded.

Like Molly, actually.

She hit a deep pothole and winced, hoping nothing was damaged. At the least, she was going to have to wash her car later, when she had more time. The road was also long and a bit creepy. Taylor wasn't in uniform, but she was packing, and that made her feel better. She wasn't scared of much, but the fact that she didn't know what she was coming up on made her cautious.

Finally, she came to a farm gate that framed another small road on her right side. A ragged metal sign hung by one screw on the post supporting it.

It read,

*No Trespassing*

It wasn't a road after all. It was a driveway—or what was supposed to be anyway.

She pulled up to it and got out of the car. Before she could shut the door, Bernard jumped out behind her, his tail tucked between his legs. He seemed to recognize the area and didn't want to be here, but Taylor could tell he also didn't want her going it alone.

"Good boy," she said.

She didn't want to go it alone, either.

She pushed the door, and the sound of it clicking shut carried through the thick pack of trees and started a chorus of barking.

That meant whoever lived here now had the upper hand. They had an idea they had someone on their property, but she didn't know who they were. Sure, she had a first name, but he could be any type of person. Way out in the Georgia sticks, you needed to be careful whose land you happened upon. Anything could happen, and you could disappear, never to be seen again.

That made her think of Lucy.

She shook it off and considered how much trouble she'd get in by knowingly trespassing. But she didn't have a phone number. And she really needed to know why he'd turned Bernard in to the shelter. To some, it might be a small and insignificant piece of information, but if Taylor was going to keep Bernard as her only constant companion, then damn, she wanted him to be settled. She felt in her gut that his previous owner could tell her something to help.

Not to mention she loved a good mystery.

She climbed the fence, and Bernard ducked under it to join her on the other side. He took his place beside her as she walked. The weather was cool, so she was glad she was wearing a light jacket, and it also covered her piece in case she didn't want anyone to see it.

They followed the driveway—or what was supposed to be a driveway—around the bend. She stopped when a small house came into view.

No signs of life, other than the dogs who were now howling their distress, somehow knowing a trespasser was trespassing even closer.

Bernard stopped and quivered slightly. He turned his nose back toward the car and then looked up at Taylor.

*Let's go back*, he seemed to implore.

"No, we're almost there. Don't be scared," Taylor whispered.

*Take in the scene, look for movement.*

She did that and saw none. The dilapidated house was quiet and looked lonely with one shutter hanging sideways. The paint was chipped and old. There were no children's toys around. No potted flowers to adorn the porch.

The only signs of decoration were a huge set of elk antlers mounted over the front door and a lone and beaten rocking chair. Hopefully, that meant he was old. Too old to be any trouble, if she were really lucky.

"Might as well get this over with." She started to take a step forward.

"STOP. DON'T MOVE," a loud voice called out.

Taylor stopped in place, cancelling the step forward as she squatted and put one hand through Bernard's collar and one on her gun. She fought the instinct to run for cover, reminding herself this wasn't a crime scene, and she wasn't chasing a criminal. She only wanted a friendly chat and some information.

A man walked out from the side of the house, holding a shotgun at shoulder level, his ease making it obvious he knew how to use it.

"What do you want?" he said.

Bernard growled low in his throat.

"It's okay, boy," she whispered, then raised her voice to answer. "I got your address from the shelter. I just wanted to ask you about this dog here that you dropped off."

The man walked closer, squinting at her, then Bernard. "Is that my dog?"

Taylor was still afraid to stand and let go of Bernard. She could feel the anxiety that raced through his body and made him quiver from head to toe. He didn't like this man.

"Well, technically it's my dog now. But I think he *was* your dog. I just wanted to ask if you had any other information on his past?"

She pulled her belt off and looped it through Bernard's collar, then stood, keeping a firm hand on it in case he bolted.

"Can we come closer?" she called out.

There was still at least a hundred feet between her and the man, and she didn't feel like wearing out her voice in a hollering contest.

"Wait," he called out sharply. "There's a trip wire less than twelve inches in front of you."

Taylor looked down at the ground in front of her and Bernard.

*What the hell? Why would he have a trip wire?*

"Okay, I'll be sure to step over it," she said. "Can I approach?"

*Never assume anything when you have a shotgun pointed at you.*

He nodded, then dropped the gun to his side.

"Come on in. The house is a mess, but I guess you probably figured that much," he said, then turned and walked back toward the house, assuming she was following.

Because of course she was. *No one ever said that Taylor Gray doesn't like to live dangerously,* she thought as she pulled Bernard behind her.

TAYLOR AND BERNARD were back in the car and on their way before dark. She didn't have the information she wanted, but she did know that Weldon Gentry wasn't the reason for Bernard's melancholy. She didn't know what was, but at least she had another clue. It was going to take some more tracking, but now she knew what to do next.

She shook her head at Bernard.

"He wasn't so bad."

Bernard scowled back.

"But I can see why you don't miss him."

Turns out that Weldon Gentry was a hoarder and a pitifully lonely man. Also, quite paranoid out there by himself, but other than that, he seemed harmless. Taylor had enjoyed his company. Somewhat. He used to be a log puller, and he told her all about how he was living off-grid what with solar panels, his own well, and a large garden that produced enough for him to can and stock up supplies in case the world began to fall apart.

He was really proud of his independence. There were a lot of people like him around Georgia, many of them higher up in the mountains with roads that would be nearly impossible to travel. With the way the world had gone to hell in a hand basket, more and more individuals were trying their hands at living off the land and staying away from others.

Weldon Gentry also regaled her with tales of his hunting trips

—his biggest prizes, his favorite dogs, and of course he'd laid out the reason that Bernard was no longer part of the pack.

Bernard had tried to save a prize chicken from a hawk attack and failed. Weldon Gentry said he'd howled as the hawk dropped nothing but feathers and flew off with its bounty.

Then he'd disappeared, and Gentry had looked for him well past dark and wasn't happy about it.

"When I finally found him, the damn fool had dug up under the chicken wire and was inside the chicken house, lying there with a clutch of orphan chicks huddled against him for warmth," he'd said, shaking his head as he looked at Bernard sitting in front of Taylor.

Bernard had stared back, guarded.

Taylor felt like he was acting brave for her sake. He hadn't relaxed until they were safely back in her car.

"So, you really are the good boy I keep calling you," Taylor said, reaching over the console to pat Bernard's head affectionately.

He stared straight ahead but let out a huff, or maybe a declaration of forgiveness. She wasn't sure. She only knew that obviously any dog with an affinity to help defenseless creatures wasn't going to be a good hunting dog, and the man's further stories confirmed that. Gentry had gone on to say that Bernard was a waste of kibble and shelter, and his lack of hunting skills had been the final straw that had got him deposited at the shelter.

Turned out Gentry wasn't too exasperated with losing a dog because he didn't have a lot of money in Bernard like he did some of his hounds. He'd gotten him from an ad in the paper advertising a free hunting dog. They were giving him up because he kept running away and they were tired of looking for him. He wouldn't play with their kids like they'd hoped, so they figured he just wanted to run and hunt, like the rest of his breed, and that it was unfair to make him be a yard dog against his will.

Taylor's stomach growled, and Bernard looked her way.

"Yeah, I'm hungry," she said. "We'll be there in a minute."

He stared back.

"Look at you, acting like you understand every word I say. I bet ole Gentry thought he'd gotten the deal of a lifetime finding you," Taylor said. "Turns out the joke was on him, huh?"

The family was going to be surprised, too, if Taylor ever found them. All Gentry had for her to go on was that he'd met them at the Tractor Supply parking lot two months before.

Taylor had eased him through the process of looking back at his personal stuff to figure out what date it was, but unfortunately, he'd accidentally dropped his phone in the lake when it fell out of his pocket while he was reeling in a big one. The new phone was clean, and the phone number and messages back and forth about the dog were lost. He didn't even remember their name.

The only thing he knew for sure was that he only looked at ads on Craigslist. It was going to take a lot of looking if it was even still there and not deleted. Hopefully she could find the archives on both.

"I'm not giving up, Bernard, but we need to wrap this day up."

He didn't argue. He looked tired. Hopefully so much so that she wouldn't have to take him for a walk when they finally got home after their last stop.

The rest of the ride was quiet, and when they pulled into the parking lot of the Bear's Den, she shut off the motor and took a deep breath. There were a few hole-in-the-wall spots around Hart County, but this one was the favored among the locals. By the count of at least seven vehicles parked around her, nothing had changed since her last visit.

"You can come in with me, Bernard. But you'd better behave, or they'll throw us both out."

He stared at her, willing her to open the car door. The delicious aroma of whatever was on the dinner menu for the night was wafting through her window, and she could see it was causing his nose to tingle with anticipation.

"I might treat you to a hamburger patty," she said. "If you can be quiet while I talk to my friend. Can you do that?"

She wasn't sure if "friend" was the right word, but it was close enough to what she felt for Cecil. He'd probably known her longer than anyone else who'd ever walked through those doors.

Time to get it over with.

She got out, and Bernard followed.

"Hey, Taylor," someone called from the other side of the parking lot.

Taylor turned.

"Hi, Chipper," she called out, seeing the man standing at the back of his truck, organizing stacks of firewood. "You doing all right?"

He nodded. "Doing fantastic! Let me know when you're ready for another delivery. I've got some good stuff right now. Seasoned red oak. I'm headed out to the sheriff's farm now to drop a load."

"I'm good for now, but I'll let you know," she replied, then waved goodbye and continued to the door.

Chipper Dayne always made her smile. His name was more for how cheerful he always was than for the fact that he made his living cutting and selling firewood across Hart's Ridge. No one even knew his real name, but everyone knew that the man could whistle like nobody's fool. Any song you requested; he could do it. Chipper wasn't a Hart's Ridge alumni, but he'd been there enough years and integrated so well that it was hard to remember that he'd once been an out-of-towner.

She smiled at the familiar sign at the door.

*No Cussing Allowed Through These Doors. One Dollar Penalty for Each Slipped Word.*

Right beside it was another sign.

*No Dogs Allowed (except service animals).*

However, Mabel had a soft heart for pups, and it was a silent agreement that if she never looked them in the eye, she didn't know they were there. So far, no one had reported her to the health department for any of the "support" animals that sometimes accompanied her favorite customers. Mabel would much rather they be safe inside under a table or beside a barstool than sitting in a hot car, a cold truck bed, or tied to the post outside.

# CHAPTER 8

*E*veryone sitting at the bar turned to look when they entered the Den, making Taylor cringe. The lights were kept up during the day then lowered for dinner, but she wished it was dim all the time.

The fire chief, Alex, held his beer mug up in a salute in her direction. "Hot damn, that's a pretty woman," he said, loud enough for her to hear.

"You owe Mabel a dollar," the guy next to him said, sliding a huge mason jar down the countertop in one graceful move.

Alex cursed again and shoved two dollars through the slot in the cap. Even in his middle age, he was a looker, and he knew it. He was also known to be a hothead—ironic, considering his profession.

In his first divorce, he was so angry that Judge Crawford was going to make him turn over his vintage Camaro, that on the day the exchange was supposed to happen, he cancelled the insurance on it and drove it down the boat ramp and straight into the lake.

He'd paid dearly for his temper tantrum—at least financially —but he'd gotten off with no criminal charges as the judge finally had a moment of empathy for him and didn't want to ruin his career. The last dirt she'd heard on Alex was his third wife was divorcing him. Hopefully he wouldn't put any more vehicles in the lake.

She ignored his comments and his disrespect.

He knew she was too smart to saddle up with the likes of him. Any sane woman would only look at that menu and decline to order the dessert. That being said, Taylor didn't like to contribute to the overabundance of attention he got from the females of Hart's Ridge.

When he turned to stare at her again, she kept an impassive expression and nodded politely, then went to their regular booth.

Cecil was already there, a plate with a huge burger and a pile of French fries in front of him. When he saw her and Bernard, a little light danced in his eyes.

He always made it clear that he looked forward to their weekly meetings.

"Girl, whatcha got there with you?" he called out, his gaze falling on Bernard at her heels. "That's the blackest dog I ever seen."

"I told you I was going to have a new man in my life soon," Taylor answered as she slipped into the booth opposite him.

Bernard curled up under the table at her feet.

"I bet he's a pretty good hunting dog, too."

Taylor laughed. "Actually, no. Turns out he's too wimpy for hunting."

"Well, that's okay. That means that God planted a kind heart in him. We need more of those to rub off on the humans around them," he said, tossing a French fry under the table. "What's his name?"

"Bernard."

"Ole Bernard, huh? Well, maybe he's good out in the field, then. I got a few baseballs rolling around in the back of the truck if you need 'em."

Taylor laughed. "I'll take one when I leave. Thanks, Cecil."

"You're welcome. And I ordered for you. They got your favorite tonight. Green beans, cubed steak, and mashed tators. Covered in gravy."

No sooner had the words come out of his mouth than their waitress Sissy was there, plunking a plate and a glass of sweet tea on the table. Taylor's mouth watered, but she grimaced internally at the thought of the gravy going straight to her hips.

But it would be worth it.

"How you doing, honey?"

"I'm good, Sissy. You? And your mom?" Taylor asked.

"We're both fine. You know Mama. She's pretty much house-bound now, but she's not going to complain much. She has Hayley to keep her spirits up. I'm supposed to take her back to Atlanta to have her pacemaker checked at the end of the week. She always tries to talk me out of it. She's so scared of that traffic."

"I don't blame her," Taylor said. "I hate it, too. I try to avoid Atlanta at all costs."

"Give Ms. Margaret my regards," Cecil said. "And keep her up late the night before your trip, and maybe she'll sleep through the traffic."

"Oh heck, I wish," Sissy said, putting her hand on her hip. "You know she'll be directing every move I make as though she herself is behind the wheel. She hasn't driven in five years, yet she thinks she should still call the shots. Then she cringes if I get within fifty feet of another car, and she wears out that invisible brake pedal on her side!"

They all laughed. Taylor could just see Sissy's tiny mama peeking over the dashboard to direct Sissy all the way to Atlanta. When Sissy used to bring her mom to the Den, Taylor had run into them a few times. The two of them were cute together. They looked alike and had a relationship that always made Taylor feel a little sad for what she'd never had with her own mother. Sissy was a single mom for the most part, though she was still on and off again with Hayley's dad. From the outside looking in, he seemed to be a good father to their toddler, so Taylor wasn't sure why they didn't just marry and parent her under the same roof. But it was none of her business, she just felt like that's what Sissy was holding out for.

"Let me know if y'all need anything else," Sissy said, then laid the ticket flat on the table.

Cecil slid his hand over it and pocketed it.

"Can you bring my boy a hamburger patty, well done?" Taylor asked, pointing to the area around her feet. "I'll pay for it separate."

Sissy looked under the table and cooed at Bernard. "I sure will give that sexy boy a treat. On the house, too."

Taylor took a big sip of her tea, watching her go.

Cecil had iced tea, too. Half sweet and half unsweetened, in a tall glass with two lemons. He was a creature of habit. Same meal and drink every week. One refill. An extra small platter for his ketchup to dip his fries and keep his main plate tidy.

Taylor dug in. No one cooked a homemade meal like Mabel did. She'd been the face of the Bear's Den since it had opened at least twenty years back. At first it was just a bar, but when the owners retired and moved to Florida, Mabel bought it and soon realized that there were a lot of people in town and around the county who had no one to cook for them and were sick of fast food or paying too much for a half decent meal.

Mabel kept quick made-up bar food on the menu, but the home-cooked meat-and-three option she changed out every day of the week was a slam dunk from day one. If you wanted to eat it at lunchtime, you had to get there before half past, or you'd find nothing left but veggies and maybe a bit of gravy. Maybe a biscuit or some cornbread to sop it up.

At least until Mabel had the dinner round ready to go at four thirty. And then it was wiped out again by six and you'd have to order from the grill.

The Bear's Den felt like home to Taylor. And Mabel was at least as old as Della Ray but wasn't slowing down as far as Taylor could see. She loved her title as the best cook in Hart's Ridge and wasn't going to give it up until she had one foot in the grave, and maybe not even then.

Yes, Mabel was the queen of her castle, and Taylor loved her spunk.

Sissy returned and bent down, holding the patty out to Bernard. He very gently took it from her fingers, bringing about more gushing baby talk from his now favorite waitress before she walked away.

"So, how're you doing?" Cecil asked.

Taylor wiped a bit of gravy from the corner of her mouth.

"I'm good. And I haven't had a drink." She winked at him over the napkin. "Yet."

He nodded. "Of course you haven't. I don't even know why you mention it."

"I like to say it out loud. Makes me feel better."

Cecil shook his head. "You know we don't have to always meet here. We could try another place."

"Nope. I like to be challenged." She looked at the bar and saw at least three men with tall, frosty mugs of draft before them. It always irritated her how they appeared to worship the drink like it was liquid gold laid before them.

More like poison.

"It's not a challenge, Taylor. You've never drunk a drop of alcohol in your life. Why do you do this to yourself?" he asked.

"Why do you do what you do, Cecil? You come here for me every week, despite some of the looks you get." Taylor had learned a long time ago to redirect conversation when Cecil asked her a question she didn't want to answer.

"Oh, you mean the looks that say what's a wrinkled, skinny old black man doing meeting a fine young officer like you here every week?'

Taylor laughed. "Deputy."

"You know what I mean."

"I don't care what they think. I need you, and I appreciate that you are still here for me after all these years," Taylor said, casting her eyes down so he couldn't see the glint of tears that popped up suddenly.

She knew he was pretending not to see. He always let her keep her pride.

"You know you don't actually *need* me, Taylor, but I'll be here until you figure that out for yourself." He tossed another fry to Bernard. "Or until I drop dead from a heart attack from eating all these French fries every week."

"Shoot, Cecil. You're a lot healthier than anyone in here. You probably walk all that grease out of your arteries in that five miles a day you do."

He grinned. He knew he was the healthiest senior citizen around Hart's Ridge. He claimed the exercise was what kept him honorable, meaning off the booze. All he craved at the end of his morning hikes were long afternoon naps and early dinners.

"So, have you heard from Lucy?"

Taylor shook her head.

Cecil knew everything about her family. He was the only person she trusted to hold all her secrets. For the few years her dad was sober, Cecil was his good friend and, most importantly, his sponsor. Cecil was a staunch advocate for sobriety. He'd been a drunk for forty years of his life and lost his wife and kids because of it. Even when he had years of being clean under his belt, they never came back.

That changed him, though he'd always been a kind soul. He'd worked for the state in the sanitation department. Kept the same job all his life. Even though he was one of the smartest people she'd ever met, blue-collar work was what he liked, and he'd never wanted anything more.

Now he was retired and spent most of his free time helping

others who also fought the fight, making amends in his own way. Taylor admired him more than she could ever say, because she knew just how hard it was to keep a habitual drunk from falling off the wagon.

They only had one rule. She couldn't talk about his family. The loss was too great and too painful for him to revisit in words.

"How does her silence make you feel?" he asked, reminding Taylor they were discussing Lucy.

"I don't know."

"I think you know exactly how you feel about it," he said. "It's just hard for you to be honest about your own feelings, because growing up, you felt it was your job to keep everyone happy. When you couldn't make your parents happy, you stayed out of their way and mothered your sisters. But you always ignored your own needs, and never showed anyone when *you* were not okay."

His words made her gaze wander to the wall behind the bar. Mabel also sold T-shirts, and one read, *Stop Trying to Make Everyone Happy. You're Not Tequila.*

She was surprised Cecil hadn't already bought it for her. He knew her so well. One day he told her that she was a brave soul, because despite having her own world crumble around her, she still wanted to save everyone else. And that she needed to find someone who would be as kind to her as she was to those around her.

He meant a romantic partner, though he didn't say it.

Taylor was introspective enough to know that being raised to have no needs or expectations had made all her adult relationships pretty much a failure. All her past significant others had told her she put up a wall between them, and not knowing what she needed made it too difficult to make her happy.

She didn't think she needed much to be happy, but obviously it was more than they could figure out because they always left.

But now she had Bernard.

At least her weekly check-ins with Cecil were better than any therapy she could ever pay for. He'd missed his calling. That didn't mean she was going to change who she was—or even could if she tried. But it made her feel better that someone in the world understood her.

"Okay. I'm worried sick about her. She's never gone this long without checking in. I'm thinking about putting out an APB on her through the wire."

An APB was an all-points bulletin with a photo and details sent out either regionally or even nationally to other law enforcement agencies, asking them to look out for someone specific.

He raised his eyebrows at her. "But technically, she left on her own, and she's an adult. Can't that get you in trouble?'

"It could. I'm going to wait another few weeks, then decide."

"Don't let your sister ruin your job, Taylor. You've worked hard for where you are today. You know how fast Lucy can tear up a good thing."

"She doesn't mean to," Taylor said quietly.

But he was right. Lucy was like a cyclone every time she came around. She wasn't a bad person—she was just damaged. Of all the Gray sisters, she felt like Lucy struggled the most. But underneath the bravado, she was just doing what she felt she had to in order to keep life from swallowing her up.

They got through the rest of the meal, and as usual, Cecil insisted on paying and Taylor tried to refuse.

"No gentleman alive lets a young lady pay for her dinner," he said again as he walked her and Bernard to the car.

His paying bothered Taylor because she knew he didn't have much, and their weekly meeting was the only time he splurged. He did especially love her old family recipe for chicken stew, though, and Taylor made a mental note to cook him up a pot of it soon. Out of the two men in her life that she fed on a regular basis, Cecil was the most thankful. It was a pleasure to bring him her simple concoctions because each time she did, he acted like he was receiving manna from heaven.

He was good to her like that. Always praising everything she did.

And by all means, she knew her cooking wasn't anything special.

Her dad confirmed it quite frequently.

The drive home was quiet. She didn't feel like listening to music, and Bernard didn't want to hang his head out the window. He was probably still reeling from his visit to his old master. They were almost at her driveway when the guilt got to her.

"I'm sorry for that, boy," she said, looking over at him.

His ear flicked slightly, showing he was listening, but he didn't turn to her.

# CHAPTER 9

*A*fter a long, hot shower, Taylor stood at the counter, waiting for her toast to pop up. It was going to be a long night. She planned to take her laptop—and her dinner of toast—to bed, and instead of putting herself to sleep with a movie, she would use the next hour scanning through more missing children's websites. Someone out there knew who Molly was and that she wasn't where she was supposed to be.

A young child didn't just drop out of the sky without anyone missing them.

She turned to see where Bernard was and spotted him in his usual place, keeping vigil for only God knew what.

That window was going to need some heavy-duty weather stripping before winter set in, if he planned to camp out there constantly.

She stretched. Her back ached, and she was just as exhausted as she'd be if she'd been in her cruiser all day. She wondered if her vitamin D or iron might be low. She really should get it checked, but that was one more thing on her list of self-care that she kept sending to the bottom.

Her laptop stared at her from the kitchen table.

Though she loathed doing it, she needed to just do it.

Quickly, she went and hovered over the keyboard.

She logged into the Sister Email Account and stood ramrod straight when she saw a tiny number one on the corner of the drafts folder. The toast popped up behind her, and she jumped. But she was no longer concerned with a light supper and early bedtime.

Lowering herself into the chair, she opened the folder.

*In Fulton County jail. Shoplifting charge. Need bail paid stat. 1000.*

Taylor couldn't stop the long sigh of relief that ran through her, releasing the anxiety and worry as it settled deep in her gut.

Lucy was alive.

She hadn't really doubted she was, but there was always that slim chance that she'd met up with the wrong person, as she tended to do. But now that she knew Lucy was safe behind bars, Taylor felt a rush of irritation. It put her in a huge bind. She didn't have the time or money for another Lucy situation. If Taylor really wanted to, she could talk to her sheriff and have him make a call, pull some strings, and bust her out.

And she'd done that before.

Twice.

She just couldn't ask him again. Couldn't face the pity that would embarrass her. Even if her savings were dwindling down to nothing, mostly because of Lucy's troubles, as well as keeping their father up. She thought about calling him and putting it on his plate. She'd done that before, too, only to have to listen to him rant that Taylor needed to use her job to do something for her sister.

He wouldn't have the money anyway.

She'd save herself the rant. It would be worse than shelling out more money she didn't have for something she didn't do. She tapped her short nails on the tabletop, wishing she'd checked the email sooner that day. Fulton County Jail was only a few hours away, and she could've made it there and back before dark.

But not now.

Damn it. Why couldn't Lucy just follow the law? Was she destined to be a lifelong, small-time criminal?

Being in the field that she was, Taylor knew that most of the time a habitual small-timer turned into a first-time felon, and some of those got hard time, depending on the crime.

She couldn't let that happen to Lucy.

She logged on to the internet and brought up the bookings page for Fulton County, then scanned through to the Gs until her sister's face popped up.

She looked sad. And so tired.

It tore at Taylor's heart.

She zoomed in and scrutinized her face, relieved that she didn't see any scabs or other telltale signs of hard drugs. Lucy was skinny, but she'd always been that way.

Taylor wished she could reach through the screen and grab Lucy's thin wrists to examine them for bruises or tracks.

She doubted normal families even knew there was such a fear out there when looking at pictures of their kids or siblings. They most likely oohed and ahhed and looked at the background to figure out what sort of fun their loved one was immersed in, not what sort of trouble they'd stirred up again. Or to see if they could spot signs of drug use.

But Lucy was *her* trouble.

Taylor grabbed the notepad and pen she kept on the table and started making a list of options, starting with just wiring the money to the jail. Or using a local bondsman. But if she bonded her out, Lucy would skip town, and then Taylor would have a bondsman breathing down her back.

It would be better to just go and get her out herself. That way, she could bring Lucy back to Hart's Ridge and try to get her to stay. She might even see if Mabel would let her wait tables.

Her little sister could always *get* a job. It was keeping it that was the problem. She knew how to make a good impression when she wanted to. Like the best con artists out there, she had a way of using her good looks and turning on the small-town charm that brought in good tips. Or at least she could when she could stay in one place long enough. But something else was always better than what she had at the moment, pushing her sister to continually pursue the mirage of happiness and end up in places that were anything but that.

This time though, Taylor would force Lucy to get some counseling.

She picked up her phone and texted Sheriff Dawkins, then nervously waited for a reply. She jumped when the phone beeped back but sighed in relief when she read his answer.

It was going to be an even longer night than she'd thought because he was going to allow Taylor to take an emergency half-day vacation the next morning.

Another text popped through from the sheriff.

It had better be worth it.

Taylor didn't know if it would or not. Lucy probably wouldn't be grateful for any longer than it took for her to retrieve her personal items and for Taylor to get her out of the parking lot.

And for that benefit, Taylor was going to work well into the night doing research on Molly and writing up a report of possible leads and direction. She didn't mind all that much, as it was either her or Deputy Clint, and Taylor didn't trust him as far as she could throw him.

A little girl's future was at stake.

"Come on, Bernard," she said, standing and taking her laptop with her as she crossed the kitchen. She pushed the button on the coffee maker, allowing her morning coffee to start now. She was going to need it.

Her dinner of toast forgotten, she headed to the bedroom. Once Bernard walked through, she locked the three locks and put the iron bar in place. The door was solid wood and couldn't be kicked in, but the bar insured the frame would stand up as well if anyone tried to enter.

She checked to make sure the baby monitor was on, letting her hear anything that happened in the kitchen and living room, then turned to find Bernard looking at her, a puzzled expression on his face.

"It's a long story," she said. "But now we can sleep safely."

# CHAPTER 10

*T*aylor drove to Atlanta and was back in Hart's Ridge in record time, due to her taking no nonsense from the aggressive drivers around her. She could hold her own, though her defensive moves also had to do with the fact that she was completely ticked off at Lucy, who had vanished again before Taylor could get to her.

She had already bonded out.

Taylor pulled into the parking lot of the station and took a minute to read the email from Lucy again. Based on the time stamp and what Taylor now knew from the Fulton Jail clerk, right after Lucy had sent her the email asking for bail, someone else had swooped in to pay it, and they'd both disappeared, back into the streets where it was nearly impossible to find someone if they didn't want to be found.

Especially in Atlanta.

When Taylor had conveyed that she was law enforcement too, the staff had been obliging with as many details as possible. Lucy had been charged with shoplifting after being caught with a loaf of bread, a jar of peanut butter, and a box of allergy meds.

Taylor couldn't decide if she thought Lucy was using the

meds to make drugs, or because she needed them. Her sister did have allergies that were mostly left untreated when she was a kid. They never had the extra money for any over-the-counter meds, much less to take her to a doctor. In foster care, they concentrated on the big stuff, not a sniffle or two.

Taylor was also able to get the name of Lucy's bonding savior. Roland Ellis.

As soon as she had a free minute, she planned to run him and see if she could figure out who the generous Mr. Ellis was and why he was helping her sister. Anyone who Lucy associated with wouldn't normally have a grand sitting around for bail money—unless they were into something they shouldn't be.

She tucked the notebook into her shirt pocket and got out of her car.

For now, she had to put her sister's situation to the side, because that morning, the sheriff had reviewed her report on Molly that she'd stayed up until three in the morning drafting. Based on a lack of real leads, he'd decided it was time for a press conference.

Since they were such a small unit, he'd texted her and told her to get her butt back there stat. She was going to be the media relations officer for the case.

Reluctantly, Taylor did as she was told. She didn't enjoy being in the limelight. She never had. That was always her sister Anna's role.

Taylor preferred to blend into the background. All that had to change during her academy training, especially since she was a woman, and her male peers couldn't help but try to step up and take on the role of leader whenever they were around. She'd had to learn to use her voice, and to gain their respect by feigning confidence even when she didn't feel it.

And she'd do the same today.

Deputy Clint passed her on his way to his car, and he gave a barely perceptible nod. Taylor returned it and climbed the steps.

She knew him well enough to know he was pouting because the sheriff picked her to lead the conference. If he only knew how hard it was for her to do, he would probably be laughing. But the joke would be on him because Taylor would stand there and answer questions, and she'd swallow her anxiety over it.

She owed it to Sheriff Dawkins. That and a lot more. While the behavior of her father had given her the ambition to go into law enforcement, her first meeting with Sheriff had solidified the dream.

She'd been an awkward seventeen-year-old, and it was during one of their bounce-back-home-from-foster-care times. She'd already graduated high school but was studying anything she could get her hands on in law enforcement from the library until she could find a way to pay for the academy.

Her sisters were still in school, and Taylor had worked two jobs between her studying. The only time she had available to go pick up groceries was after her late shift on Saturday night when she would walk from the Subway where she tossed sandwiches to the nearby grocery store. Then she'd get a taxi home because asking her dad for a ride on a Saturday night wasn't an option unless she had a death wish or wanted to see him in jail with a driving-under-the-influence charge.

One blustery winter evening, she didn't have enough money left over for a taxi, so she walked the six miles home, carrying a few heavy bags of groceries. Her feet felt like solid blocks of ice in her wet sneakers, and she still had two miles to go and a meal to make for her sisters when she got there, when the sheriff pulled up.

"Where you headed?" he asked.

"Home," she'd muttered through her chattering teeth.

At that time, she was a little afraid of anyone with a badge, even though they'd saved her mother more than a few times.

"Jump in, and I'll take you. Don't be scared. I know your dad."

Taylor had known exactly who he was, too. Everyone knew

Sheriff Matt Dawkins, aka Mad Dog Dawkins. But he didn't seem to have a bark or a bite.

He'd waited patiently while she stood looking at him. She'd never been in an official car before. She'd hesitated, but the need for warmth overrode her caution, and she had tossed her bags into the back and climbed in after them.

Sheriff Dawkins was kind to her during the ride, even though he'd given her dad a few citations for public drunkenness before he'd finally decided to keep his drinking at home.

Even as cold as she was, her face had burned with shame that he knew her father.

But there's a difference between pity and kindness. At seventeen, Taylor already knew that and appreciated that he didn't show what he was probably feeling. When he dropped her off, he told her he'd send a deputy by to pick her up the next Saturday evening, and from then on until the weather warmed up.

That hadn't lasted that long before she and her sisters were once again tossed into the system and someone else was buying their meals, but his gesture made Taylor realize that law enforcement was more than just that. They didn't always just come after the bad people. They were also doing their best to take care of the people in their community.

Taylor had never minded taking care of her sisters—and she knew that she'd feel the same about the citizens of Hart County. Somehow, the sheriff got wind that she wanted to work for him, and they awarded her a grant to cover the police academy. With one caveat.

Sheriff told her that he expected her to do exceptionally well at the academy and then be the best deputy on the force. When her father didn't show for her graduation, she buried the hurt by pretending that the sheriff was standing in. He was indeed there, looking as proud of her as any father would—or should.

And Cecil came too.

Taylor was still working on her second promise to the sheriff because letting him down wasn't an option.

He met her in the hallway as she came in the back door.

"You've got ten minutes to prepare," he said, then turned and went back to his office. "Remember, the media will get their information from somewhere. We want it to be from us. You have to feed the animals, or they'll turn on you."

"Got it," she murmured.

"They'd love to paint us as backward hillbilly incompetents if they get the chance."

"I hear you, Sheriff."

He nodded. "Good. Don't embarrass me." He walked away.

No mercy.

And she loved him for that.

Quickly, she stopped at the restroom and made sure everything looked tip-top on her uniform. In less than two minutes, she was at her desk and had pulled up her email account and the report from her sent files, then printed it.

Luckily, she was thorough with it the night before and wouldn't need to prep much. It was all there, and all she needed to do was review it.

She did so briefly. It didn't take long because they didn't have much to go on. She'd gone to sleep frustrated with herself that despite the long hours she'd put into her research, she'd found nothing about a small child matching Molly's age and description.

Taylor didn't have official training to deal with the media, and it was too late to get it now, but she'd done her own unofficial studying up on it. Just in case she was ever thrown into the predicament she was facing now. As a female deputy, she didn't get second chances. Mistakes wouldn't be forgiven. Nor forgotten.

The guys still talked about the female deputy who resigned

after taking so much crap from them about being reprimanded for a shirt she wore to a community event on her day off.

It had read, *STUPID PEOPLE KEEP ME EMPLOYED.*

Sheriff was furious with this deputy because it completely went against the relationship of service to the people he'd spent years building. But if a male officer had done it, he would've been reprimanded, then guys would've high fived him in the locker room, and it would be over.

Since she was female, the taunts went on so long and were so intense that she'd quit and gone to work as a substitute teacher in another county, probably making only a fraction of what she'd made in law enforcement.

That was the kind of crap that really ticked Taylor off.

Quickly, she emailed the photo of Molly to their central printer, then went and grabbed the printout. They didn't have the ability to do anything larger than a normal piece of paper, but the media could zoom in on it. She did have a few pieces of hard cardboard lying around, and she stapled the photo to one just so it wouldn't be flapping in the wind.

Then she concentrated on her opening statement, closing her eyes and saying it in her head. She didn't want to portray Molly as any sort of specific case, for they just didn't know if she was abandoned, lost, kidnapped, or what. Words mattered and could send everything in the wrong direction.

To be honest, she was glad the sheriff had initiated the first move. The media was a useful tool for law enforcement. For the agency, it was good to use them to inform the public of ongoing criminal activity, for their own safety. But the media could also help them find the bad guys. Or the leads they needed to solve a case. Not that she had many cases. A patrol deputy was limited as to what they could be responsible for, but luckily, the sheriff was letting her step outside the boundaries for Molly.

Taylor had to get this right. Using the media to get the public on their side was everything. As the media contact, she would be instrumental in determining what the daily reports would be and use them to figure out where Molly came from, and that excited Taylor more than anything. She'd never lie, but there were ways of reeling in what they needed by controlling what they put out there.

She was still standing at the printer, mentally practicing her opening statement, when Deputy Clint walked up and stopped in front of her, his arms crossed and a scowl across his face.

"I thought you left," she said, to cover the awkward silence.

"You'd like that, wouldn't you?" he glared at her.

"Look, I don't know what your problem is, but why don't you take it up with the Sheriff? I have stuff to do."

He nodded slowly and grinned. "Yes, you do. And when you are standing up there, I want you to look out and see me in the crowd, and just know that I'm imagining you naked."

Taylor moved around him and without a word, left him standing there. She wouldn't give him the satisfaction of knowing that all the courage she'd built up had just dissolved into a puddle at his feet.

# CHAPTER 11

*A*n hour after the press report ended, Taylor was still quaking inside. Public speaking would never be her forte, but she thought she'd done well enough. Sheriff had stood on her right and the lieutenant on her left. Both were over six feet tall and made her feel small, even standing at her straightest, chin high in the air.

She didn't let them know it.

Just as he'd said, Clint was standing where Taylor could see him. She made sure to lock eyes with him and smile triumphantly before beginning.

At first the questions were coming at her like gunfire, but once the sheriff held his hand up for calm, everyone obeyed. He was a quiet man, and the air about him demanded respect. The people of Hart County trusted him, as shown by his thirty-two years in office with elections that were always a landslide.

Taylor wasn't naïve. One day he'd have to retire, but she dreaded that day. It was a comfort knowing he was there, watching over all of them. He still exuded knowledge and control, though his face was more lined and his hair now a solid white. He never talked about stepping down, and that was just fine with her.

Taylor gave the facts as they knew them, being careful not to add any suppositions or personal thoughts about where she thought Molly might have come from. Leading anyone in the wrong direction would cost them time and effort. When she finished, the sergeant stepped up to encourage the public to contact them with any information leading to the identity of Molly, and they wrapped up.

On their way back into the station, the sheriff ordered her to meet in his office in ten.

Taylor hoped he agreed that she'd done fine, but though the office temperature always stayed at a relentless, frigid sixty-eight degrees, she sweated the next few minutes. Had he found out about her run to Atlanta and was going to chastise her for once again letting Lucy reel her in? Or had Clint ratted her out for having Bernard in her car during work hours?

When ten minutes had gone by, she wiped the sweat off her brow with a Kleenex, then reported to his office.

Lieutenant was there, too, sending little flares of alarm up her spine. She didn't have the same relationship with him that she did the sheriff. He came in knowing that there was history there, and while he didn't say anything about it, he always let her know in a silent way that there'd be no favoritism coming from him. Taylor didn't think she got any from anyone, but everyone still knew the sheriff had a soft spot for her.

Lieutenant was at his most serious and beckoned for her to take a seat.

What the hell had she done? It couldn't be about Lucy. The sheriff would never involve him in her personal problems, even if he had found out the latest.

"Sit down, Deputy Gray," Sheriff said.

Taylor slowly lowered herself into her seat, her face frozen into a blank expression so they couldn't read her anxiety.

"You did a good job out there," Sheriff said.

Taylor's anxiety dissolved from the inside out.

"But I had hoped not to let our little town draw any attention to the outside world right now," he continued. "If we don't hurry up and figure out who this kid is, someone is going to make it an evening story on a big network, and we'll be screwed."

"I thought that's what we want," Taylor said. "Get her photo out there and hope someone will claim her."

"Someone local is the hope," Sheriff said.

"We're trying to keep the department on the low side of big publicity right now," Lieutenant said. "With the big politicians doing everything they can to destroy law enforcement, for their own agendas, it's best to keep a low profile. We've been lucky. We haven't been marked for riots or looting. We have a clean record here with the public and don't want to give any excuse for the protestors to come in, because the vandals use them as a cover to give them free rein to destroy everything they can get to."

"What kind of protestors? For what?" she asked.

Sheriff shrugged. "Who the hell knows? Whatever it is they are protesting at the moment. I don't want any part of it."

Taylor nodded. She understood. For the last few years, it was hard to carry a badge in most places outside their protective borders of Hart County. So much hate pointed in the direction of law enforcement. Even the good cops took a hard rap for the few bad ones. It made their jobs so much harder.

"I'll be on every lead that comes through to see if it's good," she said.

"I know you will. And you'll have help. I put out a request to borrow some manpower for the case. Cherokee County answered. Tomorrow you'll be working to bring Sergeant Detective Weaver up to speed on what we know—or should I say what we don't know—so far."

Taylor tried to maintain eye contact but she felt herself slump. Their department was too small to pay a detective's salary, and that was the only reason she was getting to work on Molly's case at all. They all got a chance to investigate. With the press conference done now, she'd hoped to have more to go on. But he was giving it to someone else.

And wait.

Weaver? From Cherokee County?

Couldn't be.

She squirmed in her chair. Hopefully there was more than one Weaver working in Canton.

"Did you say Detective Weaver?"

Lieutenant spoke up. "Sergeant Detective Shane Weaver. He's being sent down to help since he's from here. Do you know him?"

"She knows him. Everyone in town does," Sheriff said. "Is that a problem, Deputy?"

"No, sir," she replied, struggling to hide her surprise.

"Good. Because I want you to split your shift. Do the first half on patrol, and the second half working with Weaver. Let's figure out who the hell this kid is before the FBI gets involved and I end up losing my badge. You're dismissed."

Taylor nodded. "Can I ask one question?"

"You can always ask," Sheriff said.

"Why isn't Deputy Clint getting this assignment? He's the senior deputy."

"Not anymore. Now get to work."

Taylor hightailed it out the door, down the hall, and straight into the ladies' room. In the male-dominated building, it was the only place she could be alone and try not to hyperventilate.

She went into a stall, put the toilet lid down, and sat.

*Ten deep breaths*, she told herself.

The fact that Clint was demoted was sure to make her life hell. He already hated her, and even though the sheriff hadn't given the position to her, he'd think she was up for it. He was an idiot, too. While she wouldn't turn down the promotion, she had her eye on being a detective.

He could earn his senior position back. She didn't care.

But Shane? Coming back. Sitting in her car?

She fanned her cheeks.

*Grow up*, she told herself.

Shane Weaver was the one guy in high school who was the most memorable. He was her age, and they graduated together, and he'd even been a Hart County sheriff's deputy for a year. However, he'd wanted to go where he could move up on the chain of command, and their small town just couldn't offer that with their small budget. He'd gone on to the big city of Canton only a year after he'd signed on.

Taylor wouldn't admit it, but she'd been sad to see him go.

When word came that he'd made sergeant and then detective, everyone in town was talking about it. Suddenly, the ambitious young man who wasn't that popular in school was now a town favorite.

Most humiliating was that Shane was her first kiss.

No one knew they had a thing. Well, it wasn't really even a thing. Not technically. It could've been. But it wasn't.

She hadn't dated much, or really at all, in high school because not only was she busy taking care of her sisters, but she also didn't want anyone to know about her home life. Anna and Lucy could balance the lies they told to cover the truth. They were good at pretending everything was fine.

Jo had her own group of friends. A tight clutch of girls who kept all her secrets and didn't flinch when she glossed over hard truths.

But Taylor didn't have that talent to be cleverly deceiving, and she sure didn't want any potential boyfriends feeling sorry for her.

She'd only gone to one prom and had rarely made it to the high school football games. When she did go, she felt out of place.

Like a loser with no friends. Sometimes she'd tag along with one of her sisters, who took her out of pity.

But one Friday night, when Jo and her group left Taylor sitting there watching the game, Shane approached and asked to sit with her. Turned out he didn't have a lot of buddies, either. He wasn't a football jock. Not in the band.

He didn't fit any of the high school labels. He was quiet. But not in a creepy-hope-he-doesn't-bring-a -gun-to-school kind of way.

He was a lot like her.

Anna teased her that he was invisible in school, and no one had ever heard of him. Anyone who wasn't in the popular crowd didn't exist to her. Jo thought he was cute, and of course, Lucy was ready to throw herself at him the first time she saw him.

Lucy loved older men, or so she'd always claimed.

Shane had barely looked at her sisters that night, a miracle, considering that they were all three much prettier than Taylor ever dreamed to be, and they usually got all the attention. They told her it was because she didn't do enough with her hair and makeup, that if she wanted to, she could be just as attractive. They just didn't get that she didn't want to stand out. She wanted to blend in.

Sometimes she just wanted to disappear. More often than she'd admit.

Taylor took a deep breath and stood, opening the stall door and going to the sink. The face in the mirror was still scarlet. And still just as plain as it was back in the day. It pained her that she was self-conscious enough that she wore mascara to work, and a bit of colored lip balm. But that was where she drew the line.

She and Shane became actual friends. She let him get closer to her than any other guy in those years. Of course, she didn't spill all the dirt about her family troubles, but he knew more than she usually let on, especially when they were jerked out and taken to Della Ray's house. She always called to let him know where she was on those mornings, since they were too tired from the drama the night before to be able to attend school.

He'd never pried for more information. When he got his first car—a beat-up old Chevy S10—she was the first person he gave a ride to. Her dad had gone a little over-the-top about it, so when he'd ever helped her out again, he dropped her off at the end of her driveway where her family couldn't see.

In their senior year, when she told him she wanted to be in law enforcement, he said he did, too. Taylor knew it was because he wanted to please her, or maybe even follow her. He took her home a time or two, and one afternoon in their senior year, he stopped and turned her to him.

"I've been wanting to do this all year," he'd said, then kissed her.

It was an awesome kiss, too. One that stayed with her during long, lonely nights when she repeatedly wondered why he never asked her out on an official date. Soon, she'd put it behind her. She couldn't let herself get distracted from all her responsibilities.

After a while, he found someone else, and she closed that door on the memories.

Until he showed up for work one morning in her county building.

But she was young back then, and it was okay to be awkward. Now she needed to suck it up and be a grown-up. He was probably married by now, and she'd be respectful and keep it platonic.

Completely platonic.

Damn it to hell.

Turned out he was good at law enforcement, too, no matter what the reason he'd joined up. Not having a lot of close friends in school proved to be a benefit to both of them once they'd pinned their badges on. It wasn't so hard to write old acquaintances up for tickets if you'd never hung out with them.

She looked at her watch. Six minutes in the can.

Time to wrap it up before they started talking.

She was dying to know why Clint was demoted but hadn't dared ask the sheriff anything else. No doubt, it would come out in the locker room, and for once in her life, she wished she had a penis.

There were other means of getting the information, though. It would just take her longer and force her to be chatty with Dottie in dispatch. That woman seemed to know everything that went on and couldn't keep a secret, which was why Taylor kept her at arm's length. She couldn't stand a gossiper, but this was something she had to know.

She washed her hands, dried them, then swung the door open like she meant business.

Shift was on. Time to suck it up and put on her deputy face.

# CHAPTER 12

$\mathcal{T}$aylor sat at the kitchen island in Anna's house and while they chatted, she studied the new backsplash that had gone up since her last visit. Or at least Anna claimed it was new, though for the life of her, Taylor couldn't remember what was there before.

"I really don't understand why you don't take a job elsewhere, Taylor. Like what about teaching at the academy you went to?" Anna said, her mouth pulled into that downward, disappointing half smile, half grimace that Taylor hated so much. "At least that way you could wear something other than that sorry uniform."

Anna was skinnier than even the last time she'd seen her, and it wasn't a good look on her. Next to her, Taylor felt like a cow.

"First of all, they have much more qualified teachers at the academy. Yes, I have a two-year degree, thanks to Sheriff Dawkins, but some of the faculty there have master's and such. And second, I like my job. It's interesting. But thanks for the confidence."

Taylor didn't mention her evening had been one of boring traffic stops and one shoplifting incident at the local Family Dollar. It was only a can of spam, and she'd let the old lady go, along with twenty dollars to buy her some real groceries. In between, she'd fielded calls from the press conference. A few leads had come in about Molly, and they were easy to follow up with but unfortunately had melted into dead ends.

Taylor was trying to use Anna as a sounding board, but it wasn't going too well, as usual. "If we don't get a good lead on who she is soon, the media is going to turn ugly. Sheriff will follow suit, and he'll be disappointed that I failed. He's already brought in a detective from another county, and that's embarrassing."

She declined to drop the news about Shane. The high-school Anna had been so self-absorbed that she might not even remember him. The news of his return was still too fresh, and Taylor wanted to absorb it herself before her sisters ribbed her about it.

Anna shook her head as though Taylor was a lost cause. "You put yourself under public scrutiny too much. For what? You know everyone hates law enforcement anyway. You'll never be appreciated."

"No, I don't know that. And repeating the rumor just strengthens the myth that all of us are bad. How about a little support?"

"What about supporting *me*? You could put a word in for me with Sheriff Dawkins's wife. She's the chairman in charge of the vote to add new members to the board at the country club. I want that position, but so do three other ladder crawlers." Anna sighed, then turned her attention to setting the table, laying out place mats, strikers, and even linen napkins.

"Sheriff and I don't talk about things like that," Taylor said, watching Anna fiddle with placing everything perfectly in line on the table.

It was all just too much. Why did they need all this fuss? All Taylor needed was a plate and a fork, but her sister rarely asked her to come for dinner these days, and Taylor just didn't have the heart to say, "Thanks, but your weird formality at dinner makes my skin crawl."

That, and she'd given the old lady at Dollar General her last twenty until payday, so an offer of a free hot meal wasn't something to shake off carelessly. But her sister was comparing her need to be important against the case of an unidentified child. It was crazy.

"Can I help?" she asked, deciding to just let it go, then taking the plates to the table.

Anna took them from her and waved her away.

So far, Taylor had done nothing but sit on a barstool and watch Anna finish prepping, and the kids out the window playing with Bernard. He'd perked up tremendously when they'd arrived, and right now, he was straddled over Anna's youngest who was erupting in a fit of giggles at the tongue-lapping she was getting.

"Please tell the kids to come wash up," Anna said. "They're going to have dog hair and slobber all over them, and Pete will have a fit. He should be home promptly at six, so they have ten minutes. I need to figure out which wine to have with dinner, too."

That was another thing about coming to Anna's house. Everything was about Pete. He wouldn't even allow a family pet, except for a gold fish that couldn't give snuggles or kisses. Taylor believed every child should grow up with dogs or cats, or even both, to teach them responsibility and compassion. Childhood was a lot less painful when you had something warm with a heartbeat licking your tears away. Especially for a kid who had to live in a house as pristine and perfect as Anna's husband expected it to stay.

It sure felt like a lot of pressure.

"Okay, but before I do," Taylor said, "Anna, are you happy?"

Anna stopped in her tracks, her hands still gripping the heavy stack of plates. But she didn't look up.

"Why would you ask that?"

"Um…because you're my sister, and I'm concerned. We used to talk, Anna. Now you're so laced up and tense all the time. I feel like you're going to shatter into a million pieces at any second."

Anna started putting the plates out, and the sudden stiffness in her body said volumes. "That's ridiculous. Maybe you're just jealous of my life. I'm fine."

Taylor held her hands up. "Whoa, sister. Didn't mean to ruffle your feathers. I'm just worried about you. You never smile anymore."

Anna turned to her and smiled, albeit a very lame attempt. "There. I'm smiling. Happy?"

"No. That's a fake smile. Here's a question—do you ever wish you'd gone on to finish your nursing degree? Wouldn't that have been more fulfilling than what you do now?"

The fake smile disappeared, and in its place formed a look that could kill. Taylor was saved by Bronwyn who burst through the door.

"Mom, Teague said you don't have pictures of me when I was a baby!"

"Yes, we do, sweetheart. Don't worry."

"Well, where are they?" Bronwyn whined.

Anna shook her head. "Well, I can't get them right now. They're in the cloud, or whatever they call it. Your brother knows how to do it."

The explanation satisfied her, and she turned and headed back outside.

Anna gave her a helpless look with an attempt at another smile, the nursing comment seemingly forgotten. "I have pictures somewhere. I know I do. Of course I do."

"I'm not judging."

That earned her a sarcastic grunt. "Yes, you just were. I'm happy. Let's leave it at that."

Taylor didn't know who Anna thought she was fooling.

Sure, her sister easily had it all at her fingertips. No scrambling or working odd jobs to make it happen. She had the best clothes money could buy and scheduled regular mani-pedi appointments. She also her precious country club, which she used mainly for tennis and their sauna. And still, in Taylor's opinion, she was sad. Not to mention totally closed off emotionally.

Maybe it was because she had hit her thirties. Some women found aging harder to deal with than others. Anna would probably fall into that category.

"Have you heard from Lucy?" Taylor asked, changing the subject.

Anna finished setting the table and came around to the sink to get the colander of lettuce. Then she got more salad fixings from the fridge and began to toss it all together. "No, why?"

"Just wondering." Taylor didn't dare start a conversation about Lucy being in jail and then disappearing again.

Anna had nearly no patience for Lucy and considered their youngest sister, and her failings, their family's darkest secret.

"Knowing her, she's probably in jail again," Anna said.

Taylor winced.

"You shouldn't worry about her so much, Taylor. She'll pop in or call when she needs something. She's always been like this. Remember when she was thirteen and took Dad's credit card and booked a flight to see John Lennon's childhood home?"

"Oh, I remember. Thank God she left me a note, and Dad was able to catch her before she got too far. With only ten minutes to spare before the first flight boarded, too. She'd already printed her boarding pass herself and had a plan of exactly how to get from the Bristol Airport to the old house! We should've known then that she'd never stay put in Hart's Ridge."

"Miss Independent," Anna said, laughing as she pulled a gallon of tea and a bottle of white wine from the fridge.

It pleased Taylor to see that some of their memories together could still make her smile. Though Anna was ashamed of the adult Lucy, there was no doubt that they'd all loved and spoiled the child their youngest sister had been. Taylor hoped that one day, when Lucy got her life straight, they could all build new, healthier relationships.

"How's Dad doing?" Anna asked.

"Same. You really should take the kids over there to see him, Anna. He's lonely."

That earned her the evilest look yet, but Taylor was saved from a biting remark because a car door slammed.

Anna's attention reverted fast. "Oh no, Pete's here, and I still need to get the rest of the food out. Go, Taylor. Stall him out there for a few minutes."

"What? How? I don't know what to say to him," Taylor said, feeling instantly uncomfortable. Sitting around a dinner table with him was bad enough, but to have a one-on-one conversation would be brutal.

"Talk about crime. He loves that crap," Anna said, practically flying over to the oven to remove the deep dish filled with pot roast, potatoes, and carrots.

"Fine. But you owe me."

"And send the kids in!"

Reluctantly, Taylor rushed to the door and was off the porch and out onto the driveway to run interference for her sister.

Pete gave her a half smile and paused to talk. He moved his fancy briefcase from one hand to the other, jangling the thick gold bracelet he wore, for effect, obviously. He was also wearing a suit, one tailor-made to fit him perfectly. One that probably cost her entire month's salary.

Taylor didn't care about that kind of stuff, but it irked her at how he blew money on stupid crap. Weren't there starving kids somewhere he could feed instead? Or what about his own children's college funds? Or a retirement plan? Why did he have to be so pretentious?

"Taylor, what a nice surprise," he said. "I didn't know you were stopping by. I hope you're staying for dinner."

Liar. Of course he knew she was coming. Anna wouldn't even fart without running it by him first.

"Yeah, you know I can't pass up Anna's pot roast." She searched her mind for something to say that he wouldn't find insignificant and pointless. "So, what's going on at work? Anything interesting?"

He lit up like a peacock. "Ahh, just working on some big-time mergers for a few companies. Have you ever heard of a Chinese internet company based out of Atlanta called Jung Yeong Technologies?"

"No, can't say I have," Taylor said. "Tell me more."

She tried to look like she cared.

He rambled on about takeovers, bottom lines, and a lot of other terms that made Taylor's ears nearly bleed. Then he joked about meeting with the Chinese for dinner, drinks, and karaoke starring young, beautiful women before he cut it off.

"And well, it's proprietary information, so I can't say a whole lot."

But he just had.

"Oh, okay, then. That's all really interesting. Good for you. Hey, did you see my new dog?" She pointed at Bernard with the kids, then remembered she was supposed to send them in. "Oh, you guys, your mom said to go wash up."

They obeyed immediately. Like all good Stepford children did.

Bernard tucked his tail between his legs, sauntered slowly up to them, and parked himself right between her and Pete.

"Oh. Nice dog," Pete said, his expression turning sour as he took a step back.

"Thanks. We've got some things to work through, but he's a good boy." She didn't bring up the toilet paper apocalypse. Somehow, she didn't think Pete would see the humor in it.

"Yeah, good boy. He'll be fine on the porch while you're inside, right?" He looked at Taylor nervously.

*Actually, we'd have a better meal if we left* you *on the porch*, was what she wanted to say, but instead, she caved. For Anna's sake.

"Yes, he'll be okay," she said, then turned to the house with Bernard following close behind.

She planned to sneak him a chunk of the roast as an apology. Maybe even a carrot or two.

"I'm starving," Pete said from behind her. "And wow, Taylor. Have you lost weight? You look great."

Taylor pretended not to hear him as she talked to Bernard about waiting for her. The thought of Pete commenting on her weight while looking at her backside felt completely gross, making her hurry her pace to the door.

Anna had better be ready, because that was at least five excruciatingly long minutes she wasn't ever going to get back.

Taylor needed to wrap this up and get home. She wanted to get online and see what people were saying about Molly on their department's Facebook page.

# CHAPTER 13

Taylor shut off the car and rushed up the driveway with the foil-covered plate. She went around back. Bernard trotted beside her, excited to be going to yet another new place, all in one day. At least she wouldn't need to walk him that evening, and he should sleep like the dead, especially since his belly was carrying around a super-sized hunk of pot roast as an apology for his stay on the porch during dinner.

"Don't get used to this, boy. Tomorrow you'll be by yourself again."

He looked up at her with a furrowed brow, then quickly forgot about it as he ran to a scraggly bush against the walkway and lifted his leg.

At least Anna still had a heart in there somewhere because she'd put the food together and asked Taylor to drop it by on her way home.

Her dad's place wasn't actually on the way home, but since she'd always had trouble saying no, she was going to be later getting back to work than she'd planned.

On the porch, she took a deep breath, gave two knocks, and

entered. Bernard didn't wait for approval—he darted in front of her and straight through the kitchen.

"Dad?"

It was dark in the kitchen, but she saw the dim outline of the lamp in the living room.

"What?" he called out gruffly.

She flipped the light switch and flooded the open area with light. Her dad lay back in his recliner, mismatched socks on his feet, a half-empty bottle of vodka on the table beside him.

"Sit up. Anna sent you a good supper and you're going to eat," she said, grabbing a fork from the dish drainer. She took the plate and fork to the table and set it down. "It's still warm. I'll get you a glass of water."

He put the chair into the sitting position and lifted the edge of the foil, sniffing at the food. He looked like hell—the bags under his eyes ready to pop and his clothes unkempt.

"Not hungry," he said, then sat back.

Taylor poured a glass of water and returned with it, just as Bernard popped into view, done with his appraisal of the bedroom and bathroom at the end of the trailer.

"Damn it, Dad. You're going to eat. I know you haven't had anything all day but probably tuna and crackers. If that. And why are you sitting in the dark? Aren't the races on?"

"I didn't pay the cable bill."

Taylor tried to hide the frustration that flooded through her.

"There's a dog in here." His voice sounded bored, as though random dogs appeared in his house every day.

She sat down on the couch. Or at least the edge of it. She tried to squelch her urge to pop up and head for the door, leave the depressing sight behind her. But if she didn't try, he had no one else.

"That's Bernard. He's mine."

When he heard his name, Bernard came over and sat at Taylor's feet. He gazed at her dad and wagged his tail.

"He likes you," she said.

"Well, I'll be damned. He's probably the only one in the world that does."

"Dad, stop feeling sorry for yourself. You've been drinking. Please, eat the food. You know you love Anna's pot roast."

"I'd rather see her than eat her food," he said. "If that douchebag of a husband of hers would loosen the reins, she might remember she has a family."

"They *are* her family," Taylor said. She thought about the awkward moment at dinner when Pete told Anna she'd chosen the wrong wine pairing for beef roast. "She's busy taking care of the kids, the house, and Pete, of course. You know she loves you."

"Yeah, sure she does. Just like Lucy and Jo. Haven't heard from either of them in months. They're too busy for their dear old dad."

"Well, I'm here, aren't I?" For once she'd like him to express joy to see her, instead of always wishing for his children who didn't make time for him.

"Where else would you be?" He grunted. "Flashing that badge around so you can pretend to be a big shot?"

She ignored his last statement. It wasn't up to her to try to fix the problems between him and her sisters. And it made her angry that he couldn't appreciate that she was here. That she had just put in a long day at work, an excruciatingly uncomfortable dinner at her sister's, yet *she* was here and trying to help him. Did he ever ask how she was? Or how her job was going? Or at least say he was glad to see her?

He picked up the bottle at his side.

Taylor hopped to her feet and snatched it out of his hands before he could put it to his lips. "I'm taking this with me."

"Like hell you are." He tried to stand but fell back in the chair. "Put that bottle down."

Bernard followed Taylor, getting between them. He didn't like when people acted angry, obviously.

KAY BRATT

"Then eat the damn food," Taylor said, her words slipping out through her clenched teeth. She put the bottle down, though what she wanted to do was pour it down the sink. He'd probably bought it with the money he should've paid his cable bill with. And she was running out of patience with his toddler-like attitude.

"Can you please cooperate a little, Dad? I'm tired, and I need to go home and get some work done. But I'm not going until you eat and take a shower."

"I had a shower yesterday." Her dad glared at her, but he knew when she meant business, so he picked up the fork and plate, then took a bite.

He chewed on it like it was covered in arsenic, but the next bite went in with less of a grimace. Once he got going, he ate hungrily, satisfying Taylor that at least she could sleep tonight knowing he'd had more than rot gut in his belly.

"I'll go get your pajamas and a clean towel laid out for you," she said.

There wasn't a doubt in her mind that he hadn't had a shower in at least two days. Maybe more. He didn't care about keeping himself up anymore.

"I can do it my damn self," her dad ranted at her as she walked past him to the bedroom.

"Finish your supper, Dad. And this weekend, I want you to let Cecil come visit you," she called out. "He misses his best friend."

"No!" her dad bellowed. "I don't want to see anybody."

She checked the bathroom and didn't see any clean towels, but she laid out some fresh underwear and pajama pants. On her way back to the living room, she stopped in the laundry closet and checked the dryer. It still held the clean towels she'd tossed in there to dry on her way out the last time she'd visited.

She plucked them out and tossed one through the bedroom door to land on the bed.

Her dad was plenty able to get around and keep the house up

for himself. He just didn't want to. Heck, there were men his age still working their blue-collar jobs because they didn't have any savings. He was lucky he wasn't out there trying to make a buck to keep a roof over his head. The least he could do was keep himself and his home presentable. She knew he suffered from the guilt of the mistakes he'd made in the past, ruining their childhood and sending them bouncing back and forth into foster care. She also suspected he'd never gotten over losing his wife and son to a fire. Who knows? Maybe he felt responsible.

Or maybe he regretted all the hell he'd put her through before she died. Despite his abuse, Taylor knew he'd loved her. It was sad when a man allowed his internal demons to be exorcised by abusing the ones he loved.

She bit her lip to keep from scolding him again. She'd said enough for one night. She returned to the couch with the rest of the towels and started folding them.

"I mean it, Taylor. Don't bring him up here. Cecil and I aren't close like that anymore."

"Calm down. We'll talk about it tomorrow." *When you're sober and not so angry at the world*, she didn't add.

"No, we won't," her dad said, putting the now empty plate back on the table. "I said what I said, and that's it."

Taylor finished the stack of towels, then picked up the plate and took it to the sink, rinsed it, and set it in the dish drainer.

"Come on, Dad. Let's get you to the shower." She went to the chair, and while he grumbled about not needing her help, she guided him out of it and down the hall all the way to the bedroom, then the bathroom, Bernard on their heels.

"You can go now," he said. "I'll be fine."

He did look much better with some food in him. And he hadn't stumbled much coming down the hall.

"Okay. I'm leaving. I'll try to call you tomorrow. Please, Dad, try to get some sleep."

He shut the bathroom door in her face. Literally. Like two inches from scraping her nose.

"That's a fine thank you, isn't it, boy?" she asked Bernard as she stepped back, then headed for the living room.

Bernard raised his bushy black brows in an expression of concern.

"I'm fine. That's just Dad. He's like this all the time," Taylor assured him.

She softly crossed the room and picked up the bottle of liquor and returned to the kitchen, turned on the water, and held the bottle under it. Two inches and a slosh for mixing. That was all she could get away with. She turned off the water and returned the bottle to its place, then went to the bedroom.

Bernard looked exasperated, but he took a seat on the floor at her feet while she sat on the bed and listened for her dad to start the shower, then waited until he'd turned the water off and was safely done with time added in to listen for crashes.

When she heard his grumbling start again, she stood.

"He's good. Let's go home. What do you say?" She gestured to Bernard and tiptoed out of the room.

He wagged his tail and followed. On her way out the back door, Taylor picked up the cable bill and tucked it into her pocket.

# CHAPTER 14

*A*fter a sleepless night of listening to Bernard react to every tiny creak in the house and a morning that consisted of ironing her uniform with much more care than normal, Taylor was early out the door with promises to the dog that she'd stop by in a few hours to take him for a quick walk.

In the car, she checked the mirror and grimaced at what she saw, then started the car and took off. If wishes were makeovers, she'd be looking like Emma Stone today.

Instead, the same bland face stared back at her.

She stopped at Della Ray's house first.

Molly was looking healthier and happier. And she'd started speaking, asking for snacks and toys but had said nothing useful for her case.

Taylor gave it another try, but the questioning brought up the girl's emotional wall again, so she backed off. However, she was happy to see that Molly ran to Della Ray for comfort and wrapped her arms around her legs. That was an improvement over the nearly catatonic child she'd been less than a week before at the convenience store.

Taylor left and arrived at the department early. She took the

KAY BRATT

extra time to go through the newest comments and emails but found nothing concrete to go on.

When it was time for briefing, she was the first one in the room and situated where she could watch everyone come in. A part of her wanted to gauge her natural reaction and see if the Earth moved or the lights blinked, or some kind of cosmic reaction would occur.

It didn't take long to find out.

Nothing happened, because at first, she didn't recognize him.

Shane had changed. A lot.

No longer did Taylor see the quiet, average-looking young man who had left Hart's Ridge. This Shane was confident and obviously took care of his body. He was built solid without being too thick, and under his dark hair, his face had matured into a nice shape. It made her think of the word "chiseled" that she'd heard used before, and never actually seen.

Until today.

To put it bluntly, he was hot—or whatever term they used these days. She sure wasn't in the know.

And Taylor felt absolutely ridiculous that the thought even crossed her mind. She was bigger than that. Better than that. As a result of her shame, her face and probably her ears, too, flushed scarlet when he approached her and gave her a high five.

"Good to see you again, Taylor," he said, and the pleased expression he wore made it sound genuine.

She noted that Clint wasn't there. She still hadn't gotten the story of why, either. It infuriated her that probably everyone knew but her, because despite big talk of how gender equal the force was these days, it wasn't true. The guys wouldn't share everything with her.

Once the lieutenant was through giving his notes, they dispersed, and Taylor headed for the car in the parking lot.

Halfway there, footsteps sounded right behind her.

She turned to see Shane. "What are you doing?

"We're riding together for patrol," Shane said, smiling broadly.

"Why are *you* doing patrol? I thought you'd just stay in the office."

"We can discuss the case while you show me what's new around town," he said. "Catch up and talk about old times."

Taylor's palms began to sweat. Being in close proximity with him was already going to be a lot just doing it half her shift. Now he wanted to talk about old times? She thought for sure he'd stay back and search for leads on Molly's case. Talking about old times was the last thing she wanted to do. Even though their old times were G-rated, it would still be weird. And she needed to run by and check on Bernard. Without a spy reporting back to the sheriff. But what could she say? It was clear while he was here, he had seniority.

When she didn't respond, he laughed. "Kidding. I think we need to check all the roads and ditches near where the kid was found."

"Fine, but we've already done that," she grumbled as she opened the back door and did her check of the back seat.

He did the same on the other side, then slid into the front and put on his seat belt.

"I assumed you'd want to drive," he said when she got in. He raised an eyebrow at her in a challenge.

"You assumed right. It's my cruiser, and I bet my driving record is better than yours. I remember how you drive. You got a ticket the weekend after you got your license!"

He laughed, and thankfully, it broke the awkwardness.

Taylor started the car and pulled out. "It was nice of you to volunteer to pitch in on this case. I'm hoping some good leads come in now that we've put her photo out there."

"Me too," Shane said. "But technically, between you and me, I didn't volunteer. Sending me back here is my sheriff's way of a lesson in humbleness without putting anything official on my record."

117

Taylor didn't like the way that sounded, but it could be she was just too protective of Hart's Ridge, so she decided to let it go. After all, it was his hometown too, so if he wanted to consider it punishment, that was on him.

"Oh really," she said, then turned off to the road that would lead out to the small convenience store.

"Yeah, really. I wasn't on duty when the incident happened, so I really think he's making too much of it," Shane added.

"Spill it," Taylor replied.

"My fiancée and I were downtown."

*Oh, so he's actually not married. Yet.* Not that she cared.

"We had dinner, and then we were strolling to the parking deck when a guy tried to mug me."

"Oh God. Don't tell me you shot him," Taylor said, suddenly horrified.

No cop wanted to shoot anyone.

"Hell, no," Shane said. "You know me better than that."

Taylor reddened. But he was right. Shane wouldn't shoot a simple mugger unless his life or someone else's was in danger.

"He wanted my leather jacket and Charlene's purse."

*Charlene.*

Now she had a name and felt more real.

"What did you do?"

"I made him think I was taking my jacket off, but instead I whipped out my Glock and held it to his head and told him he shouldn't go around threatening people's lives. He immediately shit his pants."

"I bet he did." Taylor laughed, though she knew she shouldn't. Anything involving a gun was serious business.

"No—I mean he *literally* shit his pants."

Taylor erupted into more laughter.

Shane talked over her chortles, and he looked like he felt guilty about it.

"Yeah, I apologized immediately. I told him I didn't expect

him to literally crap his pants when I drew my pistol. He should've known I was carrying. It wasn't cold enough for a jacket. Dumbass."

"Great detective material," Taylor said.

"Funny. But not as funny as him doing the duck walk with shitty pants and bare feet after I took his shoes, cell phone, and his wallet."

Taylor grimaced. Now he was getting to the part that got him into trouble.

"You didn't," she said.

He nodded. "Yep. I took the shoes so he wouldn't go run find his buddies to come after us, but I gave them to a guy sitting outside the homeless shelter. I also gave the guy the cash from the wallet. He was thrilled, and so was Charlene."

Taylor cringed inwardly.

"Next, the phone rings, and I answer it. Turns out he's a real mama's boy—or at least he was before I told her in detail what he'd just done."

"Ooh, that's a good one," Taylor said, laughing.

"Then I took his debit card, and surprise, it worked."

"You used his card?"

"Not for me. But for the other four cars and an RV at the nearest gas station. They were beyond grateful for the gesture of generosity."

"That's all of it?" Something told her it wasn't.

"Almost. I then dropped Charlene off at home, and I went by the club."

"The club?"

"Yeah, the one in the back streets of Canton, known as the biggest drug den in town. It was still early, but there was one shiny black beauty of a Lamborghini parked at the back door. Tinted windows, best chrome rims I've ever seen. Most likely belonged to the owner."

Taylor was now truly terrified for the would-be mugger. She

was also seeing a whole new side of Shane than she'd never seen before.

*Ruthless.*

"I put a hell of a deep scratch down the side of that beauty, then busted out the driver's window and threw the wallet in. It landed on the seat, and I left."

"You broke several laws," Taylor said, frowning.

He shrugged.

"The poor guy is probably dead by now," Taylor said.

Either that or he was wishing he were.

"Poor guy, my ass. I forgot the part where he yanked out a ten-inch hunting knife before I pulled my piece. First, if someone threatens me, they're going to get hurt. But next, if I'm out protecting my girl and she's put in that kind of danger, damn right they're going to suffer. And I never had to lay a hand on him."

Taylor had to respect that. Some of her peers might have beat the living pulp out of the guy, or even shot him. And there was one thing that hadn't changed about Shane.

He was still a gentleman. Though quite a merciless one, at that.

While they drove up and down the roads, looking for any sign of an accident or car in distress, Taylor filled him in on everything she knew so far about Molly, which was close to nothing.

"How're your sisters?" he asked when she paused.

That was a complicated question. Especially from someone who used to know her so well.

"Anna is doing fine, I guess. She's still married to Pete Chambers."

He raised his eyebrows. "Pete Chambers. That sounds fancy."

"He thinks so. She met the pretentious ass when she was working at the country club. He's a lawyer, and thankfully, as far as I can tell, their kids take after her and not him. Jo is working with a ranch-style bed-and-breakfast thing. They let her and Levi live on the property for free, and she's loving pretending she's from the Old West."

"Levi probably loves it too. What is he now? Twelve?"

"Ten. A very mature ten, I'd say. He's quite protective of his mama and the last I heard, he's embraced the cowboy lifestyle."

Shane laughed. "And Lucy?"

Taylor paused. If she even started about Lucy, she was going to open the floodgates of guilt, and he'd hear it in her voice. She was worried half to death about her little sister. Where she was and who she was with. So far, she was compartmentalizing it fine. As long as she didn't have to elaborate on her just bailed out and gone again status.

"That bad?" he said. "You don't have to talk about it if you don't want to."

"Good. I don't. And hey, I need to run by the house for just a second. Giving you a heads-up."

"No problem."

The car got silent, other than the crackling over the radio. But before Taylor could get halfway home, a call came through for a noise disturbance at a complex only a mile away.

Taylor did a U-turn.

When they got to the apartments, she parked, shut off the ignition, and turned to Shane. "This will take just a minute. Want to wait here?"

He grinned at her. "Nope. I miss these small-town policing calls. I'm going."

She shrugged. "Okay, but they might wonder why you aren't in uniform."

"Tell them I'm your supervisor, checking out how you're doing."

She stopped halfway out of the car and sat back down. "That's not happening." The glare that accompanied the words made him drop his grin.

"I see you're still a tiger behind the mask. And I was kidding. It's your beat." He got out and shut the door.

Taylor rushed to get out and take the lead.

*It was her call, damn it.*

They climbed the six stories of stairs to the third floor, found the door, and listened. She could hear a baby crying, and music, but it wasn't that loud. Then she heard a crash, and a woman swearing.

Taylor knocked.

The music stopped abruptly. Then someone came to the door, opened it a few inches, and looked out over the chain.

"Yes?" It was a young woman. No more than twenty years old, and she looked haggard. Dark circles under her eyes, hair a tangled mess, and she'd been crying.

"Ma'am, we had a call that there's a lot of noise coming from your apartment. Is everything okay?"

The girl moved a little to the side, and Taylor could see she was holding a baby, who also appeared to have just stopped bawling, judging by the sob-hiccup he let out.

"Yes—I mean, no. I…I don't know," she said, then broke out into more crying. "I thought maybe some music would calm her down. I'm sorry. Please don't arrest me."

In her peripheral view, she saw Shane's body language change. For a noise complaint, the young woman was taking it pretty seriously.

Shane stood even taller and moved in closer.

"Is someone in the apartment with you and the baby?" Taylor asked.

The girl shook her head.

Taylor lowered her voice. "Nod if you are being threatened or harmed."

Another head shake, but the tears kept coming.

"Will you open the door and let us come in and talk?" Taylor asked. She didn't want to leave the premises until she was sure the girl was fine.

The door closed, then after some racket with the chain, opened wide.

"I'm sorry. My place doesn't usually look like this. It's just me and the baby, and, well…I… She won't stop crying for more than five minutes."

"It's fine. We just want to make sure you are okay," Taylor said, stepping through the door, Shane directly behind her.

She did a visual sweep, and other than baby stuff everywhere, dirty dishes on the counters, and just all-over clutter, nothing appeared suspicious.

"Okay, let's start with your name," she said, taking out her pad.

Even for something as trivial as this, it required a report.

As she stayed to talk to the young mother, Shane crept around quietly, clearing the apartment.

"Allison," the young woman said just as the baby erupted into another ear-piercing cry. The mom limped over to the rocking chair and sat down with her. "Allison Curran. I'm so sorry. She's been doing this all night. I only slept three hours because she kept throwing up."

So that was the putrid smell permeating Taylor's nostrils.

"Can't you take her to the doctor?" Taylor asked, feeling sorry for her.

It was clear she was surviving on nothing but her willpower and was losing it fast.

"I called, and he said it's because I switched her to formula, and she'll get used to it. She wouldn't take my breast milk, and he said she needed to get something in her. I just had her last week, and my stitches are hurting so much I can barely walk, but he said not to bring her in unless she gets a fever."

Suddenly, an even worse smell began to settle around them like a dark cloud.

Allison's face fell even farther. "Oh God, I have to change her again. I'm sorry."

Taylor had seen young mothers like this one. Alone. Exhausted. Desperate. There were so many out there, and she ran into them several times a week. Usually, they were just trying to keep their heads above water—discarded by family for one slip up. Their boyfriends were usually still out living their lives while the girls they'd knocked up were doing anything but that.

Most of the young moms probably wished they could go back and rewrite the past, but they were making the best of it and trying to be a good mom.

Taylor looked at her watch. She had some time. "Here, let me. I've had lots of practice. Why don't you go take a long, hot shower? Wash your hair and put on some clean clothes." She held her arms out for the baby.

Allison didn't hand the baby over right away. Her expression was one of worry, and a little disbelief.

"You can trust me. I have a badge. And three younger sisters I practically raised alone," Taylor said, smiling at the young mother before gently taking the baby from her arms.

There was a place on the floor in the corner that had a blanket spread out, with diapers and wipes placed around it. She set the infant down gently, then knelt over her and began to unwrap her.

Shane walked up closer.

"Go," he said to Allison. "That was a direct order from Deputy Gray. Grab your opportunity while you can. Enjoy a shower and a few minutes of silence. We got this."

He reached a hand down and helped the young woman up, and she took one more look at Taylor with the baby, then disappeared slowly down the hall.

"Can I do anything?" Shane said, coming to stand over them.

The baby was still crying, but Taylor knew once she had a clean bottom, it might help her mood. It was messy, and she lifted a leg to get into a little fat flap, and instantly, the baby stopped crying and let loose a torrential spray of diarrhea.

Taylor tried to turn her head, but it got her anyway.

And it got her good.

The gulfs of laughter coming from above her didn't help the slap in the face one bit. She had to hand it to herself, though. She kept her cool. It wasn't the first time she'd been shit on—literally or metaphorically. Though it was ironic, after hearing Shane's mugger story just minutes before.

Calmly, she held the diaper over the tiny bottom, blocking the spout until it was done, then folded the diaper around the runny poo before handing it up to Shane.

Now she had to give him props.

He took it without hesitation, and surprisingly, he knew just what to do with it. As Taylor continued round two of cleanup, she heard him rustle around in the kitchen until he found a plastic bag and had the dirty diaper inside. Then he returned with it and held it open for the last dirty wipes, just in time for more crying to start.

It was ear-piercing.

"Gotta be colic." Taylor ignored the streaks of brown running down her cheek and the front of her uniform as she expertly slipped a fresh diaper under the baby and fastened it tight.

Shane tossed her a clean infant sleeper from a pile of laundry in the corner, and Taylor worked at it until the baby was buttoned up snug and clean, but still crying.

"Give her to me. You clean yourself up," Shane said.

Didn't have to ask her twice.

She stood with the baby and plopped her into his arms. Then she took the box of diaper wipes to the kitchen. The wailing was starting to make her ears ring, and the stinky situation was making her eyes water.

*I'll never have kids. Never,* she said to herself as she wiped the mess off her face first, then worked on her uniform shirt, only making it worse.

"You said we needed to run by your house anyway," Shane called out over the crying. "You can change then."

She hated that he was right. But before she could really sizzle with irritation, the crying stopped, and blessed silence took over. While it was peaceful, she ran some soapy water and tackled the pile of dirty bottles. Then the dishes.

Taylor was fast, hoping to get as much done as she could before Allison got out of the shower and the baby erupted into more cries. When her radio crackled to life, she was elbow deep in suds, and before she could wipe her hands, it clicked again, and she heard a disguised voice come over.

"Here, kitty, kitty, kitty... Here, kitty, kitty."

Fury flooded through her. It wasn't the first time someone had taunted her over the radio. It had happened other times with a male deputy and even a suspect six months ago. A crude taunt —and cowardly, too—that she was a female.

She bit her lip and prayed that Shane hadn't heard it. She had not said a word to the sheriff about the taunts. She wasn't a rat. She was sure it was probably Clint, though she couldn't prove it and wouldn't give him the satisfaction of even acknowledging his childish behavior. She'd gone through much worse in the academy, and they hadn't cracked her. His taunts were nothing compared to some of those antics.

No more than six minutes later, she dried her hands and peeked around the corner.

It was a sight that was a little too Hallmark and a lot too precious.

Shane stood in front of the window overlooking the parking lot, his feet glued to one spot as he moved his body gently in a figure-eight motion. The baby was fast asleep, her mouth wide open on his shoulder, a dark wet stain underneath it on his sky-blue dress shirt.

He turned just a tad, saw her, and smiled.

"Yep, it's colic," he whispered, then went back to swaying.

Taylor reminded herself that he was just a man. Not a superhero.

And he was also taken by some chick named Charlene.

~

"Looks like nothing's changed here," Shane said as Taylor guided the car carefully up the dirt road, missing the deepest potholes by pure memory.

She wasn't sure how to take his observation. If she were to try to see the place from his eyes, it would most likely make for a sad view. But it was home.

"I've done some renovations, but mostly inside. I hope to really fix it up one day," she replied.

*When I make more money and pay fewer bills.*

"I like it. Still rustic and calm as ever."

"Thanks." When the house came into sight, Taylor winced a little inside. Seeing it from the view of someone who hadn't seen it in years, it looked shabby and a bit pitiful.

"I'm surprised your dad let you have it," Shane said. "The land alone is worth a pretty penny."

Taylor cut the car off and opened her door.

"He didn't let me have it. I bought it to keep it from going to a stranger at auction," she said before climbing out.

Something in her tone must have stopped him from asking anything further as they walked up to the porch, scaring off two squirrels.

"They're married," Shane said, pointing at the critters.

Taylor got her key out and put it in the knob. "How do you know?" she asked as she opened the door.

Bernard came slowly out, sniffing Shane.

"Because they were eating in silence, sitting right beside each other."

"Ha ha. Is that how you and Charlene communicate?"

He looked taken aback for a second, then seemed to recover. "I suppose in the last months of our relationship, it was. Hopefully she's learned better communication skills with her new boyfriend."

So, he wasn't taken.

"I thought she was your fiancée?"

"She was. Until she wasn't anymore," he said. "That ship sailed. Without me on it."

Taylor grabbed a ball from the basket inside the door, then threw it out into the yard.

Shane was right about marriage. She'd seen it happen with her own parents.

"Get it, Bernard."

She wondered if his joke indicated he was opposed to marriage. A bachelor at thirty-two years old. Maybe he was married to his career like she was.

Bernard ignored the toss and plopped his butt down on the porch.

Shane laughed. "A little lazy?"

"No. He's depressed. Long story," she replied. "I'm trying to figure out how to help him."

"Doggie therapist?" Shane bent down and rubbed Bernard behind his ears.

He craned his neck up in satisfaction and an appeal for more.

"Sort of. He seems to be grieving. Maybe he misses his real family. I don't know, but I'm going to track it down."

"You always did want to play detective," Shane said.

Ouch.

His gaze caught on her face. "Hey, I'm sorry. I was kidding. Not funny, though. I know if you were a man, you'd have been promoted before me. You deserve it more."

"No, don't say that. I'm sure you worked hard for it."

"But it was your dream. Not mine."

She shrugged. "Someday. Now let's get him out and about so we can get back on the road before Sheriff figures out I'm doing dog duty on the clock."

Right on cue, Bernard hopped off the porch and into the yard, and squatted to dump right in front of them.

"Oh, it's dog duty, all right," Shane said. "Get it? Doodie?"

They both laughed, and the awkward moment was gone, making Taylor remember why she'd been so drawn to him years before.

Before either of them could say another word, Shane's phone beeped that he had a text message.

He pulled it from his pocket and read it, then looked up at Taylor. "It's the sergeant. Someone has come forward to claim the girl."

# CHAPTER 15

$\mathcal{T}$aylor hurried into the station with Shane following close behind. She knew it wasn't her case anymore, but this was one she was already invested in, and the sergeant wasn't going to leave her out. Not if she could help it.

She passed the bullpen and found them in the office they'd loaned to Shane.

"They haven't seen or heard from her since last week," the sergeant was telling the sheriff. "Phone goes directly to voice mail."

"What do we have?" she asked, taking the only empty seat in front of the desk.

She scanned the whiteboard that already had nearly undecipherable scribbling splashed across it. Luckily, she'd worked with the sheriff long enough to be able to understand his shorthand.

She took her pad out of her pocket and started making notes.

Sheriff pointed at the first line on the board. "Child's name is Molly Stott, and she's five years old. Lives with mother, Joni Stott, age twenty-three, in an apartment in Tampa, Florida. Father not in the picture. A family friend saw the press conference and recognized the kid, then contacted Joni Stott's mother,

Sheila Stott. She called half an hour ago and is already en route here to claim her granddaughter. She'll be here by five."

"How did the child get all the way here from Tampa?" Shane said from behind Taylor where he leaned against the doorframe.

"That's what we need to find out," Sergeant said. "Grandmother says no one has heard from the child's mother, and they knew nothing about her going out of town."

"I want to talk to the grandmother," Taylor said. She jotted down the name from the board.

"Shane's the lead on this. He'll have the numbers," Sheriff said. "You can second and start doing some of the groundwork. I want to know how Joni Stott spent every minute of the last day they saw her. Call and get the make, model, and description of her vehicle, and put out a BOLO. Find out if she's the type to abandon her kid."

Taylor nodded and kept writing. It was going to be a long day, but she hoped a fruitful one. At least they had somewhere to begin now.

"I'll touch base with Tampa PD and get them over to the residence," Shane said. "Maybe she's there, and only the kid made it to Georgia."

"Agree. That's a priority," Sheriff said, then he and Sergeant left the office, and Shane took the seat behind the desk.

"I'll also call Molly's grandmother," Shane said, surprising Taylor with his immediate assertion of his spot as lead. "You get on the social networks. See what you can find on Joni Stott and her mother, Sheila Stott."

"Fine. Can I listen in on the call?"

"I'd rather you get on the social networks. I can handle the call."

Taylor stared at him over the desk. He tapped a pen against the wood grain in front of him but didn't flinch. He wasn't the old Shane—he'd slipped into Detective Weaver mode.

"On it," Taylor said, then stood and left the office. She didn't want to push him because he could easily use another deputy to assist.

At her desk, she was relieved to see the only other deputy in the bullpen was Penner, and he rarely ever stuck his nose into anything he wasn't invited to. Out of the six of them, Deputy Monte Penner was the one who preferred the non-enforcement calls.

For him, it was a good day if he helped round up a bull who had strayed out onto the highway or got to spend his time writing blotters to submit to their local paper to entertain the people of Hart's Ridge. She had to hand it to him—he could make something out of nothing. One of his printed blotters read, *A caller was suspicious of a large round bright light shining through the woods*. It had turned out to be the full moon, but he found it amusing enough to gloss it up. Taylor suspected that Penner would make a better writer than he did a deputy, but he did his job, and that was good enough. He also helped her out with her paperwork when she was feeling exhausted.

Anyone who helps her through the daily documenting slog was all right in her book.

After logging in to the social networks under her alias, she searched for Joni Stott and found several, but only two who looked close enough in age to be her girl. One was set to private, and she couldn't see anything other than the profile picture, but luckily, her Joni's was public. It was easy from there to decide if it was her or not, because immediately she spotted Molly in multiple photos.

Taylor took it post by post, reading every comment and making notes of names who had interacted, even if it was only a like. There wasn't anything that stood out as something suspicious, but anyone could pretend to be someone or something online. If it were necessary, her list would be used to interview others. But hopefully they'd find Joni Stott, and she'd be booked on child endangerment, her case referred to social services, and that would be it.

However, something in Taylor's gut told her she was being overly optimistic.

Taylor noticed that Joni's page was fairly innocent for a young woman in her early twenties. None of the usual scantily clad photos, but a lot of inspirational memes, and tons of photos of Molly. Everything pointed to Joni being a devoted mom, despite her age. Taylor saw that Joni had tagged a sister in a few photos from several years back, but nowhere did she see the mother, Sheila Stott. She wasn't even in her friends list.

Taylor did a quick search and found her profile.

Public, thankfully. She started scrolling.

Sheila appeared to be more of a wild child than her daughter. As Taylor looked farther and farther back, she found evidence of several different men whom she was romantically involved with, but it appeared the relationships fizzled out fast.

There was a lot you could learn about a stranger from what they posted, and what Taylor immediately found out about Sheila Stott was that she was fighting growing older—tooth and nail, it seemed. She liked to dress young, loved to drink, hung out at dimly lit bars, and her memes consisted of passive-aggressive digs at unnamed individuals.

She didn't really seem like that great of a person.

It wasn't fair to judge someone on just their online footprint, but Taylor found herself wondering if Molly was going to be okay going with Sheila Stott. There wasn't one photo anywhere of Sheila with Molly. Or of Joni, her daughter. Wouldn't a dutiful grandmother be proud of having such a beautiful granddaughter and want to show her off?

She picked up her phone and dialed. He answered on the second ring.

"Wesley Wright, child services."

"Wes, it's me. Deputy Gray."

"Hi, Taylor, what's up? I have about fifty things to do before I can get out of here today." He sounded frazzled, as usual. "If it's about Molly, we haven't had any breakthroughs, despite her meeting with our therapist twice. She's not talking, and we don't want to push her before she's ready. I'm still trying to find her another placement, but between you and me, I'm not trying too hard. I think she feels safe with Della Ray."

Taylor explained to him the situation about the grandmother and her concerns over what she'd found online. When he was done scolding her for breaching their privacy, and she schooled him over the profiles being open to the public, he assured her that Molly wouldn't just be handed over to the first person who claimed her. There was a process, and once it was confirmed that Molly was Sheila Stott's granddaughter—*if* it was confirmed—there were other options they could follow if they had reservations about the child's safety.

That was a relief.

Usually, Taylor didn't get so connected in cases that involved children, but Molly pulled at her. Something about those dark, brooding eyes and her unwillingness to trust, or to act like a child her age. Children normally bounced back fast from trauma, or at least they appeared to, even when they were hiding it deep inside and letting it fester for the future when it would rear its ugly head and affect their lives.

But Molly was not bouncing fast. Or at all, really.

Something wasn't right. She was holding in a secret and was determined not to spill it.

Taylor thought of other scenarios. Grandparents battled to get their grandchildren all the time. Maybe there was a custody fight and Sheila lost, so Joni cut her out of her daughter's life. Then Sheila could've hired someone to snatch Molly, and it went awry. Of course, Sheila could very well be an upstanding grandmother and was trying to get Molly away from an unsafe environment, and Joni found out about it and ran with her daughter.

But if she wanted to keep her daughter, why would she discard Molly on the side of the road?

Or someone broke into Joni's apartment and abducted her, leaving Molly alone. But that didn't work because Hart's Ridge was a heck of a long way from Tampa.

Taylor's mind raced with possible scenarios. She looked at her watch and calculated the distance from Tampa. At least when the grandmother arrived, some of her questions would be answered immediately.

But would they be answered truthfully?

# CHAPTER 16

*I*t was nearly seven o'clock when Taylor leaned back in her seat and stretched her arms over her head to release the tension in her neck. Computer sleuthing wasn't her favorite activity, but in this day and age, it was imperative for investigation.

Shane had come out briefly an hour before to tell her that Tampa police had responded. They'd gained access to the apartment via the property manager, and nothing was out of place or indicated foul play. That didn't mean foul play hadn't happened in the parking lot outside her apartment, or after she left there for an errand or some reason, but at least they knew Molly's mother wasn't lying dead in their home while her daughter was wandering the highway.

So where was she?

They spoke to neighbors who claimed to hear nothing out of the ordinary, and the few friends they could drum up said they hadn't heard from her in ages.

They'd also gotten a description of the vehicle that Joni owned, a decade-old, Teal-colored Ford Ranger king cab. They put out a be-on-the-alert for it. According to the property manager, it wasn't in the parking lot anywhere. He agreed to turn over the surveillance from their one working camera, though it wasn't anywhere near the apartment. It faced the property trash bins but could possibly show something. He was going to turn it over to Tampa PD by morning.

In addition to her mind on overload with the case, Taylor was worried about her dad. He probably had expected her to come by, coax him to eat, and take a shower. Though he always told her not to bother, she knew he needed her, and probably a small part of him looked forward to seeing another person, even if she was usually scolding him for one thing or the other.

She'd texted Anna with hopes her sister would have a bit of compassion and go by there, but her answer was silence.

Taylor sent a text to her dad.

> Not coming by tonight. On a case. Eat something.

No reply to that one, either. He was probably rolling his eyes at the thought of his daughter being on the case of anything. He thought her uniform was for play.

She sighed and closed her eyes for a moment. Bernard took advantage of her break from the keyboard to rise to his feet and lean his snout on her knees, then look into her eyes.

"Yes, I know you're hungry," Taylor said.

Thankfully, the sheriff had gone home at four, so he hadn't seen Penner bring Bernard into the station. Calls were slow—other than a reminder call to send a traffic car out to the Baptist church the next morning so the funeral procession for one of Hart's veterans could go smoothly, and a call from a regular of the Hart's Ridge Inn saying that the manager was kicking her out because an unapproved visitor stayed fifteen minutes with the door shut. With those taken care of with a confirmation and a negotiation for one more chance, Taylor asked Penner to go give the dog a walk because she couldn't get away.

Instead, he'd returned with him, claiming that Bernard was sad and lonely, and he couldn't just shut the door on him and leave him there.

Penner was young, and he wasn't the best at following directions, but he had a good heart. He was also going to do her a solid and look up the guy who had busted Lucy out on bail. Taylor was too busy with Molly's case to switch lanes.

Shane appeared over the bullpen wall. He looked as rumpled and tired as she felt.

"Got a minute?"

"Yep." Taylor got up and followed him to his office, Bernard on her heels.

Shane closed the door behind them.

"Dinner." He pointed to the desk, and she saw a small pizza box and two Dr. Peppers.

"Oh. Thanks." She sat down, then wondered why he didn't just bring it to the break room and share with Penner, too.

It felt a bit awkward with the door shut, just the two of them. And Bernard sitting at attention, pepperoni on his mind. It was a small town, and the tiniest thing could cause gossip to stir, though thus far, Taylor didn't think anyone remembered that she and Shane had hung out some in high school.

"What the heck is taking her so long?" Taylor said, then picked a piece of pizza out of the box and slid it onto a napkin.

She grabbed the soda and popped the top, then took a long drink, practically inhaling the caffeine into her system. She'd sworn off drinking soda at least a dozen times in the last few years, but in her line of work, the caffeine was a must, and she wasn't a fan of evening coffee.

"I don't know. She's got her other daughter with her. Jessica Kurz—Joni's sister from another mister—and she's only twenty-one, so maybe that's slowing her down."

"Oh, I didn't know she was bringing anyone," Taylor said,

feeling miffed that he'd kept that detail to himself. Now she mentally listed questions she could ask the sister, too.

"You do remember that I'm doing the interviewing?"

She nodded, though actually, she'd forgotten. Now all she could think was that she hoped his interview skills were better than his communication. She was his second. He needed to tell her everything.

On that note, she filled him in about her call to Wesley at child services, and her wariness to release Molly to the grandmother without some background screening.

"It's not our call, but we can definitely assist," Shane said. Then he looked closely at her. "You aren't getting emotionally involved in this one, are you?"

"No. Absolutely not. Just being a responsible adult."

He didn't look convinced, but he softened his tone to one of kindness. "Okay but be careful. I know that with your background in foster care, you're probably more invested in what happens to Molly. You need to keep your eye on the goal here. To solve this case. Where the kid lands isn't our business."

She nodded and turned her attention to the whiteboard. In addition to the vehicle description as well as a copy of the photo Taylor had taken of Molly, he'd added some bullet points, and Taylor read through them.

*Abandonment/Deliberate Disappearance: mother dropped child and took off*

*Abduction/Foul Play: mother and child abducted, child dropped off later*

*Accident: vehicle accident, mother incapacitated, and child wandered off*

SHE DIDN'T BELIEVE Joni had abandoned her daughter, but then she reminded herself that plenty of mothers looked innocent and were later convicted of worse things than that. You never really knew someone or the demons they hold that forced them to do things people would never guess they could do. But to let your young child wander along the highway where any sicko could've picked her up?

Taylor couldn't imagine it, but suddenly, she lost her appetite and crumpled the rest of her slice of pizza up in the napkin.

"There's also the possibility that her mother is somewhere around here, and Molly got out, or was put out," Taylor said. "We canvassed the area and knocked on doors, but no one claims to know Molly."

"Which could be true since they aren't from here, but you are right. Joni may have set up a meeting with someone around here, and they've got her but sent the kid out. Not every criminal has the stomach to hurt a child."

"Woodside Apartments was closest to the store Molly walked into. I called the manager there, and he did a drive around the complex but didn't see the truck," Taylor said. "I knocked on a lot of doors but came up empty."

"She could still be there, and the truck parked elsewhere."

"Agree. We've got two deputies out looking for it now, but I'd also like to get out there as soon as we're done interviewing the women."

He turned to her sharply. "You don't give up, do you?"

She held her hands out and smiled. "Come on, Shane. This was my case, and you're still lead, but let me in. You know I've got a gut for reading people."

He rolled his eyes. "I never could tell you no. But you let me do the talking, or you're out. I mean it."

"Deal."

They both stared at the board.

"I just figured out what's been niggling at me," Shane said.

"And?"

"She looks like Lucy. Or at least what I remember Lucy looking like when she was in junior high. Dark hair, dark eyes. That sad, lost expression. There's your emotional connection."

Taylor hadn't seen it before, but now that Shane had pointed it out, yes, she could see a resemblance. Shane hadn't known Lucy when she was a young girl, but she'd pretty much kept her same look as she'd gone through school. In high school, the eyes that Lucy had hated for so long were suddenly coveted, as she'd been told they were bedroom eyes.

"I don't see it," she lied.

She wasn't giving him any reason whatsoever to think she couldn't handle working with him on this one.

"Hmm. Maybe I'm wrong—" he started, then the phone ringing cut him off. He picked it up, said a few words, then set the receiver back in the cradle. "They're here. Saddle up."

# CHAPTER 17

Sheila Stott was exactly as Taylor had pegged her, or at least that was what her initial assessment was within the first five minutes of her walking into the interview room, bringing her other daughter and the not-so-fresh scent of cigarettes right in with her.

At least forty-five but could pass for fifty-five, Sheila Stott was a nervous woman who was probably made even more so by the tall, insulated cup she carried filled to the brim with Mountain Dew over ice. Stott was skinny, but not in a good way. More in a lives-on-caffeine-and-cigarettes kind of way that wouldn't look good on anyone.

Though they'd had a long day on the road, her makeup was thick, her eyes still lined perfectly around the obviously fake eyelashes, and her hair sprayed into place with some seriously stiff hairspray.

"Oh, this is exciting," she babbled. "I've never been interrogated before."

Her festive mood was disturbing.

Shane didn't correct her and pretended not to see the wink she gave him. He let her have the floor, and Sheila didn't stop talking. Most of what she was saying wasn't useful and was more like the ramblings of a squirrel on crack than a mother worried about her grown daughter and grandchild. It was taking everything Taylor had in her not to interrupt, but she knew more than likely Shane was letting her go, hoping something important would slip out.

"Can you tell us the last time you saw your daughter and granddaughter?" he finally broke in, directing her back to a useful line of questioning.

Sheila tapped her red coffin-shaped nails against the table and fluttered her eyes at the ceiling as if waiting for an answer to drop from it.

"Your birthday," her daughter Jessica reminded her.

Only twenty-one, but the sister already gave off a better impression than the mother did, as far as Taylor was concerned. The girl barely looked like her mother, but there was some resemblance in their facial structure. Where her mother was cranked up with nervous energy, Jessica was calm. More worried about her sister than the mom seemed to be.

"Oh, that's right. February second," Sheila said, dipping forward against the table to give Shane a grand view of her cleavage.

She flipped her bleached hair flirtatiously and let it land over her shoulder, clearing the view of the wrinkled skin across her breasts. She was tanned so dark she looked leathery, a look that Taylor despised on a woman.

She didn't like her.

"It's June now," Taylor said. "And you haven't seen them since February?"

"Well, Tampa is a two-hour drive for me," Sheila said.

"They had a fight," Jessica added. "Mom ran her out of the house, and they haven't spoken since. Joni was scared to come back."

*Thank you, Jessica.*

"Oh, what about?" Shane asked.

Sheila crossed her arms tightly across her chest. "That's irrelevant. Can we just wrap this up for tonight so I can go get my grand baby?"

*Absolutely not*, Taylor thought.

"I'm sorry, Mrs., um…"

"Miss," Sheila confirmed.

"Miss Stott, yes. At this point, everything is relevant to find your daughter. And we are in contact with child services and have set up a meeting for you to talk to them tomorrow, first thing in the morning. I'm fairly sure you will get to see Molly then, too."

"Child services? Why? I want Molly now. Tonight. She needs her Gigi." She looked suddenly livid, her eyes opening obscenely wide and turning dark.

Taylor could see how she could be terrifying, even if she didn't weigh any more than a popcorn fart. Crazy was its own superpower, in a whole other league than most, and Taylor had a feeling that Mama Stott was trying to hide her cape.

"Mom, stop. They have procedures," Jessica whispered.

"Bullshit. That's my granddaughter, and if I have to get a lawyer—"

Shane held a hand up. "Hold on, Miss Stott. Let's calm down. No one is keeping Molly from you, but your daughter is right. There are procedures to this kind of thing. We can't just hand over a child to anyone who claims them. Once your relation to the child is confirmed and they've done a substantial enough background screening, I'm sure they'll allow you to take Molly into your custody. For your convenience, I've booked you a room at the Rose Cottage close to downtown. It's much more fitting for a lady than our local motel."

*A lady.*

Taylor nearly laughed at the tone Shane took. She hadn't heard him use that persuasive voice since the night of prom when he'd talked her father into believing they were going to come straight home after the event and not stop at any parties.

He'd honed it to perfection, and Sheila calmed right down.

"Screen all you want," she said. "The only thing that'll come up is a bogus charge of disorderly at a concert for Blake Shelton last year, and I'm working on getting that expunged off my record. I didn't throw that beer bottle. My friend did."

Her daughter looked like she wished the floor would open and swallow her.

"The fight was about school. Joni wants to study to be a nurse, and she wants Mom's help paying for it," Jessica said. "Or at least help paying for childcare."

Taylor jotted that down.

"I told her that if she'd graduated high school before she got pregnant, she could probably have gotten scholarships to pay her way. She made her bed, and she's got to lay in it. I'm not supporting an adult," Sheila said.

"She wasn't asking you to support her," Jessica said. "She just wanted help until after she graduates. She's applying for student loans, too. You know she barely makes enough to survive and pay her bills now. And you're paying for my college courses, so it doesn't seem fair that you wouldn't help her a little."

Sheila turned and glared at her daughter. "I don't see you with a rounded belly or a kid on your hip, either. Make that mistake and you'll be on your own, too. You'd better be grateful. I could have a vacation home for what that school is charging me. All because you think you want to be a veterinarian. And grad school is all on you. Just for the record."

"Yes, I know that. You've only reminded me a million times since I told you," Jessica said. "I haven't asked you to pay for grad school, have I? And don't forget, Dad is helping, and I have a partial scholarship, too. I'm working as many hours as I can to pay for my share. It's not like you're shouldering all of it."

Taylor wanted to reach across the table and strangle the

woman. She'd guarantee that Miss Bleached-Out-Mountain-Dew-Queen Sheila hadn't been the best example to her daughters and shouldn't be throwing stones. Whatever happened to a mother's mercy? Or compassion? How such a nasty woman had what appeared to be two decent daughters was almost as big a mystery as where Joni was hiding.

Sheila Stott came across as the kind of mother who would never consider a baby a blessing. To her, they were either a burden or a bargaining chip. Probably both.

"What does Joni do for a job now?" Shane asked after tapping Taylor's foot under the table. An obvious sign for her to keep her cool.

Taylor took deep breaths and clutched her pen harder to keep her hand from traveling the short distance to Sheila's throat.

Jessica looked from Shane to her mother, then regretfully back to Shane. "She was waitressing, but she lost her job in April when she couldn't make rent and pay her babysitter, too. With no one to keep Molly the weekend nights they wanted her to work, they fired her. She's been maxing out credit cards to stay afloat."

Sheila rolled her eyes to the ceiling and let out a dramatic sigh. "She's just like her father."

"Who is her father?" Shane asked, his pen poised in midair.

"A major screwup, that's who," said Sheila. "Why is that relevant? I've already talked to him, and he hasn't seen or heard from her either. He couldn't care less about Joni. I've told her that, too."

*I'll bet you did, you evil snake.*

Taylor took another deep breath and said a prayer for constraint.

Shane led them into answering the routine questions: description of Joni, scars, height, weight, hair color and length, glasses or contacts—the whole nine yards. They already knew some of it from her driver's license and her social network accounts, but it was always good to see what the family members had to say too. They quizzed Jessica, who appeared to be on much better terms with her sister, about any known alias or trouble with men.

"She can't keep a boyfriend," Sheila interjected.

"Not true," Jessica said, giving her mother a dirty look. "She and Josh dated the entire time they were in high school and another two years after Molly was born. He even gave her a promise ring."

Sheila snorted. "Some ring. Gaudy little purple and green thing."

"It's an emerald and an amethyst for Joni and Molly's birthstones," Jessica said. "I think it was sweet. Anyway, I'm just saying. Joni is picky about who she has around Molly. And she barely has time for herself. A boyfriend is last on her list of priorities right now. Not everyone has to have men in their lives on a rotating door, Mom."

Sheila sat up straighter and glared at her daughter. "You'd better watch your mouth."

Jessica clamped shut, and the room filled with an even more uncomfortable energy.

"Look, Officers," said Sheila, turning on the sugar again, "I know I don't seem that concerned about Joni, but I have a feeling that she's just run off with some boy. She's probably laid up in his apartment and didn't notice that Molly got out and went wandering. Now that she knows what she let happen, she's afraid to come forward. Can't you track her phone, or something like that?"

"Joni wouldn't do that," Jessica said.

"Which part?" asked Shane.

"Any of it. She's a good mom, and if she'd met someone and planned to meet them—which I don't think she'd do with Molly around—she would've told me. I think she's still in love with Josh anyway."

"She's not as great a mom as you try to preach to everyone, Jessica," Sheila said, venom lacing her words.

Jessica looked at her mother. "Not true. You're still bitter because you wanted her to turn Molly over to you once you fell in love with her, and Joni said absolutely not. You even tried to bribe her, and Joni wasn't going to sell her child."

Sheila looked like she wanted to reach out and strangle her daughter.

Shane cleared his throat. "Can we get back to what can help? So, there were no other guys in her life lately?"

"Not really," Jessica said. "The only guy she's mentioned in the last month was one she thought might buy her truck, and that was a few weeks ago."

Taylor and Shane both sat upright and leaned forward at the same time. It could be nothing, or it could be something. Taylor was hoping for the latter.

"Oh my God," Sheila said. "Are you telling me she was going to sell that thing? Her grandpa gave her that truck. It's been in the family for more than a decade."

"Mom, I've tried to tell you. She's desperate to pay her bills. You know she won't ask to come home, and she's got to live somewhere. Rent is high. Trucks get good money, and she was going to take what she got and buy a cheaper car, then use the rest to stay afloat a while longer."

"That's great information, Jessica," Shane said. "Can you tell us any more about it? Do you have anything on text message? Name or location of the interested party?"

Jessica looked at her phone and scanned through her message trail from Joni.

"No. She just said she'd listed it for sale and only one guy was interested but was giving her a hard time about the price she wanted. But she didn't mention it again, and I thought she'd decided to keep it."

"Where did she list it?" Taylor asked.

Jessica shrugged. "Not sure. Craigslist or Marketplace, I guess."

"I'll do an online search with the vehicle details and see what comes up," Taylor said.

"Miss Stott, if you know what telephone provider Joni uses, we'll work on getting the records released to us. We also need to know where she banked at so we can see what her latest transactions were."

"Verizon, and I don't think she has a bank account," Sheila said.

"Cricket for the phone, and she has an account at Bank of America," Jessica said. "The last place she worked for only paid through direct deposit, so she had to set up an account. She also puts her child support checks in there, though they are few and far between. She won't keep cash in her home, and she pays her bills online anyway."

"That leads to my next question," Shane said, beating Taylor to it even though it was on the tip of her tongue. "I need to know more about Molly's father. What's the situation? Could he have taken them somewhere? Possibly a custody dispute?"

"Not unless he's a deserter for the United States Army," Sheila said. "Josh signed up last year and, as far as we know, is still at training camp. Joni never forced him to be a father, and he's never tried to get custody. He walks all over her."

"No, he doesn't. He helps her out when he can, and they try to co-parent the best they can. She makes it easy on him so one day he and Molly can have a closer relationship, Mom. Not everyone wants to put their child through the hell of ongoing family court to haggle over money they don't have."

"You are so naïve, Jessica," Sheila said under her breath.

"Josh would never hurt her," Jessica said. "Joni still loves him."

Taylor wouldn't count on that. She knew that sometimes the person you'd take a bullet for was behind the trigger.

"Does Joni have any identifying tattoos?" Taylor asked.

"God, no," said Sheila.

"Yes," Jessica said. "A tiny sunflower on her ankle."

"Figures," said Sheila.

"I have one, too, Mom. We got them together on my birthday," Jessica said.

Sheila puffed up like a dragon, her eyebrows straight to the roof.

"Which ankle?" Taylor asked, jotting down a note.

"I'm not sure now," Jessica said. "Wait. We did opposite, and mine is on my right. So hers is on her left ankle."

"I'd like to have Molly's father's full name and how to reach him, then I think we're done here for tonight," Shane said.

"It's Joshua Greene. I'll look up his number." Jessica retrieved her phone again and found the contact information, then let Shane copy it down on his pad.

When he was done, he stood and opened the door. "Miss Rose locks the door in an hour, so that should give you time to grab a bite to eat if you haven't already, then get in and settled for the night. Taylor will text you the address to social services and the name of your contact there. We need to confirm the time, so please call in the morning."

"Who the hell runs a business by locking the door at nine o'clock at night?" Sheila muttered, then grabbed her fake purse and got up.

"Thank you, Detectives," Jessica said.

"Deputy Gray," Taylor corrected her, then nodded over at Shane. "That's Detective Weaver."

"*Detective* Weaver, where might someone stop to get a take-home drink?" Sheila asked as she smiled at Shane.

It was clear that she wasn't talking about Dr. Pepper.

"Sorry," he replied. "No liquor stores until you get to the county line, and you wouldn't make it there and back by nine."

Taylor was relieved he didn't tell her about the Den.

Sheila brushed close to him on her way out of the room, and Shane looked over her head at Taylor. She could see he was forcing politeness and ready to get her out of there.

Taylor took the lead on a beeline for the lobby and the door to the parking lot. "I'll show you out."

# CHAPTER 18

*T*his must be exactly what the walking dead feels like. Taylor finished the very last drops of her coffee and grabbed the leash off the hook. Her body was stiff, and every muscle ached, especially her neck which tended to hold all her tension.

When she'd rolled out of bed, her phone was lit up with a message from Penner.

> Your sister bailed out by Roland Ellis. Long rap sheet. Enticement of a minor, assault and battery, domestic violence in the second degree. That's just page one. Bad dude.

His report made her morning that much worse. She didn't understand how Lucy was such a magnet for the scumbags who found her. Taylor couldn't deal with it today, though. The sheriff had decided to pull her off patrol and let her work with Shane on finding Joni Stott, or at least work to find out if she was even a missing person. The only thing new they had right now was that Molly's father's alibi was confirmed. He hadn't left the training site in weeks.

Taylor wanted to get to the station before Shane and get some work done while Joni's mother and sister were visiting with Molly. No doubt she'd hightail it to them as her next stop and complain that she couldn't take her granddaughter with her that day.

Poor Wesley didn't know what was about to hit him. She had touched base with him the night before, giving him the short version of what was going on and asking him to be present with Molly and her family instead of letting a less-experienced case-worker do it, but she hoped he woke with a lot of patience. She wanted to be there herself, but that wasn't her call, and she didn't want to rock the boat.

"Come on, B." She opened the door and stepped out, immediately squinting at the bright sunlight, then struggled for the sunglasses atop her head.

She had exactly half an hour before she needed to be at the station. Switching shifts for this case had her routines and patterns all screwed up. Normally, she'd still be sleeping off the night shift at this time.

Bernard leapt to his feet and joined her on the porch, his tail pumping air at the glee of an impending walk.

"At least one of us has some energy," she mumbled, then didn't hook him, trusting that he wouldn't run. She bunched the leash up in her hand, and they took off.

Her night was more restless than usual, filled with questions about Joni Stott and worries about Lucy and her dad. Once she left the station, she'd driven home on autopilot, checked to see if she had any emails from Lucy, then dropped her clothes and crawled into the bed without a shower or even so much as washing her face.

"This way, boy," Taylor called out, then turned down a worn path behind her house.

Bernard followed, eager to explore somewhere new.

Turned out that dealing with a passive-aggressive and narcissistic woman like Sheila Stott was more exhausting than any foot chase behind all her fleeing criminals put together.

Bernard saw something in the brush and bolted.

"Whoa," Taylor said, worried it was a snake.

She was too tired, and he was much too big to be carried out of there if he got bit.

He ignored her.

"Heel!"

Still nothing. He rambled through the brush like he was digging up something.

"Heel, Bernard. *Foos*!"

Immediately, he stopped and trotted back to her, then sat at her feet.

"What the..." Taylor had used the German translation for "heel" without even thinking about it. She'd learned a few terms when she was in the academy, a study she did on her own in the hopes that one day she'd have a police dog. Unfortunately, Hart's Ridge didn't have the budget for one.

"*Platz*," she said, deciding to try another.

Immediately, he lay down.

"What about *gib laut*?"

He threw his head back and barked.

"Holy shit, Bernard. You've been trained!" Taylor couldn't believe it, though she knew just because he understood a few general commands in German didn't mean he was a police dog.

Many people thought it was amusing to teach their cues in another language. She'd lost count of the dogs she'd come across in the field who only responded to Spanish commands.

But German?

He was her first. Well, other than the dogs she'd met who really were police trained.

She was running late on time and knew they needed to get back, but she wracked her memory for one more German command. Suddenly she remembered.

"*Geh voraus,*" she said, waving her hand toward the path they'd come down.

Bernard jumped up and ran ahead, just as he was supposed to. Taylor followed and found herself full of sudden energy, fueled by excitement.

But by the time they reached the house, she realized that she couldn't just stop looking for his original owner.

What if he belonged to another police force and was lost? It wasn't completely out of the question. She'd seen alerts come across their board several times about lost or stolen service dogs. Her excitement died down when she realized that if that was the case, she'd have to give him back.

Sometimes it really sucked to always do the right thing.

At the house, she grabbed a shower, then twisted her hair up into a tight bun and pinned it. After a touch of mascara and lip gloss, she put on her uniform and shoes, grabbed a banana, and headed to the door.

Bernard sat in front of it.

"Sorry, buddy, not this time." She tried to scoot him over with her foot.

He wouldn't budge.

"Move, Bernard," she said, but then made the mistake of locking eyes with him.

He had perfected the hangdog expression, his big brown eyes puddles of emotion as he silently begged her not to leave him home alone again.

"You might be a good, disciplined boy, but you aren't on the force. You have to stay here. Want a treat?" She took one of his favorite morsels from the bag she kept on the countertop, waved it under his nose, then threw it about six feet away.

He blinked at her as though asking if she really thought he'd fall for that one.

Taylor sighed. If she let him ride with her to the station, then maybe whoever was going off shift could ride him back.

"Would that be enough?"

He wagged his tail as though he'd read her mind.

She opened the door and gave him the command to go ahead, but she wasted her breath, because before she could get off the porch, he was sitting at her car, waiting for her to open the driver's side door.

"Back seat, bonehead." She opened the back door, and he jumped in.

They were halfway to the station when her dispatch called through on the radio and instructed Taylor that Detective Weaver asked her to report to social services and observe the interaction between Molly and her grandmother.

She looked at the clock. That gave her ten minutes to get there, so that meant she'd have to take Bernard with her again. She glanced at him in the mirror and laughed. He looked like the proudest criminal she'd ever seen, his head held high and his tongue hanging happily as he surveyed the scenery going by.

"You'd better behave," she warned him, then turned off.

As she drove, the radio went off again with a call about a coyote sighting near the Forester Ranch and asking for someone to check it out. Clint picked it up, but Taylor could just see him rolling his eyes at what he'd find a waste of his time. Clint never did understand that small-town law enforcement was supposed to be there for the community and all its needs, not just criminal activity. She still didn't get why he didn't go to the big city and get a job, since he seemed to hate everything about Hart's Ridge.

Only the week before, he'd lost his cool when a call came in about someone who wanted to make an incident report against the manager of the Biscuit Barn because they'd gotten home and realized their chicken biscuit was missing the chicken.

Stupid, yes, but you couldn't go off on people for their nonsense. Dispatch had patched Taylor in to smooth the ruffled feathers of both the biscuit-eater and the manager, who were ready to come to blows not only with each other but also with Deputy McElroy for being such an ass about the whole thing.

She pulled into the parking lot, and Taylor immediately spotted Della Ray's car. You couldn't miss it as it was a pale-pink older sedan with a Mary Kay sticker on the window. Della Ray never sold for them, but one of her daughters was a successful consultant and had given the car to her mom after she'd earned herself a newer one.

On the other side of the parking lot was a fancy Range Rover with Florida plates. Taylor wished she had time to run them, but since they were all inside, she didn't want them to start the visit without her.

She parked and called in her location.

"Come on, boy." She got out and opened the door for Bernard, then they both went to the building and inside.

Jessica saw her first from the lobby. She was sitting facing the door, but her mother, Sheila, was pacing and was pointed the other way.

Taylor nodded, and Jessica smiled slightly, though it could have been at Bernard.

He followed as she waved at the receptionist and slipped quietly down the hall before Sheila could spot her and start a conversation. She already looked perturbed, and Taylor wasn't in the mood.

She stopped at Wesley's office door.

"—and they came all the way from Florida to see you," he was saying to Molly.

Della Ray was in one chair, and Molly was standing up near her, though the other chair beside her was empty. She looked very nervous, and Taylor couldn't blame her. Social services, or any government building, was a scary place for a child.

"Hi, Molly," she said, then went inside and knelt before the girl.

Bernard followed.

"Well, what a nice surprise, Taylor," Della Ray said. "And you brought Bernard, too. Look, Molly. Remember Taylor's dog?"

Over Molly's head, Della Ray mouthed the words, *She's scared.*

Taylor felt a surge of protectiveness for the girl. She'd been in her shoes too many times to count. Sometimes there were reasons to be afraid of your own family.

"No dogs allowed, Deputy Gray," Wesley said.

"He's an emotional support animal," Taylor lied.

He probably knew she was lying too and expected it. He'd never call her on it though.

"I brought him to keep Molly company for the visit."

Bernard joined Taylor in front of Della Ray and Molly, his tail wagging even harder when he saw the girl. Molly smiled gently and put her hand out. When Bernard instantly licked it, she giggled and pulled it back to her chest.

"Ooh, he really likes you, Molly," Taylor said. "How would you like for him to come with you while you visit your grandmother and your auntie?"

Molly looked up at her. "Okay. Can you come, too?"

Della Ray raised her eyebrows at Taylor, probably surprised that Molly had said so many words at once.

"I'm sorry, but it's best if Deputy Gray stays out here with Ms. Della Ray." Wesley said.

Taylor turned to challenge him but saw the look he held. He was right. She could only press her luck so far. The family had a right to a visit without feeling like criminals.

"Mr. Wright will be in there with you, sweetie," she said to Molly. "Bernard, too. And I promise, I'll be really close in case you need me. Okay?"

Molly nodded.

Wesley stood. "We'd better get this going. I think we have a few impatient people in the lobby."

His tone told Taylor that he'd already met Sheila.

"I'll be in the observation room," Taylor said, then let another lie slip. "Sheriff's orders."

He nodded, then led Molly out the door.

Bernard looked at Molly going, then up at Taylor.

"Go," she whispered. "Watch out for her."

He trotted behind them to catch up, and Taylor felt a rush of pride for him.

She followed Della Ray to the observation room that was adjacent to what they called the Family Hall. It wasn't really a hall, but it was a nice area that the town had come together and raised funds to renovate into a cozy place for children under the care of social services to visit with their family. One side held a tiny kitchen area complete with drinks and snacks available, and a few small tables to sit at. The other end was outfitted with a comfortable couch and beanbag chairs facing a television where the family could watch cartoons together.

"Has she said anything useful?" Taylor asked Della Ray.

"No, not at all. She's an extremely quiet child. And I'm not about to poke at her with questions and make her retreat further."

"That's good. At least we know who she is now. But how she got here and where her mother is remains a mystery. Maybe she'll say something to them today. I'm glad it was set up here so she can feel safe."

"You did a wonderful thing here, Taylor," Della Ray said.

"Not me," Taylor said. "It was a joint effort."

"But it wouldn't have happened without you leading it."

Taylor's face burned. She didn't need the acknowledgement.

The room had turned out well, and Taylor was proud of it. She'd spear-headed the project and had personally seen to it that it held everything that would've made it a less scary session when she and her sisters had met with their own dad on occasion.

Along the soft pastel walls were shelves of books, paper, pencils, and things to color with, as well as several stuffed animals if a child felt the need for something soft to hold.

Despite the comfortable ambiance of the room, parents were still usually outraged that they had to use it and earn their way back to being alone with their own children. It always amazed Taylor how clueless an adult could be.

Della Ray had been here many times, as many of her foster kids went through a process of supervised visits before they could be reunified as a family, and only then if the parents had gone through the court-ordered steps. Sometimes they had to finish drug rehabilitation, or parental classes, or even anger management.

The observation room, however, was just that. A small room with a table and two chairs, and a window that overlooked the Family Hall. Taylor had been in it several times, usually to watch and listen in when a psychologist was interviewing a child about any alleged abuse that he or she had been the recipient of.

She went to the window to watch for them.

Wesley brought Molly into the room and told her to sit where she liked. She chose a beanbag chair, and Bernard stayed close, settling on the floor next to her. Two minutes later, the door burst open, and Sheila came through, Jessica and Wes behind her.

"Come here, Molly," Sheila called out as she crossed the room. "Give your Gigi a hug."

Molly slowly approached, then stiffly let herself be hugged.

Taylor couldn't see her face, but it was clear that Molly was not overwhelmed with joy to see the woman.

"Hi, Molly," Jessica said. She knelt and held her arms out.

Molly entered them willingly, then clung to her aunt.

"Would you look at that," Della Ray said. "She doesn't seem too fond of her grandmother."

"Yep." But at least Molly was happy to see one of them.

Jessica rocked her back and forth, soothing her with quiet

words that Taylor couldn't quite make out. When they broke apart, there were tear tracks on both faces, though Sheila's remained dry and frozen in a jealous grimace.

She turned to Wesley. "What have you done to her? She's obviously traumatized."

Wesley gave her a look that told her she'd better zip her lip. "Why don't we sit down?"

He led them to a small table, and Molly sat on one side with Jessica. Bernard settled under the table, his nose on the child's feet. Sheila took a chair on the other side, and Wes grabbed a few color books and a box of crayons and joined them.

"Want to color?" Jessica said, then pulled two of the books over to their side. She found a page for Molly and gave her a few crayons, then joined in.

Taylor wanted to reach through the glass and pat her on the back for her gentleness, and while she was at it, she could slap Sheila. There was no doubt that Wesley had briefed them before bringing them into the room, and she knew better than to talk *over* Molly, or to say things that could upset the child.

"I've seen people just like that woman," Della Ray said. "They think because their blood runs through the child's veins, they have some sort of claim of ownership and can do and say what they want. Don't let her get you riled, Taylor."

Taylor drew a deep breath and let it out slowly. Della Ray knew her so well.

Jessica continued to try to occupy Molly with gentle talk of the unicorns they were coloring and what shade the clouds should be, and Sheila peppered Wesley with questions about where Molly was staying and how many children were there, and other things she need not know, or at least not ask in front of her granddaughter.

Suddenly, Sheila looked at Molly and slammed her hand on the table. "Molly, you tell me right now where your mother is. Who dropped you off? You know something, so spit it out."

Wesley's mouth fell open, and red crept up his neck and climbed all the way to his ears. Bernard felt the tension in the air and sat up, his ears at full attention.

Molly looked at her grandmother, an expression of terror filling her face. "I don't know."

"Yes, you do," Sheila said. "What's his name?"

"Mom!" Jessica said. "We were told not to ask her about that."

Molly began to tremble, and her eyes filled with tears.

Taylor started for the door, but Della Ray grabbed her arm.

"Let me go, Della Ray. She has no right to interrogate a child like that." Taylor shook with fury.

"Wes will take care of it," Della Ray said. "Don't make more of a scene. Molly is scared enough without seeing an officer reprimand anyone."

Wesley stood. He tried to soften his expression, but rage simmered underneath. Sheila had just made an enemy, and one thing you did not want to do is piss off social services.

"Come on, Molly," he said. "The visit is over for now, sweetie. Tell them goodbye."

Sheila jumped up so quickly that the small chair she was in flipped over backward, making a racket that caused Molly to jump.

"I'm taking her home with me. I know my rights," she flamed. "I'm next of kin and can provide a safe and nurturing environment for her until Joni comes home."

*Nurturing my ass.* Taylor couldn't believe the woman's nerve.

Jessica looked frozen in disbelief, and Molly directed her gaze to her feet.

Taylor touched the gun on her hip and took one more step to the observation room door.

Wesley opened the Family Hall door with his free hand and stood aside. "Right now, I am standing in for Molly's rights, and I feel that we need to bring in our child psychologist to talk to her before anything is decided further. She'll return to her foster home today, where she feels safe."

Sheila sputtered something unintelligible and pulled out her phone. "I'm going to call a lawyer. He'll sort this out."

Wesley nodded. "You do that, Miss Stott. That's your right. In the meantime, this visit is over. I'd like you to leave, please." He held Molly's hand gently but firmly.

Jessica squatted in front of Molly and hugged her. "Don't worry, Molly. Everything is fine. We'll figure this out and find your mom, okay?"

"Don't make her promises you can't keep," Sheila said. "Her mother is probably halfway to Mexico or Canada by now, shacking up with some criminal. She's not thinking about Molly."

"That is not true. Molly, your mommy loves you so much," Jessica said, then glared at her mother. "What is wrong with you? That is not helpful."

Taylor felt sorry for Jessica. It was clear that she was carefully balancing the beam between disgust with her mom's behavior and trying to be on her side. It was sad when the child was more empathetic and understanding than their parent, but Taylor had seen it time and again. Some mothers never grew up.

Sheila was fiddling with her phone, thumping the screen in hard, vicious pecks.

"Please make your calls outside," Wesley said, then beckoned them out the door.

Sheila mouthed off to Jessica all the way down the hall and into the lobby. Thankfully, her voice faded when they exited the building, and Wesley looked at the glass and waved for Taylor and Della Ray to come in.

"Let me go hug that child," Della Ray said, pushing past Taylor to get to Molly. "I'm going to have to get her a special treat, too."

Taylor was relieved that Sheila was gone, and Della Ray was there to console Molly, as she'd done with Taylor and her sisters so many times. Della Ray had the touch. No effort needed, and children immediately felt comforted.

"Go, Ms. Della Ray. Do your thing." Taylor was eager to go, too. Sheila Stott was anything, but grandmotherly material and she'd already had her chance to screw up two daughters, she sure didn't need another. They had to find Joni Stott—for Molly's sake.

# CHAPTER 19

*B*ack at the station, with Bernard in tow, Taylor cruised past the bullpen. Clint looked up and dismissed her without a word. She ignored him and kept going until she stood in the doorframe of Shane's office.

He didn't hear her, and for a few seconds, she observed him in full concentration mode. He was making notes on the whiteboard, and the furrows in his brow were deep and dark, his mouth in a taut line of intensity. Without his public face on, she could see the boy he used to be.

"I'm back," she finally said.

He looked up and smiled, seeming happy to see her. It was a nice change from the dirty look that Clint had shot over the bullpen wall at the sight of her.

"How did it go?" he asked.

Taylor sighed, then came in and took a chair in front of his desk.

Bernard greeted Shane with a sniff, then settled by the door.

"As expected with Sheila Stott, it was quite a shit show. She intimidated Molly, didn't seem concerned for Joni, and pissed

Wesley off in a mighty way. She'll be lucky to get within fifty feet of her granddaughter anytime again soon."

"She's probably already screaming about her rights, too." He sat down at the desk.

Taylor nodded. "Yep. She played the lawyer card again. After she left, Wesley told Della Ray and me that he's assigning Molly a court-appointed advocate. That way, she'll have someone to conduct due diligence on her behalf and depending on what we find out about her mother, make a recommendation to the judge on just what they think is best for Molly."

"Did anything helpful come up about Joni?"

"Nope. Molly was shaking and started to cry, so Wesley stopped it right there. Joni's mom thinks her daughter abandoned Molly and is on a wild joyride. Her sister is still very concerned and said Joni would never leave Molly unattended or put her in danger. Unlike their mother, Jessica seems stable and logical. Molly warmed right up to her. Anyway, what do you have?" She directed her attention back to the board.

"Tampa PD went through the apartment, and nothing is out of place, but they took fingerprints from the outer door and a few places inside. The property manager sent the only video they have, and she nor her truck was on it. He's also checked every spot on the grounds to be sure she and her truck are not there. But we do have one thing. I got the phone records coming over, but they already told me the last place her phone pinged was just out of town at a gas station on Highway 515 in Jasper. I've called them, and they have video."

Excitement surged through Taylor. "Did they tell you anything about it? Who else was with her?"

"Nope. Nothing. The manager left it for the clerk to give to me."

"Give me the address, and I'll go grab it now," she said. "If it's Jasper, it will take me an hour each way, so let me touch base with the sergeant."

"No need. I already told them we're going." Shane picked up his keys.

He stood aside and let her go out, then followed.

"C'mon, Bernard." Taylor was surprised that so far, nothing had been said about her bringing her dog into the station. Even Clint hadn't blinked an eye, missing an opportunity to throw her under the bus by stating company policy only allowed service dogs inside.

"I'll drive my car," Shane said.

They were walking past the bullpen, and Clint looked up again, this time with a knowing sneer on his face.

"I really need to take the squad car in case I get called to an emergency," Taylor said, ignoring Clint's silent insult.

Why was it when a man walked around with a man, it wasn't a big deal, but when a woman walked with a man, something was going on? The constant double standard irritated the hell out of her.

"Fine," said Shane. "Just thought I'd offer."

"You just make sure those phone records are delivered to your inbox. We also need to see who she was calling to meet her about the truck."

They got in, buckled up, and were only on the road less than five minutes when a call came in as 10-10 Fight or Disorder and 10-39 Urgent-Use Lights. Taylor listened to the address and was glad she was driving.

She told Bernard to hold on, flipped her blue light on, and whipped a U-turn. She headed to the Dairy Queen on Cold Springs Road.

"I see nothing has changed at the best ice-cream spot in town," Shane said, grinning at her as he clutched his armrest. "Always something happening."

"Well, yeah, but usually only at night on the weekends. Not midday on a Monday."

He was right, though. For some reason, when Friday night

rolled around, the parking lot of the Dairy Queen was a magnet to raging hormones driven by lifted trucks. The teenagers gathered there and sometimes tended to get out of hand. Nothing too criminal, though.

Taylor pulled in, and her heart nearly stopped when she saw a small crowd gathered around a vehicle parked next to an old pink sedan. "Oh no. I see Della Ray's car."

Shane exploded with profanity. He knew Della Ray, too. The whole town did, and they all loved her. Though he could also be cussing because the only witness to whatever happened to Joni Stott was Molly, who was obviously in the care of Della Ray. Molly was their best chance to figure out where her mother was, and Shane needed to solve the case or go back to his own town as a failure. Or at least that's what Taylor figured based on what she remembered about him and his pride.

She whipped halfway across two parking places and cut the motor, then jumped out, already trying to find Molly and Della Ray over the heads of the onlookers.

Shane followed behind her with Bernard, taking a quieter approach.

"Move aside," Taylor called out, pushing against two rednecks until they broke apart and gave her a path.

As she feared, the car the crowd appeared to be blocking in was the white Range Rover with Florida plates. Della Ray stood outside the driver's window, pounding on the glass as tears poured down her cheeks.

Sheila sat in the seat, staring straight ahead. There wasn't anyone in the passenger seat, and the back windows were too dark to see inside.

"Open this door right now," Della Ray yelled through her sobs.

"I'm here, Della Ray," Taylor said. "We'll take care of this."

Della Ray whipped around. "She followed us. I didn't see her come inside until she'd already yanked Molly away and ran out with her. I'm so sorry."

"Not your fault. Now move aside and let me talk to this maniac." Taylor clenched and unclenched her fists as she moved closer.

Seeing Della Ray in such a fright didn't sit well with her, and she couldn't imagine how terrified Molly was while in the middle of such chaos.

She used her knuckle to peck on the window. "Miss Stott, I'm giving you two minutes to open this door and exit the vehicle, or I will have to use force."

Shane moved around to the other side and pressed his face to the glass to try and see into the back.

No response from Sheila.

"Molly and Jessica are in back," Shane reported over the top of the car. "They look upset but fine."

*Thank God for that.*

Taylor leaned in again. "Miss Stott, you have less than sixty seconds to step out, or you will be arrested for kidnapping, child endangerment, and failure to comply with law enforcement."

Suddenly, she could hear Jessica shrieking from the back seat, telling her mother to open the door.

The lock clicked, and slowly, Sheila began to open the door.

Taylor planted her feet wide apart, wedged her hand in and pulled it wide open. She flipped the locks for the other doors, then jerked Sheila out of the driver's seat and threw her against the vehicle.

The side of her face made a satisfying splat against the back door.

"Wait, you can't do that," Sheila yelled and struggled.

"Watch me." Taylor could feel the cords in her neck straining, but she easily wrangled Sheila's arms behind her back, slapped the handcuffs on her, then turned around, thanked the crowd, and asked them to disperse.

Shane opened the door on the other side, and through the glass, Taylor saw Jessica climb out, then help Molly out and onto her hip where she carried her like a toddler.

Della Ray rushed to them.

"I'm so sorry," Jessica kept saying. "I told her not to do this. I swear, I told her to stop."

Della Ray took Molly from Jessica and set her on the ground behind the SUV where Taylor could see, then checked her over and finally pulled her into a tight hug.

Bernard, who Taylor had forgotten even existed and was relieved he was still with them, stood beside Molly, licking her little hands.

Molly wasn't saying a word. She clutched the hem of her sweater in her hands as she watched the ruckus, her eyes wide in fear.

Sheila continued to babble on about Molly being her granddaughter, her blood, and it was her right to take her.

"You've lost your mind," Taylor said. "Just look at what you've done to her! As though she hasn't already been through God only knows what with her mom."

Sheila let loose a long string of profanity. She was surprisingly strong for being so skinny, and Taylor had to hold on tightly as she was being verbally abused.

Another car screeched in, and within seconds, the sheriff was beside them, just in time to see Taylor hold Sheila's head against the vehicle in an attempt to shut her up.

"Deputy Gray," Sheriff Dawkins said. "Stand down. I'll take over."

Taylor looked back at him, caught off guard.

"Now," he said, his face a mask of disappointment.

At her.

Taylor let go and backed off Sheila.

Sheriff stepped in. "Miss Stott, turn around and explain yourself. Deputy Gray, go to your car and start your report."

Taylor was dying to argue back, but she bit her tongue to keep it in.

Sheila turned around. Her hair hung around her face in sweaty strands and her gaze bounced from person to person. "Did you see what she did, Sheriff? That's police brutality. I want her badge taken away."

Sheriff shook his head. "Stop making demands. You'll be lucky to leave this parking lot without a felony charge. What you've done is absolutely against the law. Do you not understand that we are in the middle of an investigation into the disappearance of your daughter? And your granddaughter could be an eyewitness to a crime."

Sheila blew a strand of hair out of her eyes. "What crime? Child abandonment? That's all this is, and it's my duty as her grandmother to keep Molly safe."

"Which is what we are doing while we figure this whole thing out," Sheriff said.

Jessica raced around to where they stood. "Please, Officer. I am—*we*—we are so sorry. It was a mistake, and please, please—"

"*Sheriff* Dawkins. Not Officer," Sheriff said. He didn't look convinced, but he let her continue.

"Sheriff," Jessica said. "My mother reacted out of worry, and she didn't mean to hurt anyone. She just wanted more time with Molly. I swear, we weren't going to take her."

Taylor almost butted back in and asked then why were people blocking the vehicle? Why was Della Ray nearly hysterical? Sheila damn sure *did* intend to steal Molly away and would've if the crowd hadn't stopped her.

Shane sidled up and stood next to her.

Sheriff saw her standing there and shot her a look that said to stay out of it.

He turned Sheila around and removed the handcuffs. "You've just won the lottery, Miss Stott, because I feel for your plight, and I think the stress of worrying about your missing daughter may have you acting out in a manner that is not usual for you. I'm giving you a pass on this one, but you'd better believe that if you do one more thing to endanger that child or impede our investigation, you'll be sitting in my jail cell, and I can promise you, it's not a luxurious place to be."

Finally, Sheila showed some sense because she kept her mouth shut and nodded humbly.

At least for a second or two, before she thought of something else. "Can I have some more time with Molly today? They barely gave me half an hour earlier."

"Absolutely not," Sheriff said. "Molly will go back to her foster home today, and you can speak to Wesley Wright later this week about future visits, and if they will even be allowed. After today's stunt, you can bet they'll be supervised, if you even get one. But that's not my call. Now get in your car and find somewhere to spend the rest of the day out of my sight."

"Thank you, Sheriff," Jessica whispered.

They both got into the vehicle, then he turned to Taylor.

"As for you, Gray, you're off the case," he said. "Too emotionally invested, and McElroy will be taking your place. You'll ride back to the station with me and write all this up."

Taylor started to say something, but he held his hand up and stopped her.

"Say one more word, and you'll be suspended."

She followed Sheila's example and shut her mouth. She felt Shane's hand pat her comfortingly on her shoulder blade, but she shook it off.

"Detective Weaver, please continue on to go pick up the video. You can take Deputy Gray's car."

Shane nodded and gave Taylor a sympathetic glance before she tossed him the keys.

Officially, she was done.

But unofficially, she wasn't giving up.

# CHAPTER 20

Taylor sat uncomfortably in the front passenger seat of Sheriff's car, Bernard directly behind her. Thankfully, it would be a short ride because she felt like she was getting picked up at school after sitting in the principal's office, and the sheriff was her dad. That was a big downfall to their relationship.

"And bringing some random dog along? What the hell has gotten into you?"

She sighed. "Random? I'm sorry, but it was your idea for me to get Bernard. He's not random. And he hates being left home alone. Seems depressed. Did I tell you that he's trained? He knows some commands in German."

Sheriff gave her a dubious look, then put his gaze back on the road. "Don't try to change the subject. Every time we get any sort of case involving a kid, you get like this, Taylor. I saw your barely contained rage out there, and you need to learn to separate your own childhood from everyone else's," he said. "You're a law enforcement officer, not a social worker. If you want to do social work, go back to school. But you can't be both."

She stared straight ahead, then remembered she needed to

call Wesley and let him know what had happened. She called, gave him the highlights, then slid her phone into her pocket.

"How did he take it?" Sheriff asked.

"Not good. He already didn't like Sheila, and now he's recommending no visits until he can get Molly in for some counseling."

"The kid still hasn't said anything useful about her mother?"

"No. And Wesley said he doesn't want anyone asking her any questions until after a professional assessment. If there's deeper trauma than being abandoned, he said it needs to be approached carefully."

They let that sink in between them for a minute or two. It was frustrating when Molly could probably tell them just how she came to Hart's Ridge and possibly what had happened for her to be separated from her mother. But Taylor knew better than anyone that a child pushed into a corner before they were ready to talk might be irrevocably damaged forever. They had more of a chance getting something useful from her if a child psychologist was involved.

"Look," Sheriff said. "I want you to get into the station and write up your report, then you're on front-desk duty until three o'clock. After that, you've got two summons to deliver. Then go home. I've decided I'm going to go ahead and give you a few days off. You need it."

Taylor's mouth dropped open. "You're suspending me?"

"Not officially. Nothing on your record, but you also won't be paid. Don't come back until Thursday, and when you do, I want you to stay away from this case. Weaver can handle it. You're back on afternoon shift, patrol only. I have a feeling this Joni girl might stay a missing person for a while. Her mother may be right, you know. Parents usually are. And if so, she'll turn up when she wants to see her kid. If we don't find any proof of foul play in the next few days, we'll charge her with child abandonment and put a warrant out for her arrest."

Taylor didn't reply, though she wanted to ask why he was

assigning Clint when he'd just reprimanded him the week before. But when Sheriff made up his mind, it would take a lot to turn it around. She'd let him simmer down after seeing her get rough with Sheila.

She did feel a little guilty because she was a strong advocate of good relations with the public and never approved of violence when not warranted. Especially in front of a crowd.

However, it was just a little shove. Sheila was really making her life miserable. Taylor was already on a budget trying to spread her money around, and three days short on her next check was going to hurt.

She thought of something then. "Do you realize that this is the third week of the month? Don't you need me on hand?"

"Nope. We'll handle it."

Taylor hoped for an even more eventful week since he was going to be a jerk about it. Half of the county's government assistance checks were coming in, and those who weren't responsible enough to spend it on living expenses would go out and buy liquor or worse. The deputies joked around the station, calling it "Happy Domestic Disturbance Day," as there were always a higher number than usual of calls related to family scuffles or fistfights, some of them over the fact that so-and-so wasn't sharing.

Luckily though, it wasn't the end of the month because then it was even more brutal when the liquor and drugs ran out and some were going haywire waiting on their next checks.

Sheriff pulled into the station and cut the engine, then turned around and gave Bernard a good once-over. "Good-looking dog," he said, then got out of the car and slammed the door.

Bernard panted, but Taylor thought it looked more like a smile.

She didn't know what Sheriff's words meant. Just a compliment, or an approval that Bernard could be with her? Sometimes he could be baffling to understand.

Well, she was going to have to take him in, because Shane had her car and wouldn't be back for at least another hour and a half. Surely the sheriff didn't expect her to leave her dog outside.

"Come on, boy. Let's go get you some water."

They got out, and she took her time, but after hitting the kitchen first to give Bernard a drink, Sheriff was still standing at the bullpen talking to Clint. When he saw her, he frowned, then went to his office.

Clint turned and looked straight into her eyes, then smiled broadly.

Taylor ignored him and went to her desk. There was a stack of papers waiting, most likely the warrants. She glanced at the names and felt relieved it wasn't anyone who was known to cause too much trouble, then set them aside for the moment.

She needed to write up the incident with Sheila.

Before starting, she clicked her computer on, and while she kept one eye on Sheriff's office door, she checked to see if any unidentified bodies had been reported found in the state of Georgia. Only one anywhere close over the weekend, and it was in Athens, but the description didn't fit Joni. Or Lucy, for that matter.

She checked Florida, and though there were several, again there were no matches.

Next, she pulled up all accidents reported within a hundred miles of the gas station where her card was used. None of them were pickup trucks.

She wondered why Molly was found wandering into the store on one side of town, but Joni had met the potential buyer at a different one. It didn't make sense.

Sheriff showed up in his doorway and looked out over the bullpen.

Taylor reached under the desk and put her hand on Bernard to make sure he didn't move. When the sheriff went back in, she shut down the website and turned to her notebook. After racing through it, she finished the report, then showed up at the front desk to get her punishment over. Some deputies loved working the front, but she wasn't one of them.

Every weirdo in Hart's Ridge's underbrush seemed to show up there every so often. One day when their admin assistant was on vacation, Taylor was doing her shift up there, and a tall, strongly built woman with a Polish accent stopped in and dropped a bundle on the desk.

"My boyfriend chased me around with this last night. I'm leaving it here," she said, then turned and tried to leave.

Taylor had to rush after her and catch her in the parking lot, and the bundle of towels turned out to be covering a rusted old machete. After some investigation and trekking out to their shack way up on the mountain, Taylor was glad to find that the boyfriend was still breathing. He was covered in bruises from the beating his Amazon woman gave him once she took the machete away, but no charges were filed, and Taylor was pretty sure he'd never mess with her again.

Then once when Penner was on duty, a car came crashing through the big glass window, and when they finally wrestled a woman out of it, she said her husband had told her if she ever thought she was being followed, to go straight to the station. Obviously, he forgot to tell her to just park the car and lay on the horn, not go straight *into* the station literally.

She was twice over the limit of intoxication and got a hefty driving under the influence charge tacked on to her five days in jail. There was no evidence of anyone following her, and eventually she lost her license because it was her third DUI offense.

You had to be alert and prepared when working the front desk. Not preoccupied like Taylor felt now. She didn't want to be here. She favored delivering warrants to known troublemakers over waiting for the unknown like a sitting duck.

While she had time at the desk, though, she began looking through free dog posts from months back to see if she could find the family who gave Bernard to Weldon Gentry. She really had no hopes of finding anything, so when she was scanning and almost passed by a photo of which she was almost positive was Bernard, she about fell out of her seat.

*Free hunting dog to a good home.*

It had a number alongside it, and Taylor picked up the county phone and dialed it immediately.

Bingo.

After a five-minute chat about the frustrations of trying to keep a dog that was constantly looking for an escape path, they promised to send her a package of paperwork that they'd forgotten to pass along with him to Weldon. The woman couldn't remember the name of the rescue Bernard had come from, but it was all in the folder. She was extremely nice and said she wished it had worked out because her kids had really wanted a dog. They'd recovered fast, though, because now they were in love with their brand-new designer labradoodle.

Taylor rolled her eyes at that, but at least she'd promised to put the packet in the mail that very day. Since she didn't have time to follow up right now anyway, she'd wait on it to show up, and maybe it would include more of his history. If not, then she'd contact the rescue and hopefully finally have it figured out.

"What do you think, Bernard? You want me to keep up this wild goose chase, or are you happy with me yet?" She looked under the desk, and he gazed up at her without lifting his head.

It was a sad look, and though she knew that he was definitely warming up to her, there was something there that she couldn't reach. An emptiness that couldn't be explained when he let out a long, heavy sigh that seemed to go on forever.

A sigh that told her nothing but said everything.

"Okay. But if this is a dead end, we need to let it go. I don't have time for a wild goose chase, buddy."

He blinked twice.

Taylor pretended it meant nothing. Things were crazy enough without thinking her dog was communicating with her on a human level.

The door opened, and their local town rambler walked in.

"How are you doing, Boone?"

He shuffled to the counter, his gaze on the floor. He wore his usual attire of a red and black flannel shirt and suspenders holding up his baggy jeans. Even in the hot Georgia summer, he never changed it up, though he did add a hat to keep the sun out of his eyes. Boone could be relied on to be consistent, if nothing else.

She noticed he needed a haircut and made a mental note to call Bessie at the Hair Place on the town square to round him up next time she saw him go by. Bessie cut his hair for free, especially because she'd been doing it his whole life, and he wouldn't let anyone else touch it. God only knew what he would look like when one day Bessie retired her shears. The tourists would be calling him in as a suspicious person, or a Sasquatch sighting.

Bernard stood, went around the counter, and sniffed at him, but Boone pretended not to notice a random dog standing in the lobby of the Hart's Ridge Sheriff's Department for the first time. He didn't rile easy.

She gave him time and didn't push. He'd get out what he was here for eventually. The locals of Hart's Ridge had somewhat adopted Boone as their own, and even though he was in his mid-thirties', he functioned at the level of a grade-school child.

Boone was never quite right after he'd accidentally shot his thumb off with a sawed-off shotgun his daddy let him take hunting when he was only eleven years old. Back then, they didn't have a very fast response team, and Boone's daddy also didn't want to take him to any specialist in the big city, so once they finally got to the hospital, they'd replaced the thumb with his big toe. As gossip had it, he hadn't even cried when he shot his thumb off, though Taylor figured that was probably a bit of a tall tale.

She remembered seeing him for nearly a year after that, his hand sewn to his chest so that the skin graft would take. It was scary for her and for her sisters. But he was harmless and now spent his days walking through town and picking up cans, or sometimes doing an easy odd job here or there. He had an old push mower he carried around on a cart when he really needed to make some bucks, and some of the residents let him do their yards, though he was known to scalp a few bushes and gardens.

Taylor didn't know what would happen to him when his parents finally passed away, but she hoped they'd made some sort of arrangements.

Bernard got tired of waiting for Boone to pet him and obviously felt he wasn't a threat because he came back around and settled at Taylor's feet again.

"Mr. Diller's grass is too high," Boone finally said. He didn't make eye contact.

"Oh. Okay. Do you usually mow it for him?"

Boone shook his head.

"Then why are you—oh! You're worried about him? You knocked, and he didn't answer the door, then?"

Boone nodded solemnly.

"Well, that's strange he's let his grass get high, but maybe he's out of town. I'll send a deputy out there right away for a wellness check," Taylor said, then logged it into the computer.

Mr. Diller had diabetes. He hadn't told too many people because he liked to pretend to be strong and healthy. It was best to send someone out to look in on him.

Boone kept standing there, but his gaze had shifted to a jar of lollipops on the desk. They were needed at times when people brought their kids in with them, and they needed to be distracted.

Taylor picked up the jar and angled it toward him. "Take them all, Boone. You did good."

He grabbed them in one big handful and shoved them in his shirt pocket.

"Anything else?" Taylor asked gently.

"Found this." He pulled out a small coin purse and laid it on the counter.

"In Mr. Diller's yard?" Taylor took the purse and opened it, surprised to see it wasn't just a few coins but also a small wad of cash. A fifty-dollar bill and three ones, which would be a small fortune for him.

"Landfill."

"Okay, then I'll keep it here in case someone calls about it. Will that work?"

Boone nodded.

"Thank you, Boone, for being so honest. If no one claims the purse within thirty days, the contents are yours."

He turned and went out the door, happy with his handful of suckers.

Taylor started to put the money back into the purse, but she saw something in the bottom. She turned it over, and a ring dropped out into her hand.

It was tarnished silver and had two stones set in it. While it didn't look expensive, it could possibly have sentimental value, so she tucked it back in and slid the cash on top, then zipped up the pouch.

She doubted though that anyone would call about it. Things ended up at the landfill all the time, and rarely had anyone called about them. Boone went out there at least once a week to pick through trash for the cans he could make money on. He'd brought other items in over the years, things he thought might have been lost accidentally. But that she knew of, this was a first for cash.

Boone truly was a good human being, and Taylor wished his life was better. But then, maybe it was just enough for him. Some people didn't need much to be happy.

Her cell phone rang, and she looked down to see Shane's name.

"Gray," she answered.

"Hi, Gray," he joked. "I'm going to stop in a minute and forward you the email file from the phone company. Can you see what numbers look out of place and try to find out who was meeting her?"

"Will do," Taylor said, already pecking her username into the computer to open her email. "But don't tell Sheriff. He's adamant that I'm off the case. You're supposed to be working with Clint."

"I know and that sucks," Shane said. "He's such an asshole, and he smells like a boy in puberty who has doused himself with cheap body spray. I don't relish riding around with that fool."

Taylor laughed. It felt good to have a comrade in arms at work. Most of the guys saw her as a threat, or as something—she wasn't sure what. But rarely did they treat her like a friend. It got lonely.

"Oh, heads-up, someone has hung fliers all over town with Joni's photo. Florida number to call," Shane said. "Every store-front and telephone pole I saw."

"Probably Jessica. I doubt her mother would do it." She relayed her searches and finds, which amounted to zilch, and Shane said he'd be here in a quarter of an hour and, if possible, would let her watch the store video with him before she left to deliver summons.

"That works. He should be leaving anytime to go to the school," Taylor said, referring to Sheriff. If he caught her analyzing video for Joni's case, he'd have her head on a platter.

"Ten-four." Shane hung up.

The county phone rang again, and she picked it up and took down the details of a complaint from a woman who said her neighbor was peeing off his back porch in broad daylight again. Just to be mean, Taylor called it in to Clint with a request to go talk to him about keeping his pecker in his pants.

Next, she called Della Ray who confirmed that Molly was fine, though extra quiet since the incident and curled up with a couple of the pups for comfort. Della Ray apologized again for almost losing Molly, and Taylor reassured her that it wasn't her fault and told her not to think another thing about it.

She checked her email again. The phone records still hadn't come through, so she tapped her short nails on the countertop and shook her leg to the beat. Sitting idle wasn't in her to do for long, and she itched to get up and out there and do something. She tried to neaten up the desk. Whoever was working it last was evidently a pig. She threw away yellow notes with scribbles marked through and an empty coffee cup, then arranged everything neatly.

Finally, she heard her email ding and looked to find a new one from Shane. She opened it and downloaded the attached file, then began combing through the dates until she found the day that Molly had walked into the store.

There were only a few incoming and two outgoing calls that entire day, which would make it easy to follow up on. Taylor started dialing. The first one was the electric company customer service line, which Joni had probably called to try to get an extension on paying her bill. The next one was Joni's neighbor, who told Taylor she'd called Joni to remind her to not leave her bags of trash outside her door, and to take them to the bin. She was immediately alarmed to be hearing from law enforcement.

While Taylor had her on the phone, she questioned her about who she had seen coming and going from Joni's apartment but got nothing useful from her.

She was on the fourth phone number when she hit pay dirt.

"Yes, as I said, I'm Deputy Gray with the Hart's Ridge Sheriff's Department, and we are investigating a missing person's case. You were one of the last people to have contact with Joni Stott before she went missing. Can you tell me about why you were in communication?"

"No shit? She's missing?" he said, his voice sounding genuinely incredulous.

His name was Bryce Kessler, and he easily admitted contacting Joni after seeing her truck advertised for sale online. He sounded nervous and claimed that he met her at the gas station on Highway 515 and looked at the truck. He said he thought it wasn't worth what she was asking, and they went their separate ways.

Taylor could barely contain her excitement. Kessler was their first person of interest and could easily become a solid suspect. She remained calm and didn't inform him that they had video of the gas station parking lot or that Molly had wandered up alone.

"She drove an awfully long way to show you a truck that you didn't want," Taylor said. "She must've been fairly sure you were going to take it."

"I know. That's my fault. I was stoked to find it for sale, but once she got it here, it just looked in worse shape than she described it to be. More than my budget can afford to put into it to get it highway ready. I felt bad turning her down. I really did. She said she really needed the money. I paid her for her gas to get back, though."

Sure he did.

Taylor kept it friendly and asked him to come to the station to make a formal statement, just so they could mark him off their list. He wouldn't know until he got here that they would most likely ask to download his phone information as well as hopefully get a mouth swab for DNA. Just in case.

"I don't really live that close to where I met her," he said. "And I have to work. Can this wait until the weekend?"

"No, it really can't."

He reluctantly agreed to come into town the next morning. He gave her his address and driver's license, and after they hung up, she ran them. They matched his name, so he was either playing completely innocent or he simply was, with nothing to hide. He was twenty-eight years old, and he supposedly had his own place, so was more of a grown-up than an overgrown kid. However, that would also make it hard for him to prove he went straight home after meeting Joni, because no one would be there to verify it.

She couldn't say that the conversation made her feel any red flags in her gut, but you never knew how well someone could cover something up. Something weird about the conversation did occur to her, though. Most probable, Molly was with Joni when they met up with Bryce at the station. Yet he didn't comment anything about seeing a child or ask about the child's welfare.

Taylor couldn't wait to get her eyes on the video. She hoped it caught the interaction between Bryce and Joni. Even without audio, you could tell a lot from someone's expressions and body language.

Quickly, she ran Bryce through the system, and that she could find, he didn't have any prior arrests. That didn't mean he would never offend—everyone started with a clean slate until their first crime. Just to be sure, she ran him in Florida, too. Nothing.

"Yes, ma'am, I'd like to report my cat up in a tree," a voice said from behind her.

She turned around to find Shane standing there grinning.

"About time you got back. I need my car to deliver summons."

He tossed her the keys and waved the video cassette. "You aren't staying for the matinee?"

She frowned. "Sheriff is still here. He'd have a conniption if he saw me in there."

Shane raised his eyebrows. "Good thing I just passed him in the parking lot, then. He's out. Clint's gone too. You're in luck."

"Okay. Let me get Penner up here. It's his shift. I'll be back there in a second."

He left, and Taylor was just about to leave the front desk and go hunting Penner when he showed up.

"Diller's mower is in the shop," Penner said, "and he was there picking it up when Boone knocked."

"That was quick. Thanks," Taylor said. "Did you have to go find him?"

"Nah. His daughter made him get a mobile phone. I have the number."

"And Diller knows how to use it?" Taylor asked.

"He knows how to answer it."

They laughed, and Taylor gave him the chair. She and Bernard headed to Shane's office to hopefully view the video. It was time to see if the Bryce guy was as innocent as he tried to sound on the phone.

# CHAPTER 21

Taylor was starving by the time she slid into the booth across from Cecil, and Bernard settled under the table. What a day it had been. First starting with Sheila's antics, then getting suspended, searching for leads to follow for Joni, and then breaking up a dog fight when Bernard refused to stand down from a set of slobbering fangs that greeted them at her last summons delivery. Thankfully, there was no blood involved, but he showed her that even if he wasn't bonding with her yet, he was all about protecting her.

"You look like you could use a nap," Cecil said.

"Ha. I'm dragging so much that I feel like I'm already tired tomorrow." She took a long swig of the sweet tea he had waiting for her and invited the sugar to do its thing.

"You aren't taking care of yourself. I bet you haven't eaten anything substantial in days."

She didn't argue, and he took that for confirmation.

"Must be on a case," he said.

"I am. Well, unofficially now." She leaned forward and began telling him about Molly and her missing mother.

She didn't talk to any other civilians about her cases, but Cecil was different. He knew how to keep his lips tight, and he was also a great one to bounce things off. Many times over the years, he had contributed helpful insight or advice. And he would never throw Taylor under the bus and talk about their conversations to anyone.

He also respected her commitment to her job. Something she wished her father could do, instead of constantly berating her for being on *their* side, as though law enforcement were enemies and not there to protect and serve.

"And you didn't see anything suspicious on the video?" he asked.

She shook her head. "It didn't show much other than her pulling her truck up to get gas and who we suppose is Bryce Kessler coming over and using his card to pay for it on the pump. They talked for a few minutes, and then she pulled out going one way, and he went the other. Plays out just like he said, but we'll see if his story changes when he talks to Shane tomorrow."

"You aren't going to be in there?"

"Nope. Turns out the sheriff wants me to take a few days off. Unpaid." She sighed.

Cecil raised his brows. "Oh? Want to elaborate?"

She told him about Sheila trying to snatch Molly, and because it was Cecil, she admitted that she could've easily let her anger get out of control if the sheriff hadn't shown up.

"I'm off the case, and Clint is on," she said.

Cecil knew all about the friction between her and Clint, though he didn't know about the kitty calls.

"Oh, he's as slick as Mama's slop jar, that one."

Taylor laughed. "He sure is. I wish he'd go on and transfer to another county."

"I keep praying on it for ya', girl. But Molly and Della Ray, they're okay?"

"Yes, they're fine. Just really shook up."

He sat back in the seat and crossed his arms. "You *have* had quite a day. I don't think you should fret over the days off. You look like you need them, and you know Sheriff won't stay mad."

Sissy showed up at the table, interrupting the conversation.

"Hello, you dark and sexy fellow," she purred.

Cecil beamed. "Well, that's a nice greeting. Hello to you, too."

They all laughed, and Sissy squatted down and stroked Bernard's coat.

Then she stood and put her hand on Cecil's shoulder. "You know you're handsome, Cecil. I don't have to tell you."

"Okay, I guess I'm not offended that you favor the pup over me, then. You can make up for it by bringing me a Cobb salad topped with chicken. Blue cheese on the side, please."

She scribbled it down then looked at Taylor.

"Mmm, the chicken sounds good, but I'm too hungry for a salad," Taylor said.

Salad was for sissies, and Taylor was not one to back away from something more satisfying.

"Mabel's got fried chicken and her squash casserole on the menu today," Sissy said.

"That's what I want. And something for Bernard."

"I'll fix him up," she said and then winked.

"Oh, can you please choose from the menu and make Dad a plate to go, Sissy?" Taylor got meals for her dad from here so often that they knew his favorites more than she did.

"I sure will, honey. I'll stick some fresh cornbread and pintos in there, too." She left them.

"How's he doing?" Cecil asked.

"It's been a few days since I've been out there, but he's as ornery as ever. He's getting worse about not wanting to do anything. Including keeping the house and himself up. I swear, if I had the money, I'd hire a caretaker to just be sure he eats, bathes, and takes his medicine. I can't run over there every day."

Cecil gave her a sad smile. "And it's not your place, Taylor.

189

He's ten years younger than I am and acts like he's a hundred. He doesn't need a nursemaid. He can choose to get up and live life."

"But he won't. And if I didn't try to keep him going, I don't know what would happen." Just saying the words made her feel heavy with apprehension.

"I want you to step back and remember your role is the daughter, not the parent. It's not your job to manage his alcoholism or his life. It's okay to care about him, and to help out some, but you need to set boundaries, and he needs to follow them. You should be able to feel free to lead your own life without guilt."

Taylor knew everything Cecil was saying made sense, but he didn't know what it was like to see her dad so miserable, or to worry that he hadn't eaten or taken his medicine. To be honest, she had a strong suspicion that guilt was killing him from the inside out. Guilt over how he'd treated her mother, and how rough he'd made life for his daughters. And that was something she was never going to be able to undo for him. He had to figure that out himself.

Sissy returned with their food and set it on the table before them, then put a small plastic plate on the floor for Bernard.

"Pulled chicken for you, buddy," she crooned. "No seasonings, just good protein."

"You're spoiling him, Sissy," Taylor said.

"I know. And that's why God put them on this Earth. Y'all let me know if you need anything else," she said, then walked away.

Taylor's appetite was suddenly gone, and she stared down at her plate.

"You cannot be everything to everyone in your family, Taylor. I've told you before, you can only do so much for those you love, and you can't save them from hard times, grief, or depression. You worry about your dad, and Lucy. And I know you think that Anna isn't happy. There are limits for what you can do, and the rest is up to them. Thank goodness at least Jo Jo seems to have her life together because I think you're stretching yourself too thin."

She smiled weakly at him. "Why did I pay for teletherapy when you know me so much better than anyone, Cecil?"

He laughed. "Because they can write prescriptions and I can't. Now eat up, girl."

They ate and spent the rest of the meal talking about other things, like Boone's worry about Diller, and Mabel's apple pie. Cecil made her laugh when he talked about how a friend of his decided to start walking with him but gave up after the first week and said Cecil must be a bionic man because a human of his age couldn't possibly be that energetic.

When they parted ways in the parking lot, Taylor felt better, both physically and emotionally. Cecil was like that for her, always a balm to her soul as he filled not only the lonely parental hole in her heart but was the best friend anyone could ask for.

Bernard must've felt the same because when Cecil bid him goodbye and went to his car, he whined as though he hated to see him go. As for Taylor, she was feeling fat and lazy. She looked forward to a bath and bed, in short order.

She was so tired that she drove on autopilot, not even registering anything but the road in front of her. When she pulled into her driveway and up to the house, she was exhausted, especially after dealing with her cantankerous dad, but something felt off. First, she could see a faint light through the window, and she was sure she hadn't left any on. She was careful about electricity and cut every corner she could to keep her bill down.

"Something's weird," she told Bernard.

She hoped it wasn't her last boyfriend, a guy who had moved to Nashville to pursue his singing career, who she found out also had a new girl waiting. She'd told him to never come back here, and he damn sure didn't have a key.

Bernard immediately perked up at her tone.

When she opened the car door, she could hear music. Someone was in her damn house!

She pulled her gun and waved Bernard to follow.

He did more than follow. He trotted ahead of her and right up to the porch, his nose to the door and then all around as he started sniffing everywhere he could.

"You smell them, don't you?" Taylor whispered. "But are they still here?"

Bernard jumped off the porch, ran around the side of the house, and disappeared for a minute, then came right back and put his nose to the door.

Taylor's heart pounded. She'd entered houses under suspicious circumstances before, but it was different when it was your own home.

Before fishing her keys out, she holstered her gun, pulled a plastic glove from her pocket, slipped it on, and tried the knob.

It was unlocked.

The music was blasting, and even if she tried to listen at the door, she wouldn't hear anything, so after placing one hand to the revolver on her hip, she turned the knob and gently opened it, gave a small push, then stepped to the side.

When nothing happened, she said a silent prayer, then went in, Bernard at her side.

# CHAPTER 22

*T*aylor cleared the living room and kitchen, then crept down the hall toward the bedroom where the music blasted the loudest. She drew her gun slowly from the holster. Bernard's hair was raised on his back and when she opened the bedroom door, he rushed in and headed straight for the master bath.

A woman screamed, and Taylor rushed to the doorway, following the direction of the barrel of her gun.

She would shoot anyone who tried to hurt Bernard.

Thankfully, she wasn't going to have to do that.

The scene before her wasn't a bloodbath of any sort, and her dog wasn't in trouble. Instead, he had his front paws up on the side of the tub, and Taylor's sister Lucy was covered in bubbles and giving him quite a love session.

Adrenaline throbbed throughout Taylor's body. She reached over to the cabinet and turned the CD player off. She should've immediately known it was Lucy by the song choice.

*"Nobody Told Me" by John Lennon.*

"You didn't tell me you got a dog," Lucy exclaimed. "He startled me."

"You didn't tell me you were coming. I could've shot you."

Lucy smiled up at her. She looked like a child with her hair all bundled on the top of her head and her cheeks scarlet from the heat of the water. A foot emerged from the water, pointed at the ceiling with bubbles on the toes. "Surprise."

"What do you think you're doing?"

"What does it look like? I'm getting ready to shave, then later you can find me between the sheets rubbing my legs together like a cricket."

Taylor expression didn't change. This wasn't the comedy club. "How did you get in?"

"Um, with the key you gave me last summer, " she said, then leaned back and began lathering a leg.

Taylor had forgotten all about that key. Lucy was only supposed to have it temporarily for a visit but had not given it back. But at least she knew why Bernard had rushed around there and then came back. He was following the scent of the path that Lucy had taken.

She took a seat on the toilet to get her breath and let her pulse slow down. A small strawberry tattoo marked her sister's ankle, one Taylor had never seen before, and it made her think of Joni.

"You scared the hell out of me, Lucy."

Lucy raised her eyebrows and smiled, then picked up Taylor's razor and started shaving her leg. "I thought cops don't scare. Anyway, your dog scared me when he came charging in here. For a second anyway. So, we're even."

"Who brought you here? Please tell me it wasn't Roland Ellis. I pray you weren't dumb enough to lead him to my home. I prefer to keep a low profile against hard-core criminals."

"Oh, please," Lucy said. "First, I see you are still using your investigation skills to check up on me. And second, you know I wouldn't do that. I took a bus from Atlanta and then a taxi from the station in Jasper. Used my last dollar, too. By the way, you have basically nothing to eat in here, and I'm starving."

Taylor didn't know whether to laugh or cry. On one hand, she was so very happy that her baby sister was in one piece and looked no worse for wear. On the other hand, she wanted to rant at her about staying so aloof and worrying everyone to death. And about going to jail. Not to mention the bad company she was hanging with.

Lucy reached up to wipe a drop of water off her eyelashes, and Taylor quickly examined her arm, noting with relief that there weren't any track marks.

"What's with all the extra hardware on the bedroom door?" Lucy asked. "You expecting the people of Hart's Ridge to revolt and come after you?"

"Real funny. I live alone. It was time to up my security," she said, leaving out the real reason she had to do it. "We have a lot to talk about. Hurry and get your butt out of there."

She stood and left the room, though Bernard stayed to hear more crooning.

Lucy called out that she was too tired to talk, but Taylor kept going.

In the kitchen, she checked the pantry and grabbed a few cans, then set them on the counter. She plucked a pound of ground beef from the freezer and popped it into the microwave to defrost, then set out salt, pepper, and chili powder. She checked the pantry again for saltines but didn't see any.

*Beggars can't be choosers*, her father would say.

With kidney beans, tomato sauce, and ground meat—plus a lot of spices—she could whip up a pot of chili to feed Lucy. Growing up, they had survived on one-pot meals, and chili was at the top of their favorites, one down from spaghetti and a Midwestern goulash that could last a few days if no one ate second helpings.

While she waited on the meat to defrost, she got Bernard's dinner ready.

He came trotting in as soon as he heard his metal bowl hit the floor, and Taylor went to her room and changed out of her uniform and into a soft shirt and sweatpants. She noticed now that a grubby-looking bag was on the floor next to the bed. She resisted the urge to search it to be sure Lucy wasn't carrying contraband into her home. She didn't have the energy for a confrontation.

As she went back to the kitchen, she pulled her hair down from the tight bun and let it fall around her shoulders, relieved to have it loose.

By the time the chili was put together, the top of it dancing in a slight simmer, Lucy finally joined her, sat down at the table, and gave her an approving look.

"You look cute, big sister," she said. "Much better out of uniform than in it."

Lucy was on her father's side and didn't appreciate or respect law enforcement. It rankled at Taylor, but she'd learned to just ignore it.

"You're wearing my favorite robe."

"Thanks. I didn't bring mine." Lucy grinned. "Mmm… It smells yummy. Is it ready?"

Taylor scooped her some into a bowl and set it in front of her, then sat down at the table. "No crackers. Sorry."

"You're not eating?"

"I ate at the Den."

Lucy took a big bite and closed her eyes in ecstasy before opening them again. "With whom?"

"Cecil. Who else?"

"I figured. Just hoped maybe you had a boyfriend by now," Lucy said. "It's just weird how you spend your free time with that old man." She got up and grabbed a glass from the cupboard, filled it under the spigot, and came back to the table.

"I have bottled water in the fridge," Taylor said. She wasn't going to discuss Cecil with someone who couldn't possibly understand the concept of loyalty.

Lucy shrugged. "I'm used to drinking from the tap. Where I hang out, we don't pay for things we can get for free."

"That's what I want to talk to you about," Taylor said. "Where have you been, and why were you shoplifting? You need to call in more often. Not just when you're in trouble, either. What have you been doing? I know it can't be good because of who bounced you from jail. He sure has a long rap sheet."

Lucy dropped her spoon into the bowl and leaned back in her chair. Her sunny optimism disappeared. "You shouldn't be getting that information and running backgrounds on my friends. And why so many questions? Which one should I answer first? Oh wait, none of them, because last I checked, you aren't my mother, and I'm not a child."

They locked into a stare that was more like a battle of wills.

Taylor broke first. She didn't want Lucy to run off again. "Dad has been beside himself worried about you."

"That's nothing new. Not my fault." Lucy rolled her eyes.

She had no idea how their dad worshiped the ground she walked on and waited for any tidbit of news on her.

"Fine," Taylor said, wishing she had the same capability to not care how others felt. "You're tired. I'm tired. We'll talk about it tomorrow."

"Or we won't," said Lucy. She picked her spoon back up and began eating again.

"The purple guest room has clean sheets if you want to stay in there," Taylor said.

"You mean *my* room has clean sheets?"

Taylor let out a long sigh. She could remind Lucy that it wasn't her room anymore because Taylor owned the house and paid the bills, but that would lead to nothing good. Sometimes her sister was a ball of sunshine and a joy to be around, and other times, she was itching for a fight. Once started, she wouldn't back down.

Taylor was too tired for those fireworks.

197

"Yes. *Your* room. Okay, Lucy?"

"Why can't I sleep in Dad's room?"

Taylor snapped. She'd had too long of a day to play games.

"Because it's not Dad's room. It's been mine since I saved this place from being sold at auction ten years ago. Dad doesn't pay the taxes and my mortgage, not to mention the upkeep this old place needs. Do you think I slid in there and got it for free? I can't even get him to come over here for simple repairs, much less contribute to paying for it." She left out the part about how she was also usually helping with their dad's bills. She wouldn't throw him under the bus like that. "And while we're on the subject of Dad, we're going over there first thing in the morning. Maybe seeing you will light a fire under his butt to get up and stop feeling sorry for himself."

Lucy didn't look thrilled about it, but she responded, which was a relief because Taylor didn't want to argue. She wanted them to be happy to see each other. To act like sisters and not like sparring partners. She wanted to be the person who Lucy could confide in and tell where she'd been and why she couldn't seem to get herself together.

Sometimes Taylor really believed that Lucy didn't understand the pressure it took to be an adult. She'd never had to pay for her own place, cover utilities or internet, or probably even knew what it meant to pay annual property taxes in addition to everything else. Lucy had been a couch surfer her entire life, and Taylor would bet that in the months since she'd seen her, nothing had changed.

But somehow, she loved her deeply.

They all did. There was a childlike innocence that Lucy couldn't shake, no matter how old she got or what terrible things she got herself into. It wasn't any wonder that out of all his girls, their dad doted on Lucy and obsessed over where she was and what she was doing. She would forever be the baby sister, and it wasn't easy to just let her be on her own.

Anna was the only one out of all of them who didn't constantly fret over where Lucy was and what she was up to.

"You want to sleep in there with me?" Taylor said. "You already know the bed's big enough for two."

Lucy smiled up at her, and everything was forgiven.

The way it always was and probably always would be.

"Can I borrow a clean nightshirt?"

"Of course." Taylor stood and picked up the bowl and glass, took them to the sink, then went into the bedroom and rustled in her drawer for an old Beatles T-shirt that came from Goodwill. It was easy to make Lucy happy, and the shirt would be sure to win her a few points.

Lucy followed, and just as Taylor thought, she practically danced with the shirt in her arms, then turned her back and dropped the robe. Taylor turned away, but not before noticing that Lucy was more filled out than usual. That was good, but it made her wonder where her sister had been hanging out to be eating so well.

Bernard curled up next to the bed and watched Lucy with an entertained expression, as though he were being treated to a Broadway show. At the end of her dance, Lucy leaned in and kissed him on the nose, and he rolled over and showed her his belly.

"He stays on the floor," Taylor warned.

Lucy gave her a pouty look. "Meanie."

"Do you want to wash the bedding clear of dog hair in the morning?"

Lucy pulled back the covers, crawled into bed on Taylor's side, and picked her tablet up from the nightstand.

"Don't break it," Taylor said, then turned and went into the bathroom.

Bernard followed her, and she shut the door behind him.

"You can stay, but don't bother me," she told him.

He settled down next to the door, his snout on his paw as he watched her.

Taylor started the water running in the tub, added some Epsom salts for her aching muscles, then undressed and got in. She thought about Molly and hoped she was doing okay. Then her mind settled on Joni—someone she'd never met but was starting to feel like she knew. In her job, she'd come across too many young women who were on their own after having a baby. It never failed to amaze her how one mistake could turn a parent against their child. Dear Sheila was the epitome of a mother failing her daughter in a crisis.

On the other hand, Joni might be like Taylor and too stubborn for her own good. Perhaps she'd decided in the beginning to do it on her own, and when she figured out she needed help, Sheila had decided to let her sink or swim.

No one really knew what went on in families.

Taylor laid her head back, closed her eyes, and began reviewing everything she knew about the case, then sighed in frustration at being kicked out of the circle. No doubt, Sheriff would punish her further by making her do more time at the front desk. She hated manning the phones and the lobby.

But at least she got to see some of the town regulars. Like Boone.

Something niggled at her.

The ring that Boone had brought in with the pouch. Something about the ring was teasing at her memory. The stones were purple and green. The two colors didn't really go that well together, but maybe the ring belonged to a teenager and the stones were her school colors. If that were the case, it wouldn't belong to any Hart's Ridge locals because they had only one school, and the colors had always been black and garnet.

Taylor wasn't sure what else it could be but— "Bernard!"

She sat up in the tub so abruptly that she sent a tidal wave of water splashing out of it. Bernard jumped to his feet, coming to full alert.

Taylor was so excited she could barely stay put.

Suddenly though, the excitement turned to dread. If her suspicions were right, it didn't bode well for Joni.

Bernard searched her face, trying to understand the source of the roller coaster of emotions he was likely picking up from her.

"Sorry, boy. I just figured out something. Remember the ring Boone brought in today? It was an amethyst and an emerald. The same stones that were on Joni's promise ring. I think ole Boone has given us our first real lead."

# CHAPTER 23

*T*aylor was waiting until first light to call Shane about the ring, but the sound of her phone going off at six o'clock startled her and made Lucy groan and pull the pillow over her head.

It was barely to Taylor's ear when Shane started talking. "They found the truck, and it was impounded two days ago. It was called in by a state trooper when he found it abandoned near Cagle just off State 515 for the second night in a row."

"Damn it." Taylor struggled to sit upright.

She also needed to tell him about the ring. She'd gone straight from the bath the night before to her computer and scrolled through every photo on Joni's social media until she found one of her showing off her promise ring years before. It was definitely a match.

"I'm glad he found her truck," she continued, "but why didn't he see the BOLO when he ran the plates and then wait for processing? It must've been a newbie, and I'd love to wring his neck."

"Um…it could be a *her*. Anyway, I have no idea. That's all I got and haven't had time to get out to the scene yet, but I got the coordinates from the owner of the impound lot."

Any evidence on or in the truck would've been compromised by whoever found the vehicle, as well as the tow company pulling it in.

Taylor could feel a sharp pain from her clenched jaw, and she tried to relax. Getting angry wouldn't work in her favor but it never ceased to amaze her how easily incompetence could run in small towns. But a state trooper—that was just insane.

"No sign of Joni, I'm assuming?" she asked.

"None."

She thought for a second. "Okay, let's assume the truck broke down, and if everything else went wrong, her phone was dead, too. Cagle is about twelve miles from Jasper, so there would've been no reason for her to start walking toward Hart's Ridge for help. So why would Molly end up here?"

"Good question," Shane said.

"I have some bad news to tell you, too." She told him about Boone, the purse, and the ring.

"And you're sure it's a match to the one she's wearing in the photo?"

"I'm positive. But we need to get her sister to confirm."

"Damn, that's not good. Listen, I'm going out to the scene and will look around where the truck was found. Then I'll go to the lot and supervise the processing of the truck. Want me to swing by and grab you?"

Taylor hesitated. She was usually a rule follower, and that was one of her attributes that kept her on the good side of Sheriff Dawkins. She was sure he'd never fire her, but he could make her life hell for defying his orders.

"I can be there in ten," Shane said. "I'm just going into the Den to grab coffee and a ham biscuit. I do need to call the sarge and tell him about the ring and let him get together a search team for the landfill."

He wasn't making things any easier for her to try to stay in her lane.

Somehow Joni's small purse had made it to the landfill. Now that her truck was found, too, that was not looking good.

"I'd bet my bottom dollar that Sarge will want to meet you at the truck before he heads out to the landfill. I can't take the chance he won't tell Sheriff. But I can meet you on scene where it was picked up. Text me the coordinates."

"Fine," Shane said. "I'll have to be back at the station by nine to meet Clint so we can interview Bryce. We'll see how he reacts when I surprise him with the news that the truck was found."

They hung up, and Taylor bounded out of bed and into the bathroom.

She emerged as Deputy Gray in the record time of five minutes, and after taking Bernard on a short walk during which she begged him to hurry and do his business, she left her personal phone and a note behind on the kitchen table for Lucy, and was on her way.

Bernard pouted, but he would be fine with Lucy. Taylor was already taking a huge chance by staying on the case, and she didn't need the extra stress.

She took Main Street on her way out to the highway. Their little town was still sleepy, and she only saw a few signs of life. Things didn't start moving until at least seven for the most part, and when it was quiet and still, it looked quite picturesque.

The fliers with Joni's photo on them glared at her from various spots, reminding her that behind almost every quaint storefront were most likely secrets and sins.

She passed the historic Tinsley House, saw a light on through the front windows, and wondered what the old woman was up to so early. Faire Tinsley was probably Hart's Ridge only claim to fame, but these days, she preferred the hermit life. At one time, she was a very well-known psychic and considered the real—or the most real—thing in the Blue Ridge Mountains. She'd worked with the FBI before and had some success in locating missing people, or at least leading officials in the right direction. But rumor had it that she'd done a bad read twenty or so years ago, then refused to ever use her so-called gift again.

Moving on, she spotted Mr. Parker standing at the side of his house, watering his garden. He would have homegrown tomatoes sitting on a table at the street in a few weeks, a pay-as-you-go mason jar set out next to the baskets to hold whatever his neighbors felt was fair for sharing the best tomatoes in town. Her tummy perked up at the thought, and Taylor could practically taste a satisfying tomato and Duke's Mayonnaise sandwich on her lips, then remembered that Shane was going by the Den. She hoped he brought her a biscuit, too.

She felt a rush of guilt for thinking of Mabel's biscuits when soon there would be a team out at the landfill, searching for Joni Stott.

The sheriff would be in charge, as he had the most experience in what would be a tricky and tedious expedition. The landfill was supposed to be organized into cells by location and date, but if the county guys had been slacking on their job, it would be more like a poke-and-hope situation. Even if it was organized as it should be, it would still be a challenge, because as soon as debris was dumped, it was soon compacted by huge steel-wheeled rollers and covered with soil to camouflage the odors as much as possible.

Despite all that, Taylor wished she could be there.

Once past the town, it wasn't too far before she got to where 575 ends, then 108 and 515 continue toward the Appalachian Highway. She followed the coordinates and took the side road Shane had indicated, then a half a mile down, she saw the county's unmarked car pulled over.

Shane leaned against the hood, a coffee in one hand and a biscuit in the other, looking like some kind of Southern mountain-boy model in his blue jeans and red and black plaid shirt.

She was amused to see he'd traded in his polo shirt and dress pants for something more fitting for Hart's Ridge, but now he looked like a preppy lumberjack who was trying too hard. It reminded her of the awkward teen he used to be.

She pulled off the road and got out, and he smiled broadly, looking genuinely happy to see her. She wished some of her coworkers felt the same way. It felt nice to be appreciated.

"You'd better have me a biscuit, too," she joked.

He handed her a bag from behind him.

Taylor peeked in and saw a cup of coffee and a biscuit squeezed in beside it.

"Mmm…" she moaned. "Thank you."

"Sausage with mayonnaise, tomato, and lettuce. Coffee, black." He smiled, and she noticed his dimples were still as deep as they were way back when, and maybe even deeper.

He was a much more handsome man than he was a boy. She always thought it was unfair that men got better-looking when they aged, and women had to fight tooth and nail to not look their age.

Taylor blushed. "You remembered."

"What kind of best friend would I be if I forgot your favorites?"

Best friend? When they hadn't talked in more than a decade?

"Well, thanks," she said.

She took a big gulp of the coffee, glad it had cooled down on the way because she needed it to jolt her system. Then she set the cup on the hood, unwrapped the biscuit, and took a monster bite.

Shane watched her, an amused expression on his face, and she felt self-conscious.

"Everything else okay? You look stressed," he said.

Taylor swallowed the bite first and rubbed her mouth for stray crumbs. "Lucy was at my house when I got home last night. I'm glad she's alive and well, but I'm not sure what's going on with her. Hart's Ridge is the last place she ever wants to be, according to her. She hasn't let on yet why she came back, but I feel like I'm waiting for a grenade to go off."

"Is that why you left Bernard behind? I was wondering where your sidekick was."

She nodded. "Yes, since she's there, I didn't feel so guilty leaving him home. I'm also afraid the sheriff might show up and be mad enough that I'm here. Didn't want to add fuel to the fire with having an unofficial dog on scene, too."

"Smart girl," Shane said.

*Woman,* she silently corrected him.

"Things are heating up," she said when she'd swallowed the bite in her mouth.

"Sure are. Sarge is working on pulling together a search team and should be at the landfill by noon. He's still going to sit in with Bryce and see how he feels about the story of turning down the truck and letting her walk. It's terribly inconvenient for him that the station they met at is only fifteen miles from where the truck was found. He could've followed her, and got her to stop, then grabbed them both."

"Right, and it might be why he didn't want to come in. He's afraid that Molly will see him and ID him, if he's the one who let her wander the highway," Taylor said. "And I'm still not totally convinced about the ex-boyfriend. I'd like to go up there myself and talk to him, and his superiors. See if they can alibi him for sure. Could be he and Joni got in an argument over a boyfriend, or child support. Maybe he decided to eliminate the problem but couldn't bring himself to do anything to his own daughter, so just set her out and hoped it would take care of itself."

Shane scowled. "Sounds cold, but I see it all the time. People can be evil. Even to their own flesh and blood."

"Do you know where the truck was found?"

He pointed about fifty feet away toward the opposite side of the road. "There's a few tire impressions in the soft shoulder there. If you finish up there, Miss Piggy, we'll go look at it together."

Taylor resisted the urge to cuss him for the insult. She gobbled the rest of the biscuit quickly and washed it down with the coffee. She did hold back a big burp, but only because she'd learned to let them out silently, not that she was trying to impress Shane.

They piled their empty cups and the wrappers into the bag, and Shane stuck it in his car. Taylor led, and he followed, both of them careful not to step before they looked, in case there was any sort of evidence miraculously left behind.

"Yep, they look like truck tires," Taylor said. There wasn't much of them to see, just a light indention in two places where the right side of the truck had settled. "No keys, I guess?"

"Nope."

"We need to find out fast if the truck could've broken down or run out of gas. That will give us a bit of a clue."

"Come on," Shane said, then held out his hand to help Taylor down the shoulder. "Let's see what's in the tree line."

"Thanks, but I got it." Taylor declined his hand.

She was a cop. Not a damsel in distress. Though internally, she thought the gesture was sweet.

Very slowly, they crept to the trees, their eyes on the ground.

Taylor saw something red and pointed it out, but when they got to it, they saw it was just the end of a fast-food cup sticking out of the leaves.

They continued on, carefully watching every step to check for evidence, but saw nothing of note. Once they'd turned back around and made the slow trek back, Shane marked the spot where the tires had left the imprints.

"I'm sure we'll come back to this," he said. "But let's hope something comes out of the interview with Bryce, or that we find evidence in the truck. Another thought just hit me. You said Boone brought the ring in and said he found it at the dump.

How do you know he's not lying? We might need to interview him."

"Boone is not a suspect, Shane. He wouldn't hurt a fly."

"You don't know that. People can fool you, Taylor. I want to talk to him."

Taylor wanted to argue, but she knew he was right. Everyone was a suspect until they were cleared. If it was indeed Joni's ring, they had to make sure Boone got it from where he said.

"Fine. If you'll take a photo of the ring at the station and send it to me, I'll text it to Joni's sister for confirmation."

He hesitated. "Let's wait on that until we see what pans out today. I don't want to get her crazy mother riled up when we tell them the ring was found at the landfill."

"We need to set up a search party here, too, if we can pull enough volunteers together. You and I may have missed something."

"I'll get on that, too," he said.

"I guess you need to go."

"Yep. And what's on your plate today?"

"I don't know. I want to be working the case, damn it."

"I know you do. How about I'll keep you updated on every little thing, and you can add your input? Sheriff doesn't have to know."

She sighed. "I'd appreciate that. Usually, I'd take the days off and get caught up on my own stuff. But I can't shake this connection to Molly, or to her mother. I've got to see this one through."

He nodded. "Well, I may need some help from my silent partner, so keep your phone handy."

"I will. But I'm going to hang out here a bit and walk a little farther. Then I guess I'll go home and take Lucy to see my dad. At least one of us can be happy today. He'll probably want to throw a party for his prodigal daughter, the Golden Child."

Shane laughed as he was climbing into the car. "Don't forget my invitation."

He didn't wait for her reply, which was a good thing because there was no way that she was bringing him around her family and then have to hear them questioning her as to whether he was single, interested, or whatever. And Lucy—she could never be trusted. She'd be all over Shane if she thought she had a chance.

Not that Taylor cared.

But she still wasn't giving her the chance.

AFTER SHANE LEFT, Taylor walked at least two hundred feet in both directions, explored a bit deeper into the tree line, and came up with nothing. She really wanted to go to the landfill and help search, or at least be part of the interview with the would-be truck buyer.

Damn that Sheila. If it weren't for her, Taylor wouldn't be standing here with her hands in her pocket, unable to do much to find her daughter.

She remembered something that Jessica had said in their meeting.

*You wanted her to turn Molly over to you once you fell in love with her, and Joni said absolutely not.*

Could there be any way that Sheila was responsible for Joni's disappearance?

But that didn't make sense because even someone as crazy as Sheila wouldn't let a child out to walk the roads. Would she?

Taylor returned to her car and started back to the house, but then felt a strong need to turn around and drive the other way, toward Jasper, the direction that Joni's truck was pointing.

*What if...*

It was a game she liked to play when she was investigating. She wasn't a detective, but she was pretty good at figuring things out, and many times, just those two words could get her thinking in the right direction.

It worked.

There was one scenario they hadn't thought of yet.

What if Joni's truck broke down and someone pulled up beside her and asked to help? And what if they said they'd give her a ride to the nearest station?

Then they didn't make it there.

Taylor drove past the place the truck was found and cruised slowly, looking for any evidence of another pullover. When she approached a stop sign, she turned right, following her gut, and crept even slower.

Suddenly, she saw what appeared to be another imprint of tires on the right shoulder. She parked just ahead of them and got out, then walked back.

Once she got close, she could see that there were several tire imprints along the shoulder, as though there were two cars parked here recently. On the highway just to the left and ahead of one of the sets, were black marks like someone left in a hurry and spun a tire.

She walked the space between the black marks, then took out her phone and made a note of the distance between the two. It wasn't as widely spaced as truck tires, so the marks appeared to belong to a car.

That still didn't tell her anything. But since she didn't really have anywhere to be and was dragging her feet about dealing with Lucy, she decided to keep walking and looking.

A whiff of a local chicken farm and the manure from it hit her, and she gagged. That was one downfall of Georgia living, and unless you'd experienced it firsthand, you couldn't imagine the stench when a farmer was spreading the valuable fertilizer over his fields. Taylor would never get used to it.

She followed the direction of the black marks and slowly investigated the shoulder as she walked, her gaze sweeping through the sparse tree line.

Nothing.

But she kept feeling like she should walk just a bit farther.

Perhaps she didn't want to go home and deal with Lucy and her father, or maybe it was just her gut continuing to lead her, but soon she was at least a half mile from her car and crossing over a small bridge.

Halfway over it, she stopped and looked over the side to the dry creek bed that lay at least sixty-five feet below.

At first, she saw nothing other than a few abandoned tires and several empty beer bottles. But then she strained to make out the edge of something black that was mostly out of sight.

It was a shoe.

A hiking boot, to be exact.

Taylor carefully made her way down to the creek bed where the boot lay. When she was close enough to see that it wasn't a man's boot, but petite enough to belong to a woman, she froze.

Not because of that revelation.

Because she suddenly knew the putrid aroma around her was not chicken shit. And because the boot was still on a foot, attached to the leg of a young woman who lay crumpled just under the shade of the bridge. It was already bloated with a group of blowflies around it, settled into the beginning of decomposition.

Taylor could see that she was still dressed, but she only wore one boot, and a tiny sunflower tattoo was visible on the ankle of the bare foot.

Shane could mark getting search parties together off his list.

She'd found Joni Stott.

# CHAPTER 24

"*I* don't think this is where she was killed," Shane said. "She was thrown from the bridge either unconscious or already dead."

Taylor had already come to that conclusion, too, but it wasn't her statement to make. Once Shane made it on scene, she'd reluctantly turned control over to him, but assisted him in documenting everything. Together, they'd marked off the area with stakes and string and a few flags. They needed to ensure no evidence would be trampled or lost.

She was just glad the sheriff hadn't told her to take off, so she was keeping as low-key as possible during the madness that was now the death scene. They still had not determined where the primary crime scene was, but she was willing to bet it would be where the truck had been found, or pretty damn close to it.

Only an hour before, it was a beautiful, peaceful morning in which Taylor still held hope that Molly's mom would be found. Now the quiet bridge she'd come upon was teeming with state police, the coroner, and other personnel, all competing to have a stake in the case now that it was a murder.

Clint was there, too. He already had a chip on his shoulder

and was prowling around, treating Taylor with indifference as though she'd stolen his thunder. He wasn't going to get any accolades for finding the body, and it obviously pissed him off. Taylor would gladly rather not have found Joni, and that she be alive and well and just off on a grand adventure like her mother claimed her to be, and soon reunited with Molly.

But Clint didn't think that way.

They were also already starting to get a few locals on scene. One farmer had stopped by and got enough bits and pieces to put out to his wife, who had run with the news that a body had been found. Now the Hart's Ridge grapevine was most likely at high alert.

Taylor had also started the logbook to keep track of who came and went on scene, but already it was getting crazy and making her nervous. Too many crime scenes or investigations were compromised by random suits not paying attention to what they were doing in their haste to get their nose into what was going on.

But she couldn't just start bossing people around unless she wanted to deal with a pack of pissed-off men.

Shane coughed into his hand. "I need to get back and start in with Mr. Bryce Kessler. The judge already approved a search warrant for his truck, and they found a bag of weed, so he's in a holding cell pending other charges."

"Did they find anything else in his truck?" Taylor asked.

"Not a thing that looked related to Joni, but the team from Jasper is processing for fingerprints and DNA. We need to take a photo over and get a positive ID from Sheila."

Taylor's stomach sank.

She'd found the body. It was her duty, and though she didn't relish telling anyone that their loved one was found dead, and especially murdered, at least she knew that it would be done with the utmost respect if she carried it out herself.

"Don't think you're invisible, Gray. I know you're here."

She turned to find Sheriff Dawkins coming up to them. He looked beyond angry.

"I'm not trying to be," she said.

"Good. You're back on. Weaver, you're still the lead investigator, but both of you will work with the state police for whatever they need. I want to get the son of a bitch who did this to that girl."

Both Taylor and Shane nodded.

"Yes, sir," Taylor said.

"I hope to God this was someone passing through and wasn't done by one of our own," Sheriff said. "But until we know, the whole damn town is going to be in an uproar."

"True," Taylor said. "I'm sure the news is making the rounds now, and we need to get a handle on just what happened."

"I saw some evidence of defensive wounds," Shane said.

"I noted a torn fingernail," Taylor said. "Hope it has some DNA under there."

"We've got the medical examiner from Atlanta coming down, and the body will be going to the state crime lab. I'm not leaving this to amateurs," Sheriff said.

"Good call," Shane said.

Taylor agreed. Their town didn't have the budget for a medical examiner full-time, and their coroner also held the position of mayor. He was a good fellow and did a fine job with accidental or illness-related deaths—and kissing babies—but murder was a different story.

"Judging by the contusion on her head, I believe she has a head injury, though I don't know if she got it from the fall or beforehand," Shane said. "I didn't see any gunshot wounds. No ligatures or other signs of strangling, either. But we'll see what the examiner finds."

"That drop from the bridge was enough to kill her," Taylor said.

"Possibly," Shane said.

215

"As soon as you're done here, I want you to go together to notify the family. Get a positive ID," Sheriff said. "That kid you got in the holding cell can sit and sweat for a few hours, so take your time. Hopefully, he'll be ready to talk when you get back. If he's the last one to see her, he knows something."

"Yes, sir," Shane said.

"Sarge is still at the impound lot, and he's making sure they don't miss anything," Sheriff said. "You don't leave here until there's not one more thing to document, gather, or photo. And get the lookers out of here stat."

Taylor nodded.

Sheriff strode off, went to his truck, and got in.

"I've already taken a few photos of the lookers," she said. "I need to finish getting names and statements. See if any of them have seen or heard anything. I'll also canvas the few houses within a couple miles' radius."

"I'll send McElroy to the houses. You meet me at the car in an hour. We need to get to Sheila Stott and Jessica before the news does," Shane said.

"I'll call Wesley and find out where they're staying. Rose called me and said she put them out after the first night because Sheila was smoking in her room and stayed up past midnight with the television blaring."

Shane shook his head. "Not surprised."

They separated, and Taylor went to where at least half a dozen locals were standing on the road, about fifty feet from the bridge. So far, they hadn't gotten close enough to see the body, and Taylor hoped the coroner and the visiting medical examiner would be able to get it into transport without a public viewing.

She approached two men standing together.

One of them was the owner of a pig farm down the road by the name of Horis Hedgepeth, but she didn't recognize the other man. Horis was a good man, a hard worker, and never gave the county any trouble.

"Horis, you've had to pass by here to get back and forth to town. Have you noticed anything out of the ordinary? Any strange vehicles? People?"

He shook his head. "Nope. But I ain't been to town in the last few days."

"And who is your friend?" Taylor asked, nodding at the man standing next to Horis.

"My cousin. He's been helping me out for a few months."

"Name?"

"Baitdigger is what they call me, but my name is Mark Jones," the man said. "I ain't been off the farm except when I was with Horis, so don't start thinking because I'm not from here that I done went and did this crime. I ain't never put my hands on no women and ain't about to start now."

"I understand," Taylor said. "This is just protocol. You aren't a person of interest at this time, but if we have questions, we may need you to come into the station. For now, I need to see your driver's license, and I'll be noting your address."

He looked terrified, but he fished it out of his wallet and handed it over. She looked, then noted down his South Carolina address.

"I'm his alibi," Horis said. "Hell, Mark hits the sack every night after dinner about eight o'clock. He ain't got the energy to do what I'm paying him for, much less get into any other trouble. Even if he did, he doesn't have a vehicle, and I keep my keys next to my pillow."

Jones shot Horis a miffed look. Obviously, he'd been under the impression he was doing a good job with the pigs.

"I swear, I ain't got a thing to do with this. I been off parole now for—"

Horis elbowed Baitdigger. "Don't say another word. Better to keep your mouth shut and seem a fool than to open it and remove all doubt."

Taylor finished with the license and handed it back. "You're on parole?"

"No. I done my time. I keep my nose clean now but can't hardly get a job with a record. That's why I'm slopping pigs."

Too bad for him. Taylor couldn't empathize. "Got it. Well, don't leave the county without letting me know. Now please, get on home. We need to clear the scene."

Horis looked like he wanted to drag his feet, but his cousin pushed him along. Taylor put a star next to Baitdigger at the top of her list. She'd told him he wasn't a person of interest, but he might be after all.

Quickly, she went through the rest of the stragglers, taking names and addresses. None of them had seen or heard anything out of the ordinary in the last week. Some of them had already given their information to Clint and weren't happy about doing it all over again. Taylor fought the urge to tell him to stop interfering with her crime scene.

It was better to work around him than to set him off.

When she finished, she'd cleared the scene of civilians and stood aside somberly while the coroner and medical examiner wrapped Joni, carried her up the ravine, and put her into the van. Taylor said a prayer for Joni's soul, and another for Molly. She was going to have a long, hard road ahead of her without a mother.

Shane was already at the car when she got there two hours later, and Taylor climbed in.

"This isn't going to be pleasant," she said.

"Nope."

"Let me call Wesley." She called, and without telling him why, found out that Sheila and Jessica were staying in the Motel Six just out of town. She let Shane know, and they headed out.

While he drove, she texted Lucy, let her know she wasn't going to be there any time soon, and asked her to take care of Bernard.

"How is she doing?" Shane asked.

"Lucy? She's...well...I guess she's fine. I haven't had a chance to really talk to her and find out what's going on."

"Is she using?"

Taylor shrugged. It didn't feel right talking about her sister's issues. Not even to Shane. "I really don't know but judging by the weight on her and her clear skin, I don't think so. She could be drinking, though. It's easier to hide."

"What're you going to do about her?"

"What do you mean?"

"I mean you have to stop thinking you can save everyone, Taylor. Your sister is how old now? Twenty-five?"

"Twenty-six, and I've no plans to try to save her," Taylor said, though she knew deep down she'd give anything she had to keep Lucy straight and put her on the road to a normal life.

"I remember in school, you even did her homework." He tapped the steering wheel, baiting her.

"I didn't *do* her homework. I helped her with it."

"Yeah, right. You also took the blame when she stole your dad's car and totaled it in the ditch," he said.

"No, I took that car. She was asleep," Taylor said.

"Oh, okay," Shane said. He looked over at her with a doubting grin. "We both know you've never broken a rule in your life."

Thankfully, before he could give her any more of a hard time, they pulled into the Motel Six and right up next to Sheila's vehicle.

"I'm assuming you should do the talking, since she's quite fond of you," Taylor said. "I have no idea how a woman like her will take this news. She could fall apart or punch you in the throat."

Shane grimaced. "Yeah, I'll tell her and get her to confirm the photo."

When they got out, Taylor saw Jessica sitting on a bench outside the office, her attention on her phone.

"Jessica?" Taylor called out.

Jessica looked up.

"Is your mom with you?"

Jessica shook her head and pointed at the room.

"You talk to Sheila, and I'll go tell Jessica," Taylor said. "It might work out better that way. I don't want Jessica to see the photo."

Shane agreed, went to the door, and gave it a few knocks. It swung open, and he went in just as Taylor reached Jessica.

"What's going on?" Jessica said.

Taylor sat down beside her. "I've got some news, and it isn't good."

"Tell me."

"We found your sister."

Jessica searched Taylor's eyes, looking for any glimmer of hope. "She's dead, isn't she?"

Taylor nodded sadly. "She is."

Jessica didn't make a sound, but as she looked at the ground, tears rained down her face.

"How?" she asked through a muffled sob.

"We don't know the details or the exact cause of death yet. We've opened an investigation, but it takes time for the medical examiner to make a ruling."

"Someone murdered her. I know it! And what about Molly? They won't even let us see her now until the psychologist gives approval, and that might be next week. Oh my God. I can't believe this is happening." The dam burst, and she let herself cry openly, the sobs wracking her body.

Taylor put her arm around her. "I am so very sorry. We are going to find out who did this. I promise you that. And you'll get to see Molly. I'll call and see what I can do about getting a super-vised visit again."

Jessica turned and looked up at Taylor. "Oh my God, what's

going to happen to her? Joni would not want my mom to have Molly."

Taylor sighed. "I really don't know what to say about that, Jessica. I'm not involved in child custody. It will be up to the courts."

"My mom is not stable, and if I have to testify and say that in front of her to save Molly, I will," Jessica said. "She is not going to ruin her life like she did Joni's. That's the least I can do for my sister."

Taylor admired the strength that came into Jessica's voice when talking about Molly, but most likely, if Sheila could pass the background checks, the courts would let her have custody. But Jessica didn't need to know that right now.

"Most likely social services will ask the court to appoint guardian ad litem to speak for the best interest of Molly. They will investigate the best options for her future and make a recommendation to a judge. But let's just take it one day at a time. I need to ask, do you know anyone who would've wanted Joni dead? A boyfriend? Molly's father, maybe?"

Jessica shook her head vehemently. "No. Everyone loved Joni, especially Josh. I don't care what my mother says. He planned to make a life for them one day. He'll be devastated. Oh God, does he know?"

"Not yet," Taylor said. "One of us will be going up to his base to talk to him."

She left out the part about looking for a positive alibi. At this point, he was definitely a person of interest.

"The guy she met for the truck!" Jessica said. "It had to be him."

"We are looking into that, too."

"Did Joni suffer? Can you tell me that?" she asked through more tears.

"I'm sorry. Until we know the cause of death, we won't know. We'll have to let the medical examiner do his job so that we have more to go on." Taylor had already given her too much information by pretty much confirming it was murder when she'd promised to get the person responsible.

Sheriff would have her badge for that slip up if he found out.

The door to the motel room burst open, and a shriek sounded across the parking lot.

Jessica took a deep breath, then stood and went to meet her mother, arms open as the skinny woman dissolved against her daughter in a puddle of hysteria.

Taylor met Shane's eyes, and he nodded.

The body had been positively identified as that of Joni Stott.

# CHAPTER 25

*B*ernard was first in, and Taylor was running on pure willpower as she followed Lucy into their dad's trailer and set the bag of groceries on the table. It had been a marathon of a day that had finally fizzled out when she and Shane couldn't get anything out of Bryce Kessler. He'd stuck to his story that he'd met Joni, declined the truck and got her some gas, then they'd separated.

Bryce was now spending the night in their county lockup because they hadn't let him make a call to get anyone to post his bail for the weed charge. They hoped a night spent cold and hungry would help open his communication.

Her dad hadn't looked up yet. He lay on the couch with his arm over his eyes and Nascar blaring on the television.

"Dad?" Taylor called out. She noticed that the kitchen was a mess. Again.

"What?" he croaked out, without looking, then shook Bernard off from painting his face with his tongue.

"I have a visitor here for you."

"Yeah, I know. He just slobbered all over me."

"Nope, someone else, too," Taylor said.

He moved his arm and peered at Lucy standing not three feet from him. For a few seconds, he just looked, as though he couldn't believe it was really her.

"Well, I'll be damned," he declared and sat up, a smile reaching across his face. "Girl, where you been?"

"Hi, Daddy," Lucy said, sitting next to him and giving him a hug.

Taylor made herself busy in the kitchen unpacking the grocery bag. It was bittersweet, but she hadn't seen him smile like that in years. She looked in the trash can and saw a pile of beer cans, which ironically, made her a bit happy. At least it wasn't whiskey bottles.

Her dad looked up toward the door. "Did Anne and Jo come, too?"

"No. Taylor called them, but Anne's kids have tennis lessons, and Jo can't get away on short notice," Lucy said, rolling her eyes.

He looked disappointed for a minute, then immediately began asking a list of questions about where she'd been, how long she was staying, and more.

When Lucy filled him in with some obvious lies, he got even more cheerful.

"I'm going to make us all some dinner," Taylor said, though no one was paying attention to her.

Her dad got up and went by her, suddenly as limber as a teenager. If he was drunk, he was hiding it well with his sudden burst of energy. Taylor didn't even try to see if she smelled alcohol. She was too tired to know.

"I'm going to wash up really quick. Don't go anywhere," he said.

Taylor winked at Lucy. They'd discussed how he had stopped caring about keeping himself up.

"Come here, Bernard," Lucy cooed, then sat on the floor.

Bernard obeyed like a champ.

Seemed everyone was on their best behavior for her sister.

Taylor thought she ought to bring Lucy in to question suspects. Maybe she could make them spill their guts.

"Want to come and help me make up the burger patties?" she asked her.

"Nope. I can't stand to touch raw meat."

"You can cut up the potatoes," Taylor offered. She wasn't a fan of raw meat either.

"Using the knife hurts my hands. I think I have early arthritis."

*More like lazy-itis.*

"Well, okay, then. Just make yourself comfortable." It wasn't any use to even suggest her sister take on dicing an onion.

"Thanks," Lucy said, not missing a beat, though she did miss the sarcasm.

Taylor quickly pounded at the hamburger patties and set them in the skillet, then covered them with seasoning. She thought about just poking the potatoes and putting them in the microwave to bake, but her dad loved fried potatoes and onions, and since she knew he wouldn't be giving her any trouble eating with Lucy here, she wanted to treat him. It wasn't a healthy meal, but it was a familiar one that reminded her of the many times they'd eaten together as a family.

She sat down at the table to peel and dice, one eye on Lucy as she turned Bernard over and began rubbing his belly. Her mind was still on Joni Stott, but she couldn't let them know it.

"What did you two do today?" she asked.

Lucy stretched her arms over her head like she was tired. "We went for a walk down in the woods. I showed Bernard our old fort. Threw him some balls. Then we had a gloriously long nap."

*Probably in my bed,* Taylor kept from saying.

Their dad came through from the bedroom, his hair still wet from the shower. He was wearing a clean T-shirt with a tractor on it, and was wearing a pair of joggers that Taylor had given him for Father's Day the year before and had never seen him in.

"So, please tell me you'll stay in town a while, Lucy Lou," he asked. He went to his recliner and sat down, then kicked it back.

Taylor waited quietly for Lucy to answer.

"Not sure, Dad," she said, keeping her gaze on Bernard.

"Well, where else you going to go? This is your home. You can stay with me or with Taylor. Maybe get a job. Settle in."

He sounded pitiful to Taylor. He'd be begging soon.

"I don't know, Dad. There's not much to do around Hart's Ridge," she said.

"Then just relax for a time," he said. "Get rested. I could take you fishing. We still got the old jon boat out there, don't we, Taylor?"

"Yep," Taylor said.

"I was twelve the last time we fished, Dad. I don't think I have the patience for it now," Lucy said.

"That's okay. We'll think of something to do. Right, Taylor?"

"Sure. Except I'll be working," Taylor said.

*Someone has to pay the bills.*

He went into telling a story about the time that Lucy caught a big bass and then it flopped into their boat, and she jumped out. Taylor hadn't heard him talk this much in years.

She didn't know what it was about Lucy. If it was that she was the baby of the family, or maybe she reminded him more of their mother than any of the others. Lucy could do no wrong in their father's eyes, and even if she told him that Lucy had just been bailed out of jail the week before by a well-known criminal, he probably would refuse to believe it. And if Taylor showed him the mug shot, he'd most likely claim that Lucy had been forced into it. That was the way it went with Lucy.

To be honest, they all sort of treated her like she was the princess. And thus far, it had not helped Lucy grow up and be responsible one bit. Could be it was time to start using some tough love on baby sister.

Taylor finished dicing the potatoes and rinsed them off in the sink. She filled a skillet with a quarter inch of oil, then let it get hot before pouring the potatoes in and hearing a satisfying sizzle, then covered them generously with salt and pepper. She turned the patties on to let them start cooking while she diced the onion over the potatoes.

She stood over the stove, turning the potatoes, while Lucy and her dad chatted. When it was done, she threw the patties on a plate, the taters in a bowl, and set them on the table.

"Eat up, y'all. I need to get home before I fall completely out," she said, then took a chair.

Lucy grabbed the ketchup, mustard, and buns, brought them with her, and sat down.

"What do you two want to drink?" Dad said.

Taylor nearly laughed. The choices were slim pickings, and she knew it.

"Water, please."

"I'll take milk," Lucy said.

Taylor was surprised but pleased. Luckily, she'd bought milk at the store in the hopes that her dad might decide to drink something to coat his stomach.

He fixed their drinks and brought them to the table, along with a glass of water for himself. He sat down and began serving himself.

She'd been asking him to drink water for months. *Years.*

She pinched a patty off the plate and passed it down to Bernard, who gulped it down with one swallow.

They all dug in, and as each bite hit her stomach, Taylor felt more tired.

Lucy and her dad chatted, but all Taylor could think of was Joni's body crumpled in the creek, and what she might have gone through before the fall. She also couldn't get Jessica's anguish out of her mind. It felt like all that girl had was her sister, and now she was gone.

"So, I hear Hart's Ridge has a murderer in the midst," her dad said with a mouth full of fried potatoes.

Taylor just about choked on her burger. Lucy's eyes widened in shock.

"Where did you hear that?" Taylor asked.

He shrugged. "Around. You know."

"No, I don't know. Good gracious, you don't leave that recliner unless it's for the couch. How can you hear something so fast?"

He looked hurt, and embarrassed, and Taylor felt bad. Of course, he didn't want Lucy to know how much he'd gone downhill.

"Really, Dad. Who told you?" Taylor asked.

"I saw it on Facebook," he said.

"Wait," Taylor said, sitting upright. "First, since when do you have Facebook? And second, that was fast. Damn town gossip mill. Were there photos?"

"Just some of the road and the bridge. Some cops standing around. Nothing of the girl. And yes, I do have Facebook. You know, old Horis has his cousin from South Carolina out there doing some work on the farm. The guy's a real loser."

"Yes, I do know that. I'm part of the investigation team. His name is Mark Jones, aka Baitdigger, and I've already talked to him. We can't go accusing him of murder just because he's not a local."

"Who was killed?" Lucy asked, all eyes.

"A young woman driving through from Florida," Taylor said. She was still shocked that her dad knew how to set up a social network profile and wondered why he'd done it. "It's an active case, and I'm not talking about it, and neither should either of you."

Her dad rolled his eyes. "Okay, Sherlock, cool your jets. I wasn't asking for insider trading tips. Just wanted to know if they have a suspect. I'm not feeling too good about you two going home alone."

"Dad. Seriously?" Taylor almost couldn't take his ridiculousness. If Lucy weren't here, he wouldn't give a fig, and she was too tired to pretend otherwise. "Look, I'm going home now. Lucy, stay or go, whatever you want, but I'm leaving."

Her dad looked beyond hurt, and Taylor tried not to look at him. He was good at slinging guilt and never acknowledging her needs.

Lucy sighed. She drained the last drops of milk from her glass and set it down. "I'm going with you, but while I have you both here, I need to talk to you."

Taylor's gut clenched.

"What's going on?" their dad asked.

"I've kind of got myself into a predicament, and I need a little money." Lucy began chewing on the edge of her finger, just like she'd done when she was a nervous child.

"I think I can find you a job," Taylor said. At least now she knew why Lucy was home.

"How much money?" their dad asked.

"Dad, you don't have any money," Taylor said. "Lucy, what's it for?"

She looked away. "I can't really say."

"I get a check at the end of the month," their dad said. "How much you need?"

Taylor shook her head. "Yes, you do, Dad, and it's not enough for you to survive on now. You can't go giving some of it away."

"A thousand dollars," Lucy said.

Taylor's mouth dropped. Her sister never asked for that much at one time.

"If you can't say," Taylor said, "then it's for something I'd put in the *not good* category. I don't have a spare grand sitting around, especially for something that's probably illegal. And Dad for sure doesn't have that kind of money. So, the answer is no. You'll need to stay long enough to work for it."

"Why are you being such a bitch?" Lucy asked. "You know I've had a rough time of it."

Dad held his hands up. "Girls, girls. Please. I don't want you to fight."

"I'm not fighting, and don't talk to me like I'm a child when I'm obviously the only responsible adult here," Taylor said. "I'm just telling her the facts. You don't have anything to give her, and I have bills to pay with my money. Mabel would probably hire her as a temporary server, and she can make the money in a month."

"I can't stay here, and I don't want to work at the Den," Lucy said. "Let's just go. I'm tired, and I want a bath."

"Fine. I guarantee you aren't more tired than I am," Taylor said, then regretted sounding like a competitive child. Her sisters tended to do that to her.

Their dad stood and took their plates to the sink. "I'll clean up. Thanks for cooking, Tay."

Taylor about fell out of her seat. Cleaning up *and* gratitude? Was it her birthday?

"You're welcome. Bernard, let's go."

Thankfully, he listened to her on the first command and didn't argue. She didn't wait to see if her sister followed because she couldn't care less if she did or not. She could always hope that her sister would be irritated at her enough to decide to camp out at her dad's house.

No such luck, because as soon as she let Bernard hop in and then climbed into her car herself, Lucy opened the passenger side and joined her.

"Well, that went well, don't you think?" she asked, then grinned as though they hadn't just sparred in their dad's kitchen over money.

Taylor threw the car into drive and took off before Lucy could fasten her seat belt.

# CHAPTER 26

"*Some people are so broken that they get mad at you for being whole.*" That was told to Taylor once by Cecil, and it was one of the few things that stuck when it came to dealing with her sisters. The crazy part of that was that Taylor probably had just as many demons as they did, but she chose to keep striving for a better path in life rather than get mired in the past. And she kept her wounds hidden and refused to bring them out and display them for the world to see.

Her drive to work was turning out to be a time of self-recrimination and second-guessing.

Lucy had staggered into the bathroom while Taylor was getting out of the shower, but her sister ran straight for the commode and threw up, and the only words they exchanged were insults about the greasy potatoes making Lucy sick.

Taylor bit back that maybe if she'd had some help, they would've been better.

Lucy gave her the evil eye, then went back to bed and was still sleeping when Taylor left a half hour later.

*"Some people don't want to be fixed because being broken gets them*

*attention"* was another Cecil quote, but one that made her feel guilty for applying to her sister.

It was always a difficult straddle for Taylor to want Lucy near so that she could watch out for her, but then want to run when her sister was being difficult.

When they got home from their family dinner the night before, Lucy hadn't wanted to talk, except about their mother. A subject that Taylor wasn't feeling like tackling. If Lucy were in serious trouble, Taylor needed to know, and she tried to get her to spill it. She sure didn't want to be unknowingly harboring a fugitive, and you could never discount that possibility with Lucy.

Besides, Lucy was too young when the fire happened to remember much of anything, so she thought of her mother in very unrealistic fantasy terms.

Yes, their mom was good to them, but there wasn't time for much other than surviving.

*And no, Lucy, they weren't tucked into bed with kisses and fairytales, but go ahead and make up whatever makes you feel good.*

Lucy wouldn't talk about her troubles, and Taylor wouldn't talk about their mother. They'd gone to bed with a bad energy in the air between them.

Taylor glanced at Bernard as he hung his head out the window. She could've left him with Lucy, but damn it, her little sister was trying to win him over, too. She already had their dad eating out of her hand. Couldn't Taylor at least keep her own dog's loyalty?

"What do you think, Bernard? Will she still be mad when I get home?"

He obviously didn't have an opinion because he continued to stare out the window as they pulled into the station and parked the car.

She got out and held the door for him.

"I should've just left you home with her. Then you two could conspire against me and discuss how totally unfair I am for not giving her a thousand dollars and you full access to your jar of treats. Same concept, don't you think? I want you to work for your rewards, too. If I gave you everything for nothing, you'd never grow up to be a healthy canine who contributes to society in a positive manner."

He didn't flinch.

She really didn't have time to worry about Lucy and her "rough time of it," whatever that meant. She had a murder to solve. Or to help solve. Of course, she was also taking a big chance in bringing Bernard back to the station, but her hope was that the sheriff would be too tied up in the case to care. She meant to leave him at home. That was the plan. Then he'd whined and looked at her with pleading in his eyes.

And she felt like he'd chosen her instead of Lucy.

That did it, and she'd folded.

"Okay, now make yourself invisible," Taylor told him as they entered the building.

Bernard took off, as though he completely understood and didn't have to be asked twice.

Taylor went straight to Shane's office.

"Hey, boss," she said.

He looked up from the computer. "Hi. Get some sleep?"

"A little. Took too long to get there because Lucy insisted on the first bath, and then she stole my side of the bed again. I went to sleep with a few colorful words on the tip of my tongue, and I think somewhere, some buddha says that's not conducive to a restorative rest." She kept out the real reason she couldn't sleep. She didn't need more questions from him.

He laughed. "I think that sounds about right."

"Anyway, what's first up?"

"I've been getting the paperwork all up to date. It's a shitload of notes, and they need to be organized."

Taylor appreciated that Shane was like her, very meticulous with his documentation. That was a trait that could make or break a case when it got to court and could be rare in her male counterparts.

"Blunt force trauma," he said next.

"Oh?"

"Yep. Just got the call. Official cause of death."

"From the fall?"

"Nope. The fall was after the head injury. She was struck hard enough with something solid to take her out immediately and was probably already deceased when she went over the bridge."

Taylor felt sick. But at least it was probably instantaneous, and she didn't suffer.

"But the biggest discovery," he continued, "is that the boyfriend was logged in as reprimanded for unapproved absence."

"No way," Taylor said.

"Yep. The only problem is that it was the two days before Molly showed up in the store. That kid couldn't have been wandering for two days, or she'd have been in much worse shape."

"Man, I thought you had something," Taylor said.

He was right. Molly hadn't looked great, but she sure didn't look like she'd been walking around alone for days.

Also, based on Jessica's remarks about the boyfriend, Taylor wasn't holding him on her list as a suspect, but technically, everyone was a suspect until they weren't.

"It could still be something. You know how many clerical errors there are in every system. What if the days were logged in wrong? I think I should go up there and investigate further."

She nodded. "I agree. I'd like to go with you. And I was think-ing, I also want to talk to the state man who called the truck in to be picked up," she said. "Maybe he saw something. You got a name yet?"

"Sure do. Greg Meyer. A thirteen-year veteran with GSP and

a hot pencil who writes a lot of tickets. I'm sure he'll love to be involved."

"Has he been notified yet that the truck belongs to a murder victim?"

Shane shook his head and pushed a scrap of paper across the desk. "Nope. Here's his number. You can have the honor if you're set on talking to him, but you'll have to get in line because he's doing a live ride along today with media out of Atlanta about self-protection for female drivers."

"Well, that's good timing."

He shrugged. "Sounds like he's a ham. Oh, I already had another round at Kessler and got nothing. I hate to say it, but he seems like a good guy. Either that or he's a hell of an actor, but either way, his dad bailed him out an hour ago."

"Damn. I wanted to have a go," Taylor said.

"Sorry. Couldn't find anything else to hold him on."

"Now he'll probably lawyer up."

"No doubt."

"I'm trying to figure out how the pouch with the ring would've gotten to the landfill. Why not just dump her things with her?" They still hadn't shown the ring to Joni's mother or sister, but Taylor felt they'd been through enough shock at this point.

Shane scratched his eyebrow with his pen. "I'm thinking somewhere in that landfill is also her wallet or at least her driver's license. Someone didn't want her to be identified too soon, so they separated any identifying articles from the body. I'm going to send a few guys out there. If they find something, it's a possibility we can pick up a print."

"We also need to keep a check and see if any of her cards get used," Taylor said.

"I've already put a flag on them. Nothing yet."

"So probably not a robbery. And it didn't appear that she was sexually assaulted, judging by her clothing being intact, though we won't know until the medical examiner says so. So that leaves a random act of violence or a personal motive." Taylor leaned back in her chair, trying to think if she'd forgotten any other possibility.

"Speaking of the medical examiner, do you have any pull there?" Shane asked. "Other than with your own coroner, I mean."

"At GBI in Decatur? Actually, I do. They'll probably have her body today, and I'll make a call to my friend there and see if they can rush the autopsy. We might get them to send the toxicology over early, but probably the best we can do on all results is bring it down from three months to just one. And that will take a miracle, but I'll see what I can do."

"Great. We need to get moving on this before I get pulled and sent back home," Shane said. He stood and began packing his computer into his bag.

Taylor made a note on her phone to call her contact. She'd never pulled the favor card from her friend at the Georgia Bureau of Investigation office yet, but she was going to call it in for this one. Seven or so years back, she had won a ticket to a fancy law-enforcement charity ball in Atlanta, and while she was there, she'd met Brandon Choi. He was a still-wet-behind-the-ears research assistant in a small lab outside of Jasper and at the party had started to make a fool of himself. His date had dumped him for the attention of a high-ranked suit, right in front of everyone when fund-raising events ended and the real party began.

Brandon hadn't liked being set aside.

It started to unravel fast, and Taylor could see him heading for an altercation that would be a career-buster. He seemed like a nice enough guy, and she'd had mercy on him, diverting his attention long enough to talk sense into him. For the rest of the night, they'd pretended to be just as infatuated with each other as his now ex and the chest-puffing assistant director of GBI.

They'd parted as nothing more than good friends, and they still talked occasionally and laughed over how they'd met. Taylor hadn't moved up in rank since then, but he had and now was a specialized forensic pathologist at GBI, a position he would've never grabbed had he followed his first instincts and taken his frustrations out on the suit at the ball, who was now his superior and had most likely signed off on the job offer.

Penner popped his head into the office. "Y'all might want to turn on channel seven."

Shane hit the remote, and they watched as a reporter held the microphone toward an officer in a blue uniform.

"Meyer?"

"Yep," Penner said, then ducked out.

Meyer pontificated on the rules of the road for women, including driving with their doors locked, avoiding dark and desolated areas, never getting low on fuel, and all the common other tips Taylor had herself recommended over the years. She just about laughed when he advised for women not to pick up hitchhikers. What era was he in? No one with half a brain cell picked up hitchhikers anymore, and for that matter, she hadn't seen a hitchhiker in at least a decade.

Taylor wished he'd talk about the more uncommon things women should know—like noticing if you were being followed and what to do, tips for highjack prevention, and how to avoid being a victim of car theft. Or how to do a vehicle safety check before setting out on a road trip alone. Useful tips that wouldn't go in one ear and out the other. Tips for this millennium.

"And remember, ladies, never engage with strangers on the road. Women attract attention just because they are women. But if you are careful enough, you will arrive alive," Meyer said, a cheesy grin stretching across his pocked face.

"Vomit," Taylor said. "So, is he inferring that if they don't arrive alive, it's their fault for being female?"

Shane laughed. "Do I sense a dislike?"

"He sounds chauvinistic. I'm surprised he didn't recommend we drive with ladies' gloves on, or let our daddies drive us. I wish we had seen what he said about the case."

"Probably not much. With thirteen years under his belt, I think he'd know to keep his lip zipped."

She wasn't so sure. Sometimes a camera in the face of an attention seeker could loosen lips, and she pegged him as someone who liked the limelight.

"I'll leave him a message to call me, then I'm going to head out to the scene. Wanna go?" Taylor asked.

He nodded and grabbed his phone from the desk.

Taylor found Bernard lounging under Penner's desk and gave him a hand wave. He popped up and followed.

"Let's take my car," Shane said.

"I'll meet you out there." Taylor went to her desk and left Meyer a message, then went by the front lobby and picked up the pouch with the ring. She wanted to take it by and give it to Jessica if they had time.

Shane was driving a dark sedan, and Taylor was glad to not be in the squad car where everyone would see them coming. Bernard hopped in the back as though he'd been in the car a million times.

While Shane drove, Taylor checked out the online page for Joni, reading through the comments to see if there was anything of value. When a text came through from Jessica, she couldn't open it fast enough. Her fingers flew over the screen, putting in her passcode.

"Jessica just texted me," she told Shane.

*Figured out Joni's password. SENTIMENTAL4U1200*

Taylor wondered briefly who the password was inspired by, then logged in as Joni and went to the messages inbox. She was looking for any correspondence that spoke of a jilted lover, secret boyfriend, or even animosity between friends. It didn't take long to go through, because despite being in the prime age bracket for social networks, Joni didn't seem to use hers much. At least not Facebook. If Snapchat was her game, then they were out of luck because nothing was saved there.

"Just got into Joni's Facebook, and there's nothing in the messages."

"Try the same password on Instagram," Shane said.

"Good idea."

She logged in there and got nothing again, other than photos of Joni and Molly. Nothing in her private messages that raised any flags.

Taylor read through a chat between Joni and Jessica, noting how Jessica had asked Joni for advice on how to deal with their mother when she was drunk and wanted to argue. Joni advised her to disengage and just leave, but Jessica came back with worry that their mother would fall and hurt herself or do something crazy in her inebriated state.

Reading the chat did nothing to help Taylor like Sheila anymore.

When they arrived at the scene, Taylor was a bit surprised to see that people had already left flowers and balloons as a makeshift shrine on the edge of the bridge. Some of it could be from Jessica and Sheila, she supposed, but it appeared to be way too much for just them to transport. She felt a moment of pride for the people of Hart's Ridge for being compassionate even to someone not their own.

"Bernard, stay," Taylor said, then got out and shut the door behind her. She didn't want him catching the scent of death and going down there.

"I'll leave it running with the air on," Shane said.

Together, they went to the shrine and examined it, looking for any notes. There was nothing personal, but Taylor saw someone had left a teddy bear with Joni's name written on a tag attached to it. She supposed they'd gotten her name from the news, but just in case, she took a glove from her pocket and took it. Never know, it could be an apology and have prints on it.

"I've got an evidence bag," Shane said. He went to the car and got a bag, then returned and held it open for the tag.

They climbed down to the creek bed and did another cursory look, though she was sure with as big of a team as they had looking, they hadn't missed anything.

"Let's backtrack again to where the truck was found," Taylor said.

Shane sighed. "I don't think it's necessary, do you? We've been over it several times."

"Then I'll go. You stay with Bernard."

"No, we'll both go. Let me get the hound." He went to the car and opened the door, and Bernard bounded out.

They walked slowly down the road toward the spot, both of them carefully examining the ground on both sides. When they arrived at the spot that had two very faint tire tracks, they stood there, not speaking.

Bernard stopped with them, his tail wagging in excitement at the impromptu adventure.

Taylor remembered the pouch in her pocket and took it out.

"Why did you bring that?" Shane asked. "That should be logged in as evidence."

"I know it's been in the landfill, and passed hands a few times, but let's see what Bernard does with it." She held it down to him, and he sniffed it.

"Taylor. You know we can't do that. Not until the case is closed. It goes back into evidence."

He was right, and embarrassment rippled through her. It was another slip of her emotions.

"Fine. But it damn well better go to her sister when this is over."

Bernard wasn't interested in the pouch, but Taylor continued to wave it under his nose while he looked away, trying to put distance between him and the object.

"Go get it," she said, tapping him on the head.

Bernard looked up at her, expectation in his eyes.

"Oh shoot, that's what I say when we play," she said. "He thinks I have a ball."

"It's not going to work, Taylor. He's not a working dog."

Shane was right. She stood and pocketed the pouch again. She was a bit disappointed. Bernard might know some commands, but he wasn't a tracker. Though to be fair, the scent trail could've been too disguised or contaminated for any dog to pick up on, trained or not.

Taylor had also brought a tape measure, and she went to work determining the distance between the tire tracks. She would compare them to Joni's truck, though she already knew they weren't a match. It was too small of a distance to be a truck. And they could be totally unrelated to Joni and her vehicle, but Taylor wanted to explore every tiny detail.

She noted the dimensions in her phone.

"Let's get back to the station and see if anything else has come in by now," Shane said.

Taylor tucked the measuring tape back in her pocket. "Come on, Bernard."

He was already ahead of her a few paces, then he dropped off the shoulder a few feet and started sniffing the ground.

"Whatcha got, boy?"

"Another dog probably peed there," Shane said.

Taylor stepped off the road and approached Bernard. It wasn't just urine.

"Nope. It's an outsole impression," she said. "Or a bit of one. I can't believe we didn't see this."

"Not much to see, and it could've gotten here today."

"Looks older than that to me. At least several days."

Shane joined her and knelt. She already had her camera out,

and she stretched her measuring tape out a foot or so next to the imprint for scale and took a few photos. Someone had been heavier on the side of their right foot, so the right outline was there, but only an inch or so of a tread pattern.

She measured the partial print and noted the details.

"Not really enough to get a manufacturer's pattern," Shane said.

"No, but I think we can determine the shoe size, and I'll blow up the photo and see if we can spot any acquired or accidental characteristics." She hoped they could because any nicks or cuts would be unique to an individual's shoe and could possibly narrow down a suspect if they had several with comparable suspicion. Since the print was from the ground and only partial, it was a long shot but at this point was about all they had.

"It's hard to believe that both scenes are so spotless, other than a body," Shane said. "And that print could be from anyone. Even the victim was wearing boots."

"Too big for her print. But yeah, evidence is just about nonexistent at this point. Maybe the medical examiner will find something we didn't see." She wasn't willing to give up hope on getting lucky. "Remember, no one can levitate in and out of a crime scene. This could be our guy. We're lucky to find pattern evidence."

"Agreed," Shane said, though he didn't sound too thrilled.

Taylor looked up at him, gauging his sudden difference in tone. He didn't seem interested.

"We need to get a cast of this," she said. "Do you have your bag?"

Every good detective carried what they needed to investigate a case, but Shane shook his head.

"I don't have casting materials. Just get some good photos, and let's go."

She didn't like it, but he was the lead, so she bit back an argument and took more photos from different angles, then jogged to catch up with him and Bernard.

In the car, she was quiet, and he was, too. Pressure was getting to both of them, she supposed. Neither of them wanted the case to be handed over to someone else.

When the silence got too heavy, Taylor couldn't take it anymore.

"Is something wrong?" she asked.

He didn't turn to look at her, but he gripped the steering wheel tighter. "Did you ever date Clint?"

His question was out of nowhere and almost made Taylor laugh.

"Clint the deputy? The creep who has made my life hell for the most part? That would be a definite no. Why do you ask?"

He shrugged. "Just something I heard him say."

"About me?"

"I really don't want to get into the details."

"Well, too damn bad. If you're asking me if I've dated him, I'd say we're already broaching the subject. Now I want to know what he said."

"Why didn't you want to date me?" Shane said, low and quiet.

Taylor didn't know where this was coming from, but it was making her very uncomfortable.

"Like, in high school? You never really asked, Shane." Sweat popped out over her upper lip. Remembering high school was never a good thing.

He kept his eyes on the road. "We hung out. I kissed you once, too. But you didn't really leave the door open for more. I just want to know why."

It's funny how two people could remember the same exact moment completely differently. They were only a few miles from the station, and Taylor was praying they'd hurry and get there. This kind of conversation made her nervous, but she wasn't about to tell her side of how she recalled their past playing out. It didn't even matter. They'd been kids!

"I don't remember closing the door, Shane. I don't remember much other than trying to give my sisters whatever sense of normality I could, considering the tumultuous life we were leading. I thought you and I were great friends. I'm sorry if you think I slighted you in any way. And this is a really weird conversation, and I don't like it."

"You never were comfortable talking about feelings. Is that why you and Nathan broke up?"

Now Taylor was past feeling awkward and making a sharp turn onto Angry Street.

"That's none of your business. And how do you know his name? Are you asking around about me? Maybe you're the one who started a conversation with Clint?"

He laughed uncomfortably, then reached over and slapped her thigh.

She stiffened.

"Oh, gotcha. I'm just kidding with you. Don't get upset." He smiled at her, his dark mood suddenly gone. "You always did like to keep everything top secret."

"That wasn't funny, Shane. You know I don't like that kind of crap."

"What? Talking about emotions? It's okay to show you're human once in a while." He winked at her.

The county parking lot came into sight, and Taylor sighed in relief, letting her breath out quietly and slowly so he wouldn't hear.

He turned in, parked, then got out first.

Taylor waited. She needed a few seconds to calm herself. It wouldn't do to face any nosy coworkers without being at her best. But as she opened the car door, a thought crept in.

How did Shane know her ex-boyfriend's name?

Clint didn't even know it. Heck, even her family had never known about Nathan.

She was going to have to watch him carefully at the station and see who he was talking to behind her back, and that disappointed her. She'd thought he was her friend.

# CHAPTER 27

Taylor went straight to her desk and turned on her computer, glad for some time alone. She uploaded the photo of the footprint into the FBI database of footwear information, hoping for a hit. If she were lucky, she'd find out the brand name and model of boot it was and could possibly help nail down a suspect—if they eventually found one, that is.

A few came close, but the tread was from a shoe that wasn't in their database.

One near miss gave her an idea, but she needed to check a few things first. She searched Google for a few shoe store numbers, then began calling.

The first few weren't helpful at all. The salespeople who answered the phone were still wet behind the ears and couldn't tell her anything beyond what she could find on their websites. Then she took another direction. If the boot wasn't in the national database, that had to mean that it was too old or too new.

Her gut told her to go with too old.

That meant she needed to find a store that had been in business for years. Maybe even before the internet.

A few more searches later, she found a Sear's Shoe Store—not related to the big chain of Sears stores—that was from a family who had come to America from Poland in the 1920s and opened a shoe repair shop in Chattanooga. As they found more success, they'd opened another in Lafayette, Georgia, then in Fort Oglethorpe.

Eventually the son, Jerry Sear, took over the business.

Taylor hoped he was still alive.

She jotted down a note and then took it over to Penner. He closed the internet page he was on when she walked up, then grinned at her.

"You look suspicious, so whatever you were doing, I'm glad I interrupted you," she said.

"No, I'm just taking one call after another from Hart's finest. Everyone is concerned there's a murderer on the loose, and they want to know just what we are doing about it."

"They could be right. Joni Stott didn't throw herself off that bridge. Anyone got anything helpful to add?"

He shook his head. "Not so far, but I'm leaning toward the boyfriend thought she was meeting a love interest, and though he didn't want her, he didn't want anyone else to have her. He followed her, and the rest is history. Weaver needs to get up there and talk to him again stat."

"That would be too easy, wouldn't it?" Taylor said, then slapped him on the shoulder playfully. "Maybe you should be leading this case, Pen."

"I'm serious. It happens every day. Different town, different names. Same old story. Anyway, whatcha got for me?" He leaned back in his chair and crossed his arms.

She handed him the paper. He might be right about Joni's ex-boyfriend, but until they had proof, she had to follow her own leads.

"I need a phone number for Jerry Sear of Sear's Shoe Store. See what you can do."

Penner loved that kind of easy work, and he turned around and got started.

Taylor called out for Bernard, and he came trotting around the corner. She took him out back and let him water the bushes, then they returned and headed for Shane's office.

Before she could get there, the sheriff stepped into the hallway.

"What's the update on the Stott case?"

"Um…well, not a lot yet. But we're working on it," Taylor said, easing from one foot to the other.

He studied her closely. "Fine. But you'd better have something good to tell me by tomorrow. The local television crew are breathing down my neck for an update."

"Yes, sir." Taylor went around him to Shane's office.

He was standing in front of the whiteboard again. This time, Joni's picture from her Facebook profile was at the top, and he was locked on it.

Taylor sighed. Joni was pretty in a very low-key kind of way. Nothing flashy like her mother. But you could see in her eyes that she was a good person. Steady.

It was such a tragedy.

He turned and saw her standing there, then went back to his desk. "I've been following up on a bunch of leads. All dead ends. Even the truck came up clean. Too clean, actually. Not a single print anywhere on the outside. Only Joni's on the inside. What about you?"

"I'm still working on the boot print," she answered.

"That's going to be a dead end, too."

Taylor was beginning to hate his pessimistic attitude. That wasn't the way to get things done. Maybe Shane wasn't the awesome detective that the sheriff thought he was borrowing.

"You never know. Don't forget about the Bruno Magli shoes."

"You watch too much true crime," Shane said, then rolled his eyes to the ceiling.

He could talk smack all he wanted, but he knew exactly what she was talking about. Everyone in LE knew of it. During the infamous criminal trial of OJ Simpson for his wife's murder, he denied ever owning the brand of shoes that were determined left bloody marks at the scene. The manufacturer had confirmed that just less than three hundred were sold in the United States. Further research showed that two pairs were sold at Bloomingdale's in New York where Simpson was known to shop. Only after he was acquitted at that trial and facing the civil court did an old photo surface of him wearing a pair of the Magli shoes. That evidence was instrumental in the civil judgement against him.

"I wish you had gotten Kessler to bring in the shoes he wore when he met up with Joni," she said. "We might have to get a warrant and go get them."

"Good luck with that."

Finding out more about the boot left at Joni Stott's death scene might lead to nothing or might be a clue that convicts. Taylor wasn't taking any chances on letting it go. There was something else, too.

"I want to look at the footage from the gas station again," she replied.

"I've already studied it several times. It gives us nothing."

"Humor me. At the least, we can note what kind of shoe that Kessler is wearing."

Shane didn't look pleased, but he hit the space bar to bring his computer back to life, then clicked a few things until the video popped up.

"You want my seat, too?" he asked sarcastically.

"Actually, yes." Taylor needed to be able to see it well.

When he saw she wasn't kidding, he stood up, and with a flourish of his arm, moved aside and let her slide in. Bernard scooted under her legs and curled up under the desk, and Shane hovered behind her.

Taylor started the video and moved it to six fifteen in the evening, the time they already knew that Joni pulled in.

"What are we looking for? I mean, besides the shoes."

"Just wait," Taylor said, peering closer. "I saw something the last time, and I want to see it again. Might be nothing."

She watched as the truck pulled to the side of the parking lot. She already knew Joni wouldn't get out of her truck until Kessler was there, so she forwarded it.

When his truck pulled up beside her, Taylor watched Joni lean toward the back seat of the cab, where she was obviously talking to Molly, then get out and shut the door.

She and Bryce walked around the truck, and he kicked a few tires. It was hard to see clearly, but it appeared that he was wearing black or brown shoes. Or boots.

"Can you zoom in?"

He reached over her and used the mouse to zoom as much as he could, but it just made the photo blurrier. All Taylor could tell was that they weren't sneakers. They could be boots, or they could be some sort of Dockers.

Back at the driver's door, Kessler pulled it open and reached in to pop the hood lever.

Taylor could see in Joni's body language that she was insecure, though she wasn't sure if her unease was because Bryce was a nice-looking guy around her age, or if she was so desperate to sell the truck that it was anxiety. Either way, after he looked under the hood, he got into the truck and started it, but not before Joni ran around to the other side to open the passenger side door and put her hands on Molly.

*Good mom,* Taylor thought.

Joni was making sure if Bryce—who was supposedly a stranger to her—got a notion to take the truck, he wouldn't be taking Molly with it.

After he let it run for a minute or two, he apparently cut the motor, climbed out, and shut the driver's door.

Joni did the same on her side and then came around and joined him.

Taylor wished so hard that they could hear what they were saying, but if Kessler were telling the truth about the sequence of events, it made sense.

In the footage, he looked apologetic but was shaking his head, then pointed at the gas pumps. Joni moved from foot to foot, then you could almost see the disappointment go through her body in the slump of her shoulders before she climbed back in her truck and shut the door.

She drove it over to the gas pump, and Kessler walked over and used his card to pay and pump it into her truck. When finished, he went to her window and said something, then held a hand up as a parting gesture and went back to his own truck.

Joni pulled out of the parking lot going north, and Kessler pulled out going south.

"See. That's it," Shane said.

"Hold on. I want to note every car that drove the same direction as her in the same time period." She didn't point out that Kessler could've turned around and came back to follow Joni.

"That's going to take a while. There's three hours of footage there." He went around and sat in the chair in front of the desk.

"There wasn't that much traffic out there on a Sunday night. I'll just keep forwarding until I see a vehicle, then pause it to get the details." She pulled her pen from her shirt pocket and grabbed a piece of scrap paper from a pile on the desk.

"You can't see plates."

"I know. But we can see color and car model and guess the make."

"I feel like you've got a hunch you're not telling me," Shane said. He was rubbing his eyebrow like he always did when he was trying to analyze a problem.

"I might. But just let me run with this first. Please."

He settled lower in the chair and folded his hands over his stomach, then closed his eyes.

The first car came into view, and Taylor paused.

White Nissan Altima, four doors and probably a 2018 model. She made a note and then thought of her dad. He'd always had a habit of calling out a car's make and model when they were on the road. It used to irritate her and make her wonder why he thought he was so special because he knew his cars. Crazy how it had become an integral part of her job in law enforcement to know with a glance the make and model of a car. Or at least something close.

"I'm going for coffee before you put me to sleep," Shane said, then got up and left the office.

Taylor kept going, forwarding in short bursts so she wouldn't miss anything.

A few more vehicles went by before she got the first hint that her hunch might just be right. She didn't write anything down. Before she let Shane or anyone else in on it, she needed to be sure to have something to go on. If not, it could cost her career.

Just as she'd remembered, the next car to go by was the one that got her attention. Still could be nothing.

But nothing could always be something.

She wrote down the minimal details she could see, then got out of there before Shane could come back.

Back at her desk, she spotted the scrap of paper she'd given Penner, but with a phone number scrawled at the bottom and a few words.

*He's old as dirt. Better hurry and call.*

She smiled at Penner's advice and dialed the number.

After four rings, Taylor was sure it was going to roll over into voice mail, but on the fifth, he picked up. She identified herself and informed him that she was working on a case, then asked him if he had email so she could send him a photo.

"I might be old, but I'm also a businessman," he replied, then rattled off his email address. "I'll wait for it, then call you back."

Taylor sent the photo of the boot tread, or at least a partial of a tread, then waited. She tapped her short nails on the desktop. When her phone rang, she just about jumped out of her seat.

"Hello?"

"Not much to go on there," Mr. Sear said.

She slumped in her chair. "I know. Well, I thought I'd try."

"Now hold on, young lady. I didn't say I was done. What I was going to say, if you'd give me a minute, was that luckily you reached out to probably the oldest shoe expert in Georgia, and to beat that, one with a photographic memory. I know that tread."

Taylor got so excited that she jumped up and began pacing in her cubicle. "You do? Can you tell me what it is and where it was sold?"

"Well, I'm not a magician," he said, then went into a long series of coughing before he continued. "What I can tell you is that the boot was first released around 1988 by a company in Carson City, Nevada. They were popular for a while because they were so lightweight. You see, the boot was built on a Puma sole like what they use for softball shoes. Men who had to wear them all day found them easier on the joints. They also took a good shine, if I remember right."

Taylor had no doubt his memory was on point. "This is fantastic information, Mr. Sear. Did you carry them in your store, too?"

"I did, until something better and more popular came on the market."

Taylor quizzed him some more, noting down approximate dates and a few more details. Unfortunately, he couldn't track customer sales from more than a few years back, but the bit he'd told her was helpful.

As soon as she hung up, her phone rang, and Brandon Choi's name flashed across the screen with the words *Forensic Contact* behind it.

"Hi, Brandon. You got anything?"

"Actually, yes. I found something you might think is very interesting."

What he told her next lit her up inside. The piece of evidence that he'd found on Joni's body went well with the path Taylor's gut was taking her down.

"And you're sure?" she asked him.

"Yep, the dye used on the piece of thread was discontinued a decade ago after only being used for that specific item."

Taylor grinned. With the information about the boot tread, and now Brandon's discovery, she might just have something.

Maybe.

Hopefully.

"Oh, and one more thing," he said. "I think I know the name of her assailant."

She almost dropped the phone. "What? How?"

"You may not have seen it under her long hair, but on the side of her forehead it said Ed."

"Ed? What do you mean? Written on there?"

"Pounded on there, more like it. I'm thinking a mono-grammed belt. Maybe a keychain. Not sure, but whatever it was, he hit her hard enough with it to leave the outline of the letters."

The thought of what Joni had gone through sickened Taylor, but she thanked Brandon.

He added that if he needed to be an expert witness in an exciting case, he would be all for it so he could build his resume. She promised she'd let him know and hung up feeling a bit of hope for the first time.

He'd given her good stuff to go on.

*Ed.* Who was that?

Bernard must have felt the energy and came out from under

the desk, and Taylor gathered him against her legs and hugged him close.

"What do you say we go get you something good to eat? I think we've earned it."

His tail wagged furiously.

It was a good day's work, and if she was on the right track, the puzzle pieces should start falling together quickly. If not, then she'd be back to square one. If that happened, she hoped Shane was also onto something he wasn't telling, either. She would love to be the one to solve the case, but overall, she just wanted someone to be brought to justice, no matter who brought them.

For Molly's sake.

# CHAPTER 28

*W*hile juggling the contents from her mailbox, Taylor struggled to get into the door. The plan was to grab Lucy, go get takeout from the Den and take it to their dad's home to have dinner together. First, she needed to check the voice mail that had come through from Meyer while she was driving.

She dropped the bag off on the table and looked closer at the big manila envelope, then set it aside. She listened to the voice mail, and Meyer, the state man who had tagged Joni's truck, told her that he'd stop by the station first thing in the morning for a quick meeting before he reported to his area. It was going to be early, but that was all he could do.

With that settled, Taylor checked her text messages. Penner had sent her a few, both about a few phone calls they'd gotten about someone linked to the case. They were enough to raise her eyebrows a bit, and she'd check them out as soon as she could.

Next, she opened the manila envelope. A rusted old rabies tag fell out along with a sheaf of papers and a fat white sealed envelope.

The smaller white envelope had TO ADOPTING FAMILY scrawled across it in nearly illegible handwriting.

"Oh, this is your stuff," she mumbled to Bernard. "We'll look at that later."

She dropped it on the table next to the bag, then called out for Lucy.

No reply.

She realized the house was too quiet. No music blaring.

Quickly, she went through it and straight back to her bedroom. Her bed was still unmade, not surprisingly, but she didn't see her sister anywhere.

A quick peek into the bathroom, and she knew it then.

Lucy had bailed.

Bernard was looking for her too, and he gazed up at Taylor with a questioning expression.

"She's gone, boy."

Taylor wasn't sure how she'd gone anywhere without a car, but all her things were gone. Makeup, clothes, and even the grungy flip-flops that had been lying in the way.

"But you know what? She didn't have the money for a taxi. Or a bus." Taylor got a bad feeling, and she went back to the kitchen.

She opened the cabinet under the kitchen sink and pulled out her lard can—the fake one behind the real one. They were just old Folgers' canisters, and she was shaking when she peeled the plastic lid up.

"Damn it!"

There was a note on top.

*I'm sorry but I'll pay you back. Don't try to find me.*
*Let it be.*

Taylor fumbled to see what was left under the note, but it was mostly dollar bills and a few fives. She sank to the floor, her back against the cabinet. She felt like a fool for leaving it unsecured, but through everything, her sister had never stolen from her before.

There was a first time for everything because Lucy had taken her emergency fund, or at least the bulk of it. A thousand dollars, to be exact.

Money that had taken her months to save up.

And when Lucy wanted to disappear, she did it like a pro. She'd never see that grand again.

So much for a nice family dinner.

Finally, she struggled to her feet.

"We still have to eat," she told Bernard. "And we might as well pull the Band-Aid off for Dad while we do it. Come on."

She was too tired to change clothes first, and they slipped out to the car. Her dad would just have to deal with seeing her in her uniform. She truly dreaded telling him that his favorite child was gone again, but as usual, she'd have to be the bearer of bad news. She was almost tempted to pick up a bottle of booze to take along with her to soften the blow, but her common sense stopped that train of thought.

The ride to the Den was quiet. Taylor didn't even want music. She had to admit that the house had felt more alive with Lucy's energy in it. Even though she could be a brat, when she was under the same roof, Taylor could relax in knowing she was safe, too. Underneath the bravado, her sister had a big heart. Now Taylor had to go back to worrying about what Lucy would get into next.

To top her evening off, when she pulled into the Bear's Den parking lot, Alex was getting out of his truck. Like her, he'd neglected to change out of his uniform. Unlike her, Taylor knew he loved the attention being the fire chief brought him, so he wore his to dinner often.

She waited in the car for a minute or two, but when it

appeared he wasn't getting out any time soon, she opened the door and let Bernard hop out first.

Of course, then Alex decided to exit his truck.

"Hi," he called out, then approached her. "Nice dog."

"Thanks. His name is Bernard."

Alex bent down to give him a pat, and when he straightened, he smiled at Taylor. "I think it's fate that we showed up at the same time. Want to have dinner together?"

Internally, Taylor cringed.

Outwardly, she shook her head politely. "I'm picking up food to take out to my dad's."

Just as the words were out, one of Alex's buddies showed up from around the side of her car, making it more awkward than she intended it to be.

"Ooh…burn, man. Strike," he called out.

Alex turned red. "Go screw yourself."

The buddy went into the building, and Taylor started to follow.

Alex reached out and grabbed her arm, stopping her.

"Hey, what are you doing?" she said, shocked that he'd put his hands on her.

Bernard let out a low growl.

"Not so fast. First, I want you to tell me why you keep turning me down. I know a dozen women in town who would like to have my attention."

Taylor narrowed her eyes. "First, I want to tell *you,* get your hands off me before I kick you so hard that I make you into a eunuch."

Bernard growled louder, and his hair on his neck stood up.

Alex let go instantly.

"And secondly, I wouldn't go out with you if you were the last man on Earth," Taylor continued. "Want to know why? First, in case you forgot, you're still married. Then we have the problem of your arrogance. I like my men humble. And clean. Those dozens of women you mentioned—you've already been through them and probably more."

If she thought his face got red before, now it was more of a purple hue.

He stepped back and glared at her. But he blocked her way inside to the Den.

He lowered his voice to a hoarse whisper. "You stupid bitch. Who do you think you are talking to? I'm the frigging fire chief in this town."

"And that makes it okay for you to harass every woman you lay eyes on? What would your wife think? Oh wait, I'm sure she already knows and is getting ready to take you for what your previous wives left behind."

He looked her up and down. "You don't know nothing, and on second thought, I wouldn't call you much of a woman, either. Why don't you do something with yourself? Let your hair down. Slap on some makeup? You look like some sort of she-man in that uniform. Going around town like you're Sherlock Holmes when you're more like a stuck-up Barney Fife. At least your little sister was friendly enough when she climbed in my truck for a ride today. *If you know what I mean.* But she asked me not to tell you that."

The wink he followed up with did it.

Taylor didn't even think it through. When her right uppercut made impact, solid satisfaction streaked through her before the pain.

Alex staggered back, then he lifted his own fist.

Bernard erupted into a half snarl, half bark, ready to pounce.

Taylor grabbed Bernard's collar before he could. "I dare you, you filthy piece of shit. One step closer, and I'll let him go."

Alex lowered his fist, and they stared each other down. After a full minute, he visibly relaxed his stance.

"I'm going to let you off tonight because I need a warm meal and a cold beer," he said. "But this ain't over. And don't think I don't know why your family left Montana. I got contacts everywhere in the fire family, and if I ran my mouth, you wouldn't be walking around so proudly in that uniform."

Bernard was still growling, and he'd put his body between her and Alex.

"And I lied. You dog is butt-ugly, too," he said, then turned and slammed his way into the Den.

Taylor knelt and hugged Bernard, praising him for his bravery. She didn't want to make Alex think she was too scared to go in behind him, so once her heart rate slowed down, she took some deep breaths and followed.

He wasn't running her off from anywhere in her town. Especially Mabel's.

She took a seat at the bar, only five stools down from him. Sissy seemed to notice something was off when she approached, so she quietly took the order and then disappeared into the kitchen to get it ready.

While she was gone, Taylor watched Alex in the mirror across from them, her expression deadly. Her knuckles were throbbing, but she wouldn't dare look at them. The thought of Alex touching Lucy in any way made her sick, but she was going to tell herself that he was a lying son of a— Well, anyway... He was a liar. He'd even admitted he was a liar. Lucy might have gotten a ride from him, but that was it.

Even Lucy had standards.

But what was he talking about when he'd mentioned Montana? The fact that they'd left a tragedy behind wouldn't garner the sarcasm in his voice.

He looked back at her once or twice, but for the most part ignored her and downed two tall ones in quick succession. It would serve him right if she followed him once he left and then pulled him over for driving under the influence.

She wasn't in the mood for it, and he had planted something in her head that she needed to get straight with her dad.

Sissy returned with the bag of food and set it down.

"I added dessert along with something for your sexy boy," she said. "And it's on the house. Mabel said I could because I told her it looks like you've had a really shitty day."

The gesture of kindness just about broke Taylor's tough façade.

"Thank you, Sissy," she whispered.

She got off the stool and didn't even have to say a word to Bernard. She walked as tall and nonchalantly as she could, and he followed her out the door.

HER DAD'S house was dark. Usually there was at least one light shining through the curtains at the living room window, but tonight, it wasn't there. They got out of the car, and after Bernard did his obligatory sniff and pee along the path, they climbed the steps to the back door.

Taylor knocked, but when he didn't answer, she went in.

One day, he was going to regret always leaving his door unlocked. She just hoped it wasn't tonight. She always worried over what she'd find when she entered his house.

Inside, the house was dark. She flipped the kitchen light and got nothing.

She wanted to scream in frustration, but at least now she knew why it was so dark. The living room curtains were open, and with the moonlight shining in, she could see her dad's silhouette lying on the couch.

Bernard trotted over there and got close.

"Dad? You okay?"

"I would be if you'd train your dog to keep his butt-licking tongue off my face." He sat up and wiped his face with the back of his hand.

"Didn't pay the utilities again?" she asked.

"I'll pay it Friday. Don't lecture me."

She wanted to. She wanted to do it so badly, but with the evening she'd had, she felt if she started, she might end up screaming.

"Where's the lanterns I got you last time?" She went to set the bag of food on the table and bumped into a kitchen chair.

She cursed—very unladylike, too—when the pain reverberated through her knee. Now it matched her punching hand.

"There's furniture in there. Be careful."

"Very amusing, Dad." She set the bag down.

"The lanterns are right behind you on the counter. Batteries are dead."

"On both of them?" She remembered she carried a flashlight on her uniform, and she pulled it down and turned it on, then shined it at the counter.

"Yep. Dead as doornails. Where's Lucy?"

"Bernard, stay." She ignored his question and went back down the hallway and out the door.

At her car, she popped the trunk and fumbled through her storage basket until she found a pack of batteries. She was hungry and not in the mood, but she couldn't leave him without any way to see. With her luck, he'd fall and get hurt.

When she came inside, she saw her dad hadn't moved, but Bernard was now on the couch beside him. Leaning into him, to be accurate. And her dad wasn't complaining.

Taylor got busy putting new batteries into the lanterns. When they had light again, she pulled the containers out of the bag.

"You need to eat. And Sissy sent dessert, too." She peeked at the first small container which was heaped high with peach cobbler. The second one held a perfectly seared piece of cubed steak, without gravy or seasoning.

"You didn't answer my question. Where's Lucy? You two fighting?"

"Bernard, come eat." Taylor put the meat on the floor without a plate.

It wasn't like his floor was clean anyway. It would be up to her to run a mop over it as soon as she had time again. She would try to squeeze it in over the weekend.

Bernard didn't have to be asked twice. He was there in an instant, and two seconds later, the meat was gone.

"I bet you said something to hurt her feelings, didn't you?" her dad said.

He still hadn't moved to come get his food, and it was irritating Taylor to no end. She wished she had someone to think of her and bring food occasionally. Especially paid for. But he took it for granted.

"No, Dad. I didn't. Got home a while ago, and she was gone, along with all her things. Left me a note to not look for her. Don't tell me you're surprised. She always does this."

She left off the part about stealing the money. She'd take that up with Lucy next time she showed up looking for love.

"I'm not hungry," he said.

Taylor didn't even turn and look at him. She knew if she did, she'd see his head hung low. Probably in his hands now. And as much as it hurt that he loved Lucy so much more than he did her, it still shattered her to see him sad.

She put her container back in the bag and tied it up, then turned to him.

"I'm not going to beg you to eat. I'm exhausted and have had a rotten day. I'll just eat mine at home. Where's the utility bill?"

He shrugged.

"Dad, you know where the bill is. Just hand it over so I can pay it. Stop acting like a child." She was going to have to do some creative juggling with her own finances, especially with her savings now gone, but he needed electricity.

Once again, she wished he'd put his finances as priority over his whiskey.

He stood and glared at her. "I said I don't know. I haven't checked the mailbox in days. And I don't need you paying my bills. I'll do it when I get my check."

"You don't get your check for almost a week. You can't live without electricity that long. You can't even flush your toilet or take a shower because there's no power to the well. And I'm not even going to look at what might be rotting in the fridge by now," she threw back, glaring at him.

She wanted to remind him that if he kept putting off the bill, the overdue charges would just keep adding too. It was a vicious circle, and if he'd just pay them on time, and stay off the bottle, he could handle it, and she wouldn't have to. But he was her father, and if he hadn't even walked out to the mailbox in days, that meant he was depressed worse than usual. She wouldn't browbeat him when he was down.

"Fine. I hope you get some sleep." She headed for the door. "Come on, Bernard."

She and her father would play the game they always did. She'd find the bill from the mailbox and pay it quietly.

She remembered something and stopped before she got to the door. "Before I go, I have a question."

He sighed loudly and rubbed his face. "Another one?"

"Why did we move here from Montana?"

His head jerked up as though tied to a puppet string. "Why are you asking me that? You know why we left."

"Tell me again."

"Because I wanted to give you girls a fresh start. That's why."

She hesitated and wondered why he suddenly looked nervous. "And that's it? Nothing else you want to tell me? Anything about the fire?"

"Nope. Not a damn thing."

They glared at each other.

He came toward her, then picked up a lantern and shuffled

toward his bedroom. "I'm not listening to any more of your questions. I'm going to bed."

Just before he got to the door, he spoke again. The anger was gone from his voice. "Did Lucy leave a phone number or say where she was going?"

"No, Dad. She didn't."

He closed the door soundly behind him.

# CHAPTER 29

Taylor slept fitfully all night with chaotic dreams about Lucy, her father, and a fire that bearing down on all of them. When she woke and discovered she was out of coffee, it put her butt into high gear to get to the station early enough for a few cups before Meyer got there. She wanted to be fully awake and ready to ask all the right questions.

While stumbling into the kitchen, she passed by the stack of mail she'd pulled from her dad's mailbox. She didn't have the mental energy to go through it yet.

She let Bernard out, fed him when he returned, then went to get dressed.

She was good on time when she hit the road. It was a quiet ride as she planned out how she'd start the interview.

*So much for good intentions*, she thought when she pulled into the parking lot at five minutes past six and saw the state patrol car already there. She looked it over, then when she saw Clint's cruiser, she cursed. He was the last person she wanted to see when she'd rolled out of the wrong side of the bed.

Bernard seemed to sense her mood, looked over, and whined at her.

"I'm fine. Just need coffee," she assured him, then parked and led him to the back door.

She was reaching for the handle when it swung open, and Clint was in her face.

"Oh. Sorry," he said.

He had someone behind him, and judging by the uniform, it was Meyer.

They stepped out, and Clint immediately shifted from foot to foot nervously before speaking. "This is Officer Meyer. The one who tagged the Stott girl's truck. I already took his statement."

Now she was more than just crabby. She was incensed. But she needed to hide it. This was too important for her to screw it up.

Bernard took a seat at her feet, filling the space between Taylor and the men.

Meyer looked Taylor up and down and nodded without offering a handshake. "You must be Officer Gray." He smiled at her and tilted his head.

If she were male, his eyes wouldn't have traveled farther down than her badge. She mentally noted that he carried the creep factor times ten.

"I am. I thought we were on for six thirty?" She returned the full-body appraisal, taking in his spotless hat, starched uniform, and all the way down to his shined boots before she smiled in satisfaction and nodded back.

Two could play at his game.

"I'm habitually early," he said. "Can't help it after nearly two decades doing this job. And your partner here took care of things. Wasn't much to report. I passed the truck once, then on the second pass a few hours later, I tagged it. I saw no one, noted nothing strange or out of place, and figured someone left it there because it quit running or was out of gas. Happens all the time out that way."

"What about your dash cam? Can I see it? Maybe there was something you didn't notice," she said.

He shook his head. "It's clean. Believe me, once I heard about the girl, I played it back at least a dozen times. Nothing to see, and really nothing to tell."

Clint nodded and patted the notebook that was in his pocket. "Yep. I got your statement right here." He looked at Taylor. "I'll write it up after my next interview later today. I had a talk with Weaver last night, and we're both liking the ex-boyfriend for the primary. We're going to make a trip up there this afternoon. If all goes well, we'll announce it by tomorrow in a press conference."

Taylor ignored Clint's blustering and kept her gaze on Meyer. If there was a press conference scheduled, she'd know it, considering she'd be the one giving it. The fact that he was gunning hard for a promotion to detective was so blatant it was ridiculous. And he was willing to play dirty to get it.

"He's not my partner. And if you don't mind, I'd like to ask you a few questions myself," she said.

Meyer smiled down at her apologetically. "Negative. I really don't have time for a second run at it. I need to hit the road. He can get you up to speed, ma'am."

"It's Deputy Gray," Taylor said, then swung past them into the station.

Bernard shot through just before the door closed.

Clint was saying something about no dogs allowed in the building, but Taylor didn't look back. He could kiss her backside. She could just imagine the two of them looking at each other and raising their eyebrows. Probably remarking something about her flouncing off or having no idea why she was infuriated. Sometimes she wondered why she'd chosen to go into a male-dominated industry.

"Go lie down somewhere," she muttered to Bernard, and he headed for her desk area.

Clint was really stepping over the line. He knew damn well

that she'd come in early especially to talk to Meyer. He didn't usually come in until close to eight o'clock anyway. But like he had always done, he made it a point to step on her toes. He probably hadn't even talked to Shane the night before as he'd claimed. Shane would've told her if he were that serious about Josh as a suspect. He'd send her to do the interview. Not Crazy Clint.

She paused. Wouldn't he have? What if her gut was wrong? And Jessica was wrong? Maybe the boyfriend really did get jealous and follow Joni, then make her pull over after the meeting. They argued. He lost his temper. The unimaginable happened. He tossed her and ran back to the base before anyone missed him.

But what about Molly?

Surely, she would've mentioned her own daddy if he were involved. And for that matter, even if she wouldn't, what kind of father would set his own child out on the road?

Taylor didn't believe it for a minute. Her gut was telling her that someone else was responsible. It was even telling her *who* was responsible. Now she just needed to find the evidence that would make Shane and the sheriff listen to her. Shane was starting to feel like a stranger to her, and that unsettled her more than she liked to admit.

In a way, she'd be glad for him to return to his own town and leave Hart's Ridge to her.

She breathed deeply to calm herself and went straight to the coffee station.

At least someone had just brewed a fresh pot. She pulled her own mug from the cabinet and poured herself a cup, added a pink sugar to it, and took a sip. Instantly, she felt her blood pressure going down.

Behind her, the back door opened and shut. If it were Clint, he'd better think again before coming at her about her dog. Or about anything right now.

She took her coffee and joined Bernard at her desk, then powered up the computer.

Something more was needed to calm herself down, so she called Della Ray, who she knew would be up early preparing breakfast or putting down her first pot of coffee herself. Taylor didn't let on that she was upset, and Della Ray sounded happy to hear from her.

"Hello, sweetheart. How are you doing?"

Della's slow, sweet tone eased Taylor's shoulders down so they were no longer around her neck. She was able to take a deep breath. "I'm okay. Just checking on Molly."

Once they got through discussing Molly and how, after her traumatic near abduction by Sheila, she'd backslid a bit and closed herself off again, Della Ray assured Taylor that she'd work with her more until she felt safe again. Then she asked about the case.

Taylor told her they were making headway, though she wasn't exactly sure of that herself. Della Ray knew not to ask for details, and by the end of the half-hour call, she had Taylor feeling anchored again. She was one person who always had confidence in Taylor's abilities to do her job.

After she hung up, she finished up some lingering paperwork, then while she had time, she searched the internet about the evidence that her forensic guy, Brandon, had found. She went through fifteen pages of searching different online hits before she agreed with him. The dye color was only used for one thing, then retired. That gave her the first glimpse of optimism for the day.

But it was only one piece of the puzzle.

She opened the log from the day before to check and see if any new tips had been called in. After a few that looked to be nothing, she saw one marked as anonymous, but it came from the telephone number of the Department of Public Safety Headquarters in Atlanta. When she read it, she took a note with her phone, then shut her computer off.

An email chimed through on her phone, and she read it. It was from Shane.

*I'm still looking at Greene for primary but heads-up-- new discovery just in. Joni's mother has an ex who has a prior arrest for possession with intent to sell. What if Joni hooked up with him to make some money, and the deal went bad? We need to interview him. I'll be in shortly, and we can talk about it.*

Taylor pushed back from her desk. It was ten o'clock, and she thought about replying to Shane to let him know where she was going, but she remembered the look of triumph on Clint's face when he said they'd talked the night before and already picked a primary. She wasn't telling anyone anything until she nailed down a few more details.

TAYLOR PULLED into the edge of the small town, impressed at their *Welcome to Historical Calhoun* sign. The only thing that Taylor knew about Calhoun was that it was where some of Sherman's heaviest fighting went on during the war and was where the Trail of Tears officially started.

Those two facts were the only ones that she still retained from her eighth-grade field trip but made absolutely no effect on her opinion of the town as she drove into it now.

Calhoun was nice, though she didn't think it compared to Hart's Ridge. She'd taken her time on the drive so that she could kill an hour or so. At the slower speed, she'd noted the nice rolling hills and how they were set against a lush backdrop of trees and some wide-open pastures.

She passed a beautiful entrance with another sign that read *Copper Creek Farm* and advertised things like a sunflower fest, corn maze, wagon hayrides, and even talking watermelons. That was new since she'd been there as a kid. She was sure there was no such thing as a talking watermelon, but a part of her wanted to pull in and see what it was all about just to be sure.

She drove on, though even Bernard looked like he knew they were passing on something fun as he gazed out the window.

Calhoun wasn't a big town, but it was much larger than Hart's Ridge. Taylor had never heard of the restaurant she was looking for, but she'd plugged the address into her GPS and eventually, she found it and turned.

A half mile on the left, Dub's High on the Hog was right where the flag on her computer had said. Taylor hoped that the person who gave the details was sure about the scheduling of their waitstaff because she didn't have time to waste.

There was no mistaking the building. As described, it was made of a red cedar with a faded red metal roof. Two long benches sat out front with the word DUBS carved into the front of them. Like many small diners and restaurants around Georgia, it claimed the best pork BBQ and fall-off-the-bone ribs in the state.

Taylor wasn't that fond of either, but she was going to have to order something to not look suspicious.

She lucked up with a parking space right in front of the door. She turned to Bernard. "Sorry, buddy. You have to stay this time."

He sniffed and turned his head away.

"I swear, I'll be less than five minutes," Taylor said. She left the car running and went inside.

"Hey, how are you?" The hostess was already standing there waiting.

"I'm fine. You?" Taylor looked at her name tag and breathed a sigh of relief to see that it read LeeAnne.

This was her girl.

"I'm good. Table for one?"

"Um…no. I just want to order something for takeout."

LeeAnne nodded and handed her a menu, then pointed to a bench a few feet away. "You can order and then wait there."

Taylor scanned the menu quickly, then ordered chicken tenders and a side of okra—both things that she could pick at as she drove. She considered picking up an order of fried tomatoes for her dad, but decided they'd go bad before she got them to him. She added a sweet tea to it then handed the menu back, along with her debit card.

LeeAnne took the order down and disappeared with the card.

Taylor sat down and waited for her to return the card, nervous about starting the conversation she'd planned. She looked around. The interior design was very country-inspired. Lots of wood everywhere, from the paneling to the tables set into wooden booths with puffy Georgia-red shiny cushioning. They were obviously proud football fans, judging by the stone Georgia Bulldog statue that sat proudly next to the hostess stand. A real stuffed boar's head hung on the wall; its mouth open in a salacious-looking grimace with big teeth visible. Rusted-out bicycles hung from the ceiling. Then she noted what must have been their mascot—a pig in overalls that was scattered around in pictures and as a three-foot statue.

Two minutes later, a waitress went by carrying a tray that was laden with three plates, all of them the same, heavy with a pile of pulled pork, a round pile of potato salad, a bowl of baked beans, and a slice of Texas toast on the side. Taylor had to admit, it smelled delicious, but she couldn't see how anyone could eat something that heavy for a lunchtime meal.

She got up and went to the doors. She could see Bernard

sitting in the front, sitting straight and tall as he stared at the restaurant door.

Taylor gave him a wave, but he didn't react. She went back to the bench, but she didn't sit. She tapped her nails against the frame of the bench. Then she bit at a hangnail.

When she looked at her phone again and saw she was at four minutes in, LeeAnne returned and handed her the card, but moved her attention quickly to a group of four linemen who waited to be seated. They nodded politely at Taylor, then followed LeeAnne to a table. She gave them menus, took their drink orders, then disappeared again.

*Damn it. Bernard was going to be antsy.*

Taylor stood and went to back the door, looked out, half thinking Bernard might be standing there waiting on her to open it.

He wasn't. In the car, it appeared that he hadn't moved a muscle. His gaze was unflinching, and he looked worried.

LeeAnne returned, stationed herself behind the hostess stand, and leaned over it toward Taylor.

"Looks like it's going to be a busy day," she said, smiling.

She was friendly. A pretty one, too. Especially when she showed the deep dimples. Taylor would guess her to be no older than nineteen or twenty.

"Sure does," Taylor replied, then went to the stand. "Actually, I'm not here just for the carryout. I'm here because I'm working on a case, and I heard you might have something of interest for me."

"Like what?" She narrowed her eyes. Her smile disappeared.

Taylor leaned in and quietly told her what she was there about.

LeeAnne straightened, then looked from side to side, before answering.

"Are you in your patrol car?" she finally asked.

Taylor nodded.

"Take it and park in back. I'll tell my boss I need to run your food out to you when it's ready. I'll only have a few minutes, but I'll tell you what I know."

"Thank you. I appreciate it," Taylor said, then went out the door.

Bernard bounced around, his tail thumping against the door panel when she got into her car. She checked the county computer, thankful nothing was pressing. As instructed, she pulled around to the back of the building. Her stomach cut flips in anticipation of what LeeAnne had to tell her. She prayed this wouldn't be a dead end.

Ten minutes later, LeeAnne came with a plastic bag tied at the top and a cup.

"Thank you so much," Taylor said, then reached for it and set the bag on the seat beside her. She took the tea and popped the straw into it.

"Listen," LeeAnne said, leaning down to the window. "I was told to keep my mouth shut, and after some of the things I found out later, I did just that. I don't want any trouble."

"You won't get any," Taylor assured her. "But this is important."

LeeAnne looked around the parking lot, then took a deep breath, leaned in, and started talking. As promised, less than five minutes later, she'd said her piece and was headed back inside.

# CHAPTER 30

*T*aylor decided that nothing good ever came from jumping the line of seniority, so now she was in the hot seat in front of Shane's desk listening to him completely disregard the investigation she'd done so far and what it had led to.

"There's no way in hell I'm going to Sheriff with that. Do you even know how out of line you are? What will happen to our careers if you go forward with this crap?" He picked up the report Taylor had suffered over and balled it up, then threw it at his trash can in the corner.

He missed and his scowl grew darker.

"It's all there, Shane. It fits. If I can get the search warrant, I'll prove it to you."

"If we ask for the search warrant, all hell is going to break loose. If you're wrong—and I guarantee you are barking up the wrong tree—you can kiss your career goodbye. I also have every intention on following up on the lead about Joni's mother and her convict friend. Like I said, this is just the sort of thing that happens with a drug transport gone bad."

"I will not believe that her daughter would involve herself in dealing drugs."

"You heard the sister, Taylor. She was hurting for money. People do crazy things when they get buried in debt."

"Just listen to me, Shane." Once again, she repeated what the shoe man, Sear, had told her about the shoe print and how it fit her theory. She went over her conversation with the hostess from the diner and listed the several calls that had come in over the last two nights that they'd first thought had amounted to nothing. Then the smoking gun—the forensic evidence that Brandon Choi discovered. It pulled it all together.

"There's no match on the DNA," Shane said.

"First time crime. Or else he's never been caught."

"Oh, come on in," Shane said, looking over Taylor's head. "Gray here is giving me the lowdown on her theory."

Taylor looked up and around to see Clint standing in the doorway.

"Yeah, I heard," Clint said, his voice dripping with sarcasm. "I think she's lost her mind."

"*She* is right here, and you can talk directly to *her*," Taylor said, her tone calm and professional. She wouldn't let them push her into acting anything less.

Clint took the chair beside her, falling into it as though his legs had suddenly lost all strength. He let out a long, frustrated sigh, reminding Taylor of a teenager reporting to the principal's office.

"The baby daddy is our guy," Clint said. "I talked to Stott's mother today, and she told me all kinds of things about the toxic relationship the two of them had."

"And the sister, who knows Joni better than the mother, denies that," Taylor said. The sudden pain in her jaw reminded her to try to relax. She really loathed Clint. Even the cheap cologne he reeked of was disgusting. She wished she could move her chair another few feet away, but she didn't want them to call her dramatic.

Clint acted as though she hadn't said a word. Didn't even look at her. "All we need to do is prove he found out Stott was meeting someone. He left base and either went to her apartment complex and followed her from there, or he knew where they were meeting, and he hid out until she left, then got her to pull over."

"It does sound feasible," Shane said. "I've also done the math. If they logged his unexcused absence in on the wrong day, it works."

"And you really think the guy set his own child out on the road in the country, where a bear or coyote or some sicko could get her and just drove away?" Taylor said.

Clint turned toward her. "You know nothing about him. If he was any kind of father, he'd still be there for his kid. So maybe he's the sicko. That's where the trail leads and where we need to pick it up."

"Hold up, McElroy," Shane said. "I want to give Taylor—I mean, Gray—another chance to convince us."

Taylor hated that she had to say a word about her investigation around Clint, but she took a deep breath and dug in.

The entire time she talked and laid out every piece of her puzzle, Clint refused to look at her and sat staring at Shane, arms crossed across his chest.

"I want to get your forensic guy on the phone," Shane said.

At least he was finally listening.

Taylor dialed Brandon's number and prayed he'd pick up. When he did, she put the phone on speaker and set it on the desk.

Shane led the questions, and Taylor was proud of Brandon. He was direct and forthright with his answers, and very convincing.

She owed him another beer.

When the conversation was over and Brandon hung up,

Shane sat looking at the whiteboard, his hand over his chin as he stared at Joni's photo.

Clint tapped his foot irritatingly on the floor, but at least he didn't interrupt. Finally, Shane looked at them both, then directly at Taylor.

"This is what we're going to do. We'll hold off announcing a prime suspect because I honestly think it's the ex. I'll go to the sheriff with what you've got, Taylor. If he thinks it's worth pursuing, we'll get the search warrant. If he thinks you're out of line, then you drop this theory, and hopefully, it doesn't get out. Deal?"

Taylor wasn't happy with the way he said he'd go to the sheriff, implying it would be a private conversation, but she nodded anyway. She couldn't get everything she wanted.

"Deal."

Clint huffed heavily, then got up and left the room.

Shane shook his head. "You'd better be right on this, or he's going to make sure you lose your job."

Taylor agreed.

One hundred percent.

IT ONLY TOOK a record time of four hours before Taylor and Shane had the search warrant in hand and were pulling into the driveway of the residence where they'd conduct their search. Clint declined to ride along and was on his way to the base where Josh Greene was stationed, with full plans to interrogate and investigate, then return with everything he needed for an arrest warrant.

Taylor wished him well and thanked the heavens she wouldn't have to deal with him anymore that day. He would not have approved of sitting in the back with Bernard anyway.

On the drive up, they'd gone over every detail of the phone call tips, the clues of the tires and footprint, and Brandon's discovery. The longer they discussed it, the more it seemed like Shane was on her side, and the weird friction between them during the last few days was slipping away, and their camaraderie was coming back. She had to admit, it felt good having a friend again.

"This is it," Shane said, glancing at the paper and then back at the number on the mailbox.

Her suspect's car was in the driveway, parked alongside an older model white suburban. They had plans to take measurements and photos of the car, but that would have to wait until the interior of the home was searched.

Taylor scrutinized the house. It was nice, but nothing spectacular. Definitely upper-middle class, and she wondered what his wife did for a living that they could afford it.

She felt so antsy that everything in her wanted to jump out of her seat. She'd never been along on a search warrant, though she'd studied every guideline and doctrine and knew exactly what they could and couldn't do.

She wasn't about to mess this up.

Shane parked the car and turned to her. Friend mode was gone, and in its place was Cocky Shane. "Let's leave the dog in the car."

"I don't think that's a good idea," Taylor said. "It's hot. And we might need him."

"Damn, Taylor. You're bound and determined to get us into trouble. Fine, but I'm lead on all points, and you keep him leashed."

"Absolutely."

He gave her a look like he didn't believe for a minute she'd comply. "First, we'll knock and announce. If they let us in, we'll do a full sweep inside and gather anyone in there to the front room. Then you'll stay with them while I search and collect. I'll do the inside first, then the garage and any outbuildings. You good with that? If not, say so now."

"Of course. I know you're lead." It really ticked her off how he was acting, but she had no illusions of who was in charge. She was lucky to even be here. "Just make sure to get any boots you see. And I'm looking for his flashlight, too."

"If they don't open the door, I'll do the forced entry."

She hoped they didn't have to do that. No sense making it more dramatic than it already was.

"Let's do this," Shane said, then climbed out of the car.

Taylor and Bernard were right on his heels when they approached the front door and it opened.

They both stopped abruptly, and she pulled up on the leash, making Bernard sit.

"He's in there, and he's been acting like a crazy man since he got the call," a woman said.

She was middle-aged and wearing yoga pants that didn't do anything for her fluffy outline. She was covered in perspiration and looked terrified.

Shane drew his gun and stood to the side. Taylor did the same.

"Someone let the cat out of the bag," Taylor whispered.

Shane ignored her comment and directed his gaze at the woman. "Is he armed?"

"Of course he's armed," she said.

"Are there any other occupants in the house?" he asked.

"No. Just us and our bird. We have an African gray parrot. Our son is in college, and our daughter lives on her own."

"Did he threaten to hurt anyone or hurt himself?" Shane asked.

"No, not yet. He's furious, though. Said your division is going to ruin everything he's worked so hard for, and everyone will be talking about us. I told him that one day he was going to run into trouble because of the way he is. He brought this on himself."

"Go wait in my car," Shane said. "My partner and I will see what we can do to calm him down."

She scurried toward the car, and once she was secured, Shane took another step toward the front door.

"Wait," Taylor said. "Don't you think we should call for backup?"

"Not yet. I can understand his anger. I think I'll be able to talk to him and let him know that we can do this quietly. If he has nothing to hide, we can move on, and no one needs to hear about it. We call for backup, and it's all over the news."

Taylor's stomach tied itself into knots. She didn't agree with Shane about doing it on his own, but he was lead.

He entered the house and moved from the foyer into the living room, where they had a view of the entirety of it as well as the kitchen and a short hallway that led to a back door.

It was quiet now, and they didn't see or hear him.

"It's time to feed Louie," a voice shrieked from behind them.

They turned, only to see it was the parrot on its stand in the living room.

"This is Detective Weaver out of Hart's Ridge, and we just want to talk to you," Shane called out.

State highway patrolman Greg Meyer stepped out of the pantry in the kitchen and laid his gun on the smooth gray granite of the island.

"I'm not dangerous," he said.

Shane put his gun away.

Taylor wasn't ready yet.

"I know you aren't. Thirteen years on the force with a spotless record. Why would I think you're dangerous?" Shane said, then relaxed his body language. "We just want to talk."

"First of all," Meyer said. "You don't just want to talk. You've got a search warrant in your back pocket. McElroy gave me the heads-up. At least *he* has some loyalty to a brother in blue. And next, you probably think I'm dangerous because my wife can't keep her damn mouth shut and told you a pack of lies."

"She didn't tell us anything," Taylor said.

"You shut the hell up," Meyer said, glaring at Taylor. "Why are you here? You shouldn't even be carrying a badge. You women will say anything to protect each other."

She raised her eyebrows but didn't engage. He was just one more chauvinistic asshole in her profession, and she was used to that.

Shane held his hands up. "You're right. We do have a search warrant. Just doing our job, Meyer. Like you do yours. We've only got a few items to take into custody. If you show us where they're at, we can be out of here in fifteen minutes or less, then we can move on to the next suspect on the list, and no one needs to know anything about this."

"Don't treat me like an idiot," Meyer screamed, and slammed his hand down on the counter next to the gun.

The sound of the piece bouncing against the granite sounded like a cannon in Taylor's ears.

They both went rigid again.

Shane looked at her and shrugged.

The parrot squawked. "Time to feed Louie. Time to feed Louie."

When it stopped, Shane spoke softly. "Look, man. I know you're upset. I would be, too. Sucks for you that you were the one to tag that truck. You should've known you'd be looked at closer. Let's just get this over with and if you're innocent, you're scratched off the list. How about that?"

Meyer put both hands flat on the island and leaned forward. A vein in his forehead bulged and looked like a blue river.

"What about you ruining my reputation? My grandfather was a state man. My father, too. This is in our blood. And you want to try to take it away?"

"No one is taking it away, Meyer. Listen, I need you to step away from the gun now. I want you to put your hands up and walk toward me," Shane said.

"You can kiss my ass," he replied.

"You got your boots from your dad, didn't you?" Taylor asked. She couldn't help herself. "Kept them in the family. A symbol of dedication."

"Taylor…" Shane warned, his voice coming out between clenched teeth.

"It's true. You can't get the brand of those boots anymore. His father kept them meticulous, and Meyer honored him by wearing them, too. Walking in his daddy's shoes like a good little boy. Size nine, right, Meyer? You know what they say about small feet."

"Fuck you."

"And what about that patch you wear of your father's? The red dye on the threads was only used on State Highway Patrol patches for the year he entered the force, then retired after that batch was done. They went to a more vivid color. Did you know in the scuffle with Joni that a thread from your patch transferred to her shirt?"

Meyer lowered his head, his panicked eyes on his gun.

She was on a roll now. Anger clouded her good judgement. Anger for Joni. And for Molly, who now had to live life without a mother whom she adored.

"Oh, and I talked to LeeAnne Gillespie, Meyer. She told me how it almost happened to her, too. You pulled her over after her shift and then told her to follow you down another back road. After you got her out of the car, you stood there for two hours talking to her. Didn't do anything illegal, but you scared her half to death, didn't you? She had to play along because she was terrified. How many other women did you stop and make passes at? Scare them out of talking?"

"Taylor, that's enough. Save it for the interrogation," Shane said.

"Some of them called in to our help line. I bet you didn't count on that," Taylor added.

"SHUT UP!" Meyer screamed, then grabbed his gun. "I didn't touch any of them."

Bernard shifted his body until he was between Taylor and the line of fire. At least from the waist down.

"Whoa, there," Shane called out. "Drop the weapon. Now, Meyer."

Meyer wasn't pointing the gun at them. He held it to his side as he stood there, shaking with fury. The cords in his neck stood out, dark red lines of rage. "We were just talking. I didn't touch that girl, and I wouldn't have. But she ran her mouth. Told me she was going to report me the next day for harassment and find out who my wife was and let her know too. She wrote my badge number down," Meyer screamed. "She was going to ruin my reputation and my marriage!"

"And now she's dead, and here we are," Taylor said, her voice steely.

He'd taken an innocent life, and for what? Some ego trip? It pissed her off that he represented the law but thought it shouldn't apply to him.

"Like, what did you think," she continued, "a beautiful young woman like Joni Stott was going to go for a creepy old sucker like you? Why don't you show us your flashlight? If you still even have it, which a smart man of the law like you wouldn't likely be dumb enough to keep. I'll bet you a dollar the brand was an EDCL LED."

Bernard growled.

"What the hell are you talking about?" Shane hissed back at her.

"He hit her with it and left the letters ED imprinted on her forehead."

Meyer shifted, and Shane stiffened even more.

"Meyer— I SAID PUT THE GUN DOWN!" Shane yelled. "Taylor, shut the hell up!"

"And what about the kid?" Taylor said. "Did you kill her mother in front of her? How does that give you any honor? And last question. How many men did you put behind bars in your *stellar* career? You ready to be reunited with some of them?"

"The girl was sleeping," Meyer said, suddenly much quieter.

Something shifted in his eyes, and suddenly it looked like all the breath in his body left him and he could barely hold himself upright. Taylor wasn't sure if it was realization, or maybe resignation she saw before he looked down.

But when he lifted the gun and locked eyes with her, there was no time to do anything.

Bernard charged, the leash flying out of Taylor's hand, his body suddenly two feet off the ground as he lunged at Meyer.

The blast was louder than any she'd ever heard.

The mess was worse than anything she'd ever seen.

Whether it was shame or guilt that made him pull the trigger, they'd never know.

But she wasn't leaving without his boots.

# CHAPTER 31

*T*aylor stood by the sheriff as he rambled on at the microphone, leading their last press conference on Joni Stott. Shane stood on the sheriff's other side, ordered to be there in case any questions came up that needed his input. It was a celebratory day, and though the rest of her life was in shambles, at least this moment could be counted as a win.

However, Meyer wouldn't face justice—he'd taken the coward's way out, but Joni's family would at least know how and why she was killed.

To top it all off, Taylor felt vindicated. All her hunches had been on point, and because she'd talked the sheriff into asking for the search warrant, they'd solved the case.

There hadn't been time for her to talk to the sheriff, but she looked forward to it. Finally, she felt like she'd lived up to the expectations he'd set for her so long ago. The icing on the cake was that McElroy was immediately relieved of his duties for putting their lives in the path of danger by giving Meyers a heads-up that they were coming.

"It always leaves a bad taste in our mouths when a law enforcement officer goes bad, and we hope that you understand it's not the norm or the majority," Sheriff said, then outlined what could be shared about how they came to look at Meyers as a suspect.

They couldn't tell all the details in case his wife tried to fight the charges or sue for defamation. It wasn't likely, as from all the talking she'd done in the interview, she'd known for years that he was being too friendly with the ladies and trying to use his badge to influence them. To Taylor, it didn't seem like she was too surprised that he'd crossed the line and then tried to protect himself from ramifications.

Sheriff reached out to pat Shane on the back.

"We also must thank the sheriff of Cherokee County for sending one of their top-notch detectives down here to Hart's Ridge to help with this. Without his expertise and strong ethics, we may very well not have followed the lead that led us to Meyers, and the Stott family would've never gotten the answers they needed because this story has more twists than a pretzel factory."

Taylor's pulse quickened. She chanced a sideways glance at Shane. He was puffed up like a peacock.

"What was the most damning evidence against him?" a reporter called out.

"Weaver has a list going, and you know we can't give you all of it. Just let it be said that our lead detective followed his instincts, and it's a true test of his skills that despite a lack of evidence in the beginning, he kept digging and was able to work with our forensics team to put together a scenario that ultimately proved to be true."

*What the hell?* Taylor's blood rose to her throat and burned her ears.

Shane hadn't believed her about Meyers. He'd claimed that it was normal for Meyers to be passing by the gas station at that time, though Taylor had talked to her contact at his dispatch, and she'd said it wasn't. She'd also relayed that Meyers had gotten several complaints from young women about his overly flirtatious stops in the past, which proved a pattern.

The red thread found on Joni should've been a big deal, too, but Shane said it could've been simple transference if he'd pulled Joni over, which then would be circumstantial evidence. Taylor reminded him that Meyers claimed he'd never pulled her over. He'd only seen the truck abandoned and called it in.

As for the boots, Shane argued that there was no possible way those boots were the very ones that were used back in the day that Meyers's father was in the force. That they would've fallen apart.

That wasn't true either.

Taylor had proven to him that the distance between the tire treads at the scene and Meyers's cruiser was the same.

He said many cars had that same distance.

Meyers' obsession with his reputation proved motive.

She had it all. The absolute only thing she could hand to Shane was that he'd decided to give her theories a chance and had gone to bat for the search warrant, but in the hopes of proving her wrong.

"While we never want anyone to end their life the way that Craig Meyers did, his act confirmed his guilt and inability to face the consequences of his actions. After that incident, the murder weapon was found and still held the DNA of Joni Stott. There are other items of evidence that took Detective Weaver some real skill to tie together, making this a solid case that gives me confidence Meyers was indeed guilty."

Taylor put her hands behind her back to hide the shaking, but she couldn't do anything about the tic in her jaw. No wonder Shane had wanted to be the one to give the report to the sheriff. He obviously took all the credit, too.

She looked out at the crowd gathered around them.

Sheila and Jessica were near the front, one of them somber and the other looking angry. She'd had a chance to talk to them earlier and had furtively slid the small pouch containing Joni's ring into Jessica's hand. Sheila was too busy to notice, as she took the opportunity to run her mouth again about getting an attorney to get custody of Molly. Jessica didn't look like she was too supportive of the idea.

Boone was there, looking lost and messy, but obviously wanting to be included in whatever was going on. Taylor needed to remember to give him a McDonald's gift certificate or something. No one ever appreciated him or his contribution to the town.

Alex, the fire chief, was out there too, leaning against the tree. Taylor made the mistake of making a nanosecond of eye contact, and it felt like he was shooting invisible daggers at her.

She shot them right back, then looked away.

"...and now I'd like to announce that the county has approved for Hart's Ridge Sheriff's Department to finally add a full-time detective position to our masthead," Sheriff began.

That got her attention.

"And Detective Weaver has accepted the offer to transfer here to Hart's Ridge permanently," Sheriff said.

The rest of the press conference was a blur after those words. When it ended, she walked stiffly off the front steps and straight to her car, wishing she hadn't left Bernard at home for a day of recovery. She needed his quiet companionship.

In the car, she turned off her radio, disconnecting from dispatch. They'd wonder why she'd gone dark, but at this point, she didn't care. They could fire her if they wanted to. Once again, she was betrayed. And it was worse this time because Shane was supposed to be her friend.

She pulled out of the parking lot and on instinct headed home.

It wasn't fair. She'd been thinking of forgiving Shane for asking questions about her ex-boyfriend. She had to admit that a part of her had fantasized that maybe he was interested in her.

After seeing him with the baby on their first day out together, she'd easily imagined him as a stable family man, or at least partner. But this—no. She couldn't just ignore that he'd taken credit for her case. That showed a serious lack of morals and ethics.

Would she never be able to tell the jerks from the gems? She remembered something that Cecil had told her before about betrayal. To release the disappointment at once so the bitterness wouldn't have time to take root. That was proving impossible for Taylor to do. She wanted to chew on it, get it perfect, then spit it back in Shane's face.

It was going to take her some time.

Clint—he was an asshole who hated women in the force, and anything he did to deter her in her career was expected.

Shane had really fooled her at first, presenting himself as a friend and a gentleman. He'd treated her like a colleague. An equal.

He knew that was what she longed for at the station, and he'd used it against her.

She paused at the end of her driveway to grab the mail, and that reminded her of her dad's mail. She needed to get that power bill paid to get his lights on.

When she approached the house, she could see Bernard perched on the chair looking out the window. He wasn't barking, so he recognized the sound of her car, and that nearly made her smile.

She climbed out of the car, and feeling like she was at least eighty years old, went to the door and let him out.

He sat down right in front of her and looked up, scrutinizing her face.

"What? Don't you want to go pee?"

His tail swished back and forth against the concrete like a windshield wiper against the glass.

Taylor picked up a ball from the toy basket and tossed it into the yard.

"Go. Fetch. Be a dog or something."

He ignored the ball, but he walked off the porch and lifted his leg against her favorite Azalea bush, then returned, looking like he'd lost his best friend.

"You are so weird," she said. "I wish I knew what it is that puts you into your moods."

She thought about the packet that had come with his information. She needed to go through that, too.

Bernard followed her into the house. She slipped off her shoes, then her belt. Relief flooded through her as the weight lifted off her hips. Then she noticed the roughed-up roll of toilet paper perched on the dog bed next to the fridge. It was tattered too much to put back on the dispenser.

"Damn it, Bernard. How did you get that off there?"

He dropped eye contact and looked embarrassed.

She took a seat at the table and tossed her mail down, then pulled her laptop close to her. Quickly, she checked her email, going to the drafts folder.

Nothing.

Obviously, Lucy was intent on punishing her for not loaning her the money and was going to stay silent.

She picked up her dad's stack of mail. The utility bill was on top, and she opened it and was happy to see it was less than usual. It wouldn't hurt her checking account nearly as bad as she'd feared.

Before she could forget, she called the number she already had in her contacts and used the automated selection to pay it with her debit card. She hoped they'd turn the switch immediately.

Next in the pile was an envelope that really piqued her interest.

The return address was from the Montana Prison for Women.

She felt something shift inside her stomach. What had her

father gotten himself into now? First he was exploring Facebook and now had a pen pal in a prison?

She opened the envelope expecting a letter, but only a small slip of paper fell out. She picked it up. It was a receipt for a money order voucher for payment made on the account of inmate number 070895 for one hundred dollars.

Taylor leaned back in the chair, letting out a long and frustrated breath.

She wondered how long he'd been sending money there. At least that answered her question about where his money was going. But how had he connected with a prison inmate? Prisoners couldn't have social network profiles. The bigger question though—was her dad being scammed? Phished, as it was called?

She was tempted to call him up and ask him outright, but she knew that wasn't how to get anything out of her stubborn father. She'd have to be sneaky and investigate on her own when she wasn't feeling so deflated and drained.

Her dad wouldn't get his next check for a few more days, and that would give her time to stop him from sending more money when she could confront him with details of who he was really being a sugar daddy for.

"I'll call them and get a name to go with that inmate number tomorrow, and then we'll see what she's in for," she said to Bernard. "But let's change lanes and see if there's anything useful in your stuff now."

She flipped through the stack until she found the packet. She didn't know where her letter opener was, so she used her fingers to make a mess of it, but finally she peered down into the contents.

There was a faded old collar and a few envelopes inside the packet. One envelope had a return address from the rescue that had fostered Bernard before he'd been adopted out. Someone had scrawled on the front of it.

*Sorry—this should've gone with him to his first home.*

When she flipped it over, it didn't appear to have ever been opened. Or if it was, it had sealed itself back seamlessly. It was probably more receipts. Or maybe it was some sort of report that could give her some insight into some of his issues and how to help him.

Suddenly more fatigued than she'd realized, she took the envelope to her bedroom and crawled onto the bed. Bernard followed, but she quickly told him no, and he pawed at her carpet until he circled then settled next to the bed.

She ripped the envelope open and inside found a letter with a sticky note on it.

*For the family who adopts my dog.*

She unfolded it and started reading.

It was only one sheet of paper, and when she opened it, she could see it wasn't anything official. It was written in barely better than doctor chicken scratch and was going to be a slow read.

*To whomever adopts my dog:*
*I wasn't going to write this letter, but this is my last night with my best friend, and I can't sleep. I've been sitting here watching him curled up beside me, snoring so loud it could wake the neighbors, content in knowing he is safe and loved. I could just drop him off and let the chips fall where*

they may, but something deep inside me knows that this is going to be so hard on him. And if a little insight I can give will make his adjustment better, then why the hell not write a letter?

First, his name isn't Bernard. I don't know why I said it was, other than the fact that I didn't want the people working to place him make him feel they were getting familiar, just to ship him off to a new location. His new family should have the honor of using the name that I took so long to pick for my best friend.

His name is Diesel.

The reason I picked it is because, more than anything else he knows, riding up in my jeep is his favorite thing. As soon as he even gets close to it, he inhales as though the diesel fuel is the most enticing scent ever.

He will only go in through the driver's door, and then he almost looks human as he rides shotgun with me, his eyes watching the road for his favorite spots.

So please, take him on rides. Long rides with country music playing on the radio.

Some days, I'd just pick a field and pull over, then throw the ball as hard as I could and watch him run, gracefully and powerfully until he reached the ball, then turned around to obediently bring it back.

Every. Damn. Time.

And swim! If you want to see his inner puppy come alive, take him to the river. He loves the water, and he'll sleep like a rock later, so use the river runs on days you plan to leave him for an evening out.

Tricks. He knows a lot of the usual ones like sit, stay, and down.

But one fun trick I taught him is Snake! Before you call it, be ready. You'll need to balance yourself, hold out your arms, and bend over slightly. Then prepare for seventy pounds of dog to jump onto your shoulders because that's what you'll get.

Don't drop him.

Now for the good stuff. Diesel is smart. Loyal. And he has no fear when it comes to protecting me. But he'll be just as happy being a family dog. Hopefully.

Quirks. Just one. He loves toilet paper. He won't eat it, but he will disperse it through the house, and if you let him, he'll use it like a security blanket.

Hunting: This might surprise you considering his breed, but Diesel doesn't like to hunt. He loves all creatures, even the baby rabbits that he found under our porch. He even had a hummingbird pal for a while. It hung out around our porch, and for months, when we came out for our evening walk, the bird played around Diesel's head, and he liked it. I guess something weird happened in his genetic makeup, so he won't be searching or killing critters, so just mark that off the list.

He's a good dog.

No, scratch that. Diesel is the best damn dog in the world. And that's why when it was time for my third deployment, I decided I can't keep doing this to him. The first two times were hard enough. Diesel needs to find a new person who won't leave him confused and sad when they take off for months at a time. He also needs someone who isn't damaged. Someone who knows how to laugh and how to fill the house with the sound of others. Maybe some kids, as long as they don't tease him or pull his tail.

Diesel deserves better than I can give him. And it kills me to say that.

If you are reading this, you were chosen by what I'm told is the best lab rescue group in the state. That means you've been vetted, and you are going to help Diesel forget about me and learn to love again.

To trust again.

Give him an ear rub for me. And just before bed every night—and this is going to sound very unmanly, but hell, I don't know you—grab him by the ears and pull his face to yours. Then, touch *noses and tell him to sleep. That's the signal that he's safe, or off duty for the night, as he probably prefers to think.*

*Signed,*
*Samuel G. Stone, Diesel's first dad.*

Taylor sniffed and wiped at her face. It was going to need a major cleanup and some moisturizer. She also needed a tissue. A sleeve wasn't going to sop up all the tears that were running amok.

She folded the letter and held it to her heart.

Poor Bernard.

*No, not Bernard.*

"Diesel," she whispered.

He was already in a light sleep next to the bed, his low snore getting ready to ramp up another level.

"Diesel," she said again.

His ears stood up, and he turned to look at her, his eyes questioning.

"Come here, boy," Taylor said, feeling another tidal wave of emotion coming. "Come, Diesel."

He heard her loud and clear that time. He climbed out of his bed, his whole body quivering as he approached.

"Up," Taylor said, patting the bed.

He looked confused.

"Diesel, up. It's okay. You're invited this time."

He jumped up, and Taylor put her arms around him.

"I'm so sorry about you losing your best friend, buddy," she whispered into his ear, pulling him onto her lap. "Good dog, Diesel."

He nuzzled into her chest and whimpered, then went slack against her. Taylor felt the anguish he carried. The sadness and grieving. He was still, but the pounding of his heart against hers told her all he couldn't say.

She cried silently, not wanting to distress him. No, right now, this was about comfort. And her guilt. Why had she not thought about how he could've lost someone? How he might be grieving? Grown dogs didn't just drop out of the sky. Of course they have a history.

"Such a good boy, Diesel," she said softly, rubbing behind his ears.

Finally, she pulled apart from him. When he prepared to jump off the bed, she touched him lightly.

"Stay, Diesel," she said, then patted the place beside her.

She went to the bathroom, opened the cabinet beneath the sink, and pulled out a fresh roll of toilet paper. She brought it to the bed and tucked it beside him, then pulled off her uniform, stripping to her underwear before she joined him.

He still looked ready to leap off the bed, but when he looked to her for confirmation that she wasn't going to send him packing, he curled up next to her. She pulled the sheet over them both.

She nuzzled into his soft ear. "You've been looking for your person, haven't you?"

There was no question of what she had to do for him. Especially because as outrageous as it sounded, other than a recovering alcoholic who was old enough to be her grandfather, Diesel was her only real friend.

Taylor pulled the covers up over her legs, then put her arms back around Diesel. She leaned in and put her nose to his. "We'll fix this. But for now, just sleep."


THE END

∼

READY for more Hart's Ridge? Check out book two, LUCY IN THE SKY, at this link:

DOWNLOAD *LUCY IN THE SKY*

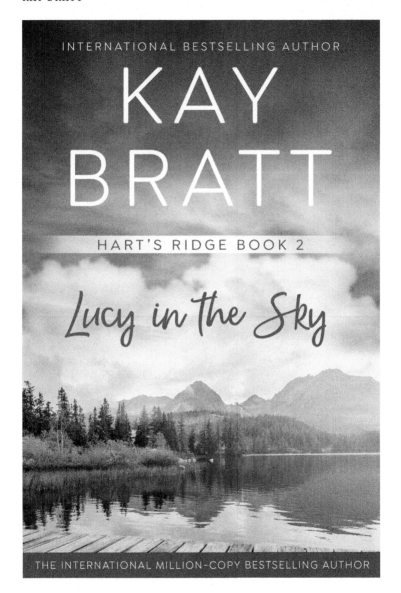

INTERNATIONAL BESTSELLING AUTHOR

# KAY BRATT

## HART'S RIDGE BOOK 2

*Lucy in the Sky*

THE INTERNATIONAL MILLION-COPY BESTSELLING AUTHOR

DOWNLOAD *LUCY IN THE SKY*

Lucy Gray doesn't always start trouble, but it's sure to be there when she arrives. This time, when she runs from her hometown, she's determined to undo her biggest mistake yet and finally hits some good luck. But her sister, Taylor, has always told her that if it looks too good to be true, it probably is. This time, she might be right.

Deputy Taylor Gray grew up wanting to solve crime, but she never dreamed of taking on a case that could change her family forever, either bringing them together in a healthier dynamic or shattering any hope of ever fixing the many fractures within. With this one, there's no other option—she will get to the truth.

Featuring a true crime element, the *Hart's Ridge* series is built around Deputy Taylor Gray, a young woman carrying the world on her shoulders as she does her best to solve mysteries while simultaneously piecing her fractured family back together, one bit at a time.

**Lucy in the Sky is book two of the new Hart's Ridge small-town mystery series, written by Kay Bratt, million-copy best-selling author of Wish Me Home and True to Me.**

PLEASE JOIN my monthly newsletter to learn more about myself and the Bratt Pack, and to be notified of new releases, sales, and fantastic giveaways!

JOIN KAY'S NEWSLETTER HERE

# FROM THE AUTHOR

~

Hello, readers! I hope you enjoyed the first book in the *Hart's Ridge* series. The plotline of Joni's murder was inspired by an episode of *Forensic Files*. In 1986, before the gift of DNA analysis was discovered, a university student named Cara Knott was pulled over and then killed by a state trooper for resisting his advances and threatening to expose him.

My sincere condolences go out to Cara's family.

As for the letter from Sam Stone about Bernard—ahem...*I mean Diesel*—it was inspired by an article going around the internet about a veteran who left a similar letter with his dog when he was shipped out and didn't return. It brought me to tears, so of course I wanted to give it a bigger story than just a post on Facebook. Taylor won't give up until she finds out all she needs to know about the dog who has become her best friend.

The cozy town of Hart's Ridge is taking up such a huge space in my imagination that I can barely keep up with what I want to write next. There's so much for you to find out in this series! Don't you want to know if there are more mysterious reasons that Jackson moved Taylor and her sisters from Montana? What exactly was he running from and who is he sending money to?

And for Lucy to steal money from her own sister—well, there's a reason for it. I can promise you that. You'll want to follow her as she once again begins a new life in a strange place. She legitimately tries to stay out of trouble this time, only to find it as impossible as it's always been.

Also, I'm sure you aren't liking sister Anne very much right now. Or her arrogant husband, Pete. But try to withhold judgement until you learn more about her, because things aren't always what they seem.

Remember Faire Tinsley? Don't you just love that name? I saw a very similar name on a plaque in front of a historical house here in my small town in Georgia, and immediately my mind was spinning on what kind of person would live in such a grand home. I know I barely mentioned her in this book, but she's the town medium who, due to a terrible mistake, no longer wants to be recognized. I'm so excited to delve into her personality and backstory a bit.

Also Jo Jo, Taylor's sister who works on a ranch, will have her own story. Sissy and her mother, Margaret, along with Della Ray and Mabel, may also pop in a time or two in the next books. Y'all, I love true crime. This series will give you a crime to ponder in each book, inspired by a true story but nestled within the fictional world of Hart's Ridge. Yes, I have so much more in store for you in the upcoming *Hart's Ridge* books, and I hope you continue to follow along. You can download book two, LUCY IN THE SKY, right here at this [link].

Can I ask a favor? I'd be overwhelmed with gratitude if you'd care to post an honest review for the books. On Amazon especially—and BookBub and Goodreads if you're feeling exceptionally generous. It's a big ocean of books out there, and mine need all the help they can get to be seen. Please recommend it to your bookworm buddies in online book clubs, too!

And lastly, if you are a long-term fan, I want you to know I appreciate your picking up this book, which is a bit of a detour from my usual stuff. If you are new to my work, thank you for taking a chance, and I hope I didn't let you down! Come find me in my private readers' group, Kay's Kindness Krew, where I'm known to overshare with stories of my life with the Bratt Pack, and all the kerfuffles I find myself getting into.

Until then,

Scatter kindness everywhere.

Kay Bratt

# AUTHOR BIO

Writer, Rescuer, Wanderer

Kay Bratt is the powerhouse author behind over 30 internationally bestselling books that span genres from mystery and women's fiction to memoir and historical fiction. Her books are renowned for delivering an emotional wallop wrapped in gripping storylines. Her Hart's Ridge small-town mystery series earned her the coveted title of Amazon All Star Author and continues to be one of her most successful projects out of her more than million books sold around the world.

Kay's literary works have sparked lively book club discussions wide-reaching, with her works translated into multiple languages, including German, Korean, Chinese, Hungarian, Czech, and Estonian.

Beyond her writing, Kay passionately dedicates herself to rescue missions, championing animal welfare as the former Director of Advocacy for Yorkie Rescue of the Carolinas. She considers herself a lifelong advocate for children, having volunteered extensively in a Chinese orphanage and supported nonprofit organizations like An Orphan's Wish (AOW), Pearl River Outreach, and Love Without Boundaries. In the USA, Kay served as a Court Appointed Special Advocate (CASA) for abused and neglected children in Georgia, as well as spearheaded numerous outreach programs for underprivileged kids in South Carolina.

As a wanderlust-driven soul, Kay has called nearly three dozen different homes on two continents her own. Her globe-trotting adventures have taken her to captivating destinations across Mexico, Thailand, Malaysia, China, the Philippines, Central America, the Bahamas, and Australia. Today, she and her soulmate of 30 years find their sanctuary by the serene banks of Lake Hartwell in Georgia, USA.

Described as southern, spicy, and a touch sassy, Kay loves to share her life's antics with the Bratt Pack on social media.

For more information, visit www.kaybratt.com.

Printed in Great Britain
by Amazon

37239698R00182